This book would have remained an idea without the encourageme: friends and family; a special thank you goes to Mark for putting up with my artistic efforts and to Lisa for continuing to be my valued "reader".

My thanks also goes to Lynn and the team at Zimmer & Rohde for all their help, support and advice about the world of interior design.

To Maureen
I hope you enjoy all the shopping bits!
Ann x

This is a work of fiction. Names, characters, businesses, places, events and incidents are either the products of the author's imagination or used in a fictitious manner. Any resemblance to actual persons, living or dead, or actual events is purely coincidental.

© 2011 Anna Hutton-North. All rights reserved.
ISBN 978-1-4478-0897-8

Chapter 1

The church stood tall and solid as the dull persistent rain fell on the huddled congregation; the top of the spire was hidden amongst grey swollen clouds. Around the newly dug grave the funeral party shivered as the damp seeped through their clothing. Josie watched numbly as the coffin of her husband was lowered into the hole, unable to summon up any emotion other than continued disbelief at what was happening. The news had come as a sudden shock; it wasn't something she had been ready for. Waking up to a pale faced policeman standing in her mother's sitting room telling her that Nick was dead. They had told her that Nick had died in a car accident down one of the country lanes. It was an image that haunted Josie during her sleep, wrecking her dreams with its sudden appearance. She would see Nick driving along the unfamiliar roads in the dark visibility lessened by the blanket of rain, and then the abrupt screech of the brakes and the metallic splitting of the crash as the vehicle skidded off the road and collided, the sound drowning out the driver's screams. The urgent but futile attendance of the emergency services to deal with the already dead driver.

The shrill ring of the telephone broke into Josie's thoughts, transporting her back to reality. Tentatively she put out her hand to pick up the receiver; since Nick's death she had shut herself away, trying to make some kind of sense of the situation.
"Hello?" Her voice sounded strange to her ears after being quiet for so long.
"Josie?" The booming voice down the phone bought instant comfort. "Is that you?" Tara, her best friend, the one person who had been absent when Josie had needed her the most.
"Yes it's me."
"How are you? No, cancel that question. It's obvious how you'll be feeling." Her voice softened. "I've only just heard. We landed this morning and I've only just listened to our answer phone. I'm sorry love."
"Don't worry."
"Don't worry! I told Jeremy if he ever took me on a six week cruise again when my friend needed me – I'd kill him. Ohmigod, I can't

believe I said that. If I bring a bottle of vino round will you forgive me?"
"Of course." Josie laughed, everything suddenly seemed a little less awful.
"At least if I've got a mouthful of wine there won't be room for my foot as well." Tara said ruefully.

Despite it being a mission of mercy Josie knew Tara well enough to know that it would take her at least 30 minutes to select the right outfit for consoling, apply her already perfect make-up and to select just the right bottle of wine for the occasion.

Looking round she was glad for Tara's foibles. She hadn't done anything to the flat since she had been told of Nick's death. Gazing round the sitting room she wondered how it had come to resemble this. The once pristine minimalist décor had been transposed with accessories of dirty plates, discarded clothing and... what was that? A baby's blanket? Oh yes, she grimaced at the recollection of being so distraught after the funeral that she had picked up her niece's pram blanket thinking it was her pashmina.

Thirty minutes later and both the flat and Josie stood transformed. For the first time in weeks she had tidied, washed and blow dried. As she stood contemplating her reflection she realised that her weight had plummeted since Nick's death. Like every woman Josie always wanted to be a bit taller and a bit thinner, but now that she was thinner she somehow looked less attractive. She'd always joked about her slight roundness being far more attractive to men than the stick women she called her friends – but deep down she'd envied them. So now she had joined their ranks why wasn't she out celebrating? The door bell rang announcing the arrival of Tara; opening the door Josie found herself enveloped in a huge woolly hug.
"I'm so sorry I wasn't here." Tara said, her voice sounded muffled to Josie through the layers of wool.
"Well at least you are now." Josie's muffled voice came back dampened by the fluffy mohair that was now starting to tickle her nose. Luckily Tara unclasped her and she stood back objectively, assessing her friend before starting to laugh. "Oh dear."
"What?"

"Think you'd better look in a mirror."
As they both gazed at Josie's reflection it was as though she had just been through a snow storm. Tiny white flakes clung to her damp face and black shirt. "I should never have worn this jumper." Tara lamented.
Brushing herself down, Josie led the way to the sitting room and as Tara brandished the promised bottle, a cheeky little Chablis with a hint of gooseberry, Josie went out to the kitchen for the glasses.
"The amazing thing," Josie reflected "was that half an hour with a friend and life didn't seem so hopeless." They had gossiped about friends, Tara had regaled her with stories of the awful people they'd met on the cruise; "awful darling – loads of lovely cash but not a taste-cell amongst them! One of them even wore a cardigan to dinner at the Captain's table. I'm not a snob – but there are some things that men should never wear!" Not one mention of Nick until now when Tara gently enquired "So tell me what happened" and suddenly all the emotions that had lain hidden under the disbelief bubbled their way to the surface and she felt the hot flow of tears cascading down her cheeks. Tara calmly provided a flow of tissues as in between the sobs Josie told the story of how she had been visiting her mother for the weekend when Saturday morning they had been woken by a policeman who had broken the news that the previous evening her husband had been killed in a car crash.

As the emotions receded Josie gave a little hiccup and she tried a weak smile. "That's it really. I have to say that I still can't quite believe it."
"So why didn't Nick go with you to your mother's. He loves going there – I reckon he was the only man who liked his mother-in-law."
"I think it's because he missed out on having his own – what with being brought up by his father for most of his life."
"So why did he stay behind – was it work?"
"Noo..." Josie's voice sounded uncertain. "I'm not quite sure now. He said something had cropped up at the last minute, which he seemed concerned about. He was distracted. He took me to the train station and said he'd see me after the weekend, and then kissed me on the cheek and walked off."
"I wonder what it was?" Tara's brow furrowed as she thought on it.
"Well whatever it was I hope it was important."
"I guess we'll never know." Josie mused.

Josie reflected on the day as she was getting ready to go to bed; the double bed she'd spend months persuading Nick to buy. "You want to spend how much on a bed?" He'd spluttered. "Do you realise you could get a car for that much money Josie." He had prevaricated for months before secretly buying it on their first Christmas in the flat. "Well I knew I'd never get any peace until you had it." He said pointedly "And now we have it, we'd better christen it!" Now it had suddenly lost all its appeal, it felt lonely lying there all by herself, in the vast expanse of space. The sheets were cold and unwelcoming without Nick's warming presence. Turning away from it she walked into the bathroom. "I wonder what Nick had been doing that weekend?" She asked her reflection as she brushed her teeth – but it didn't matter how long she stared at her own image there was no answer forthcoming. Wearily she climbed into bed, plumping up the pillows when all of a sudden the phone rang. Perplexed she checked her watch wondering who would be phoning her at this hour.

"Hello?"

"It's only me love," Tara's voice boomed down the line. "Just checking that you're ok."

"Yes I'm fine."

"Are you in bed yet?"

"Yes, just waiting for Brad Pitt to come over." She joked.

"Well tell him not to waste his time on you, and send him over to me. Give me a call tomorrow morning and we'll go out. Now try and get some sleep."

'Some hope.' Josie thought as she said goodbye before trying to shuffle down into the bed covers, picturing her friend archly telling Jeremy that it was never to late to phone friends. Grimly she closed her eyes and waited for a fleeting sleep to finally descend.

"Yes Mum I'm fine." Josie lied wearily, "No, there's no need to visit; no it's not that I don't want you here, but you hate London and I need to get a few things sorted." She looked down at the letter she had received earlier that morning, its official stamp now covered with tiny doodlings of ornate flowers and intricately winding leaves and stems. "Look I'll give you a call later." She turned away from the window and walked across to the two leather sofas that dominated the sitting area of the flat; standing in the middle she suddenly felt the silence to be oppressive, as though she were the only person left on the earth, and that somehow everyone else had slipped away unnoticed. Turning the radio on a woman presenter's voice echoed into the space energetically as she espoused the virtues of using ancient Hebrew dancing as a daily exercise regime for keeping the body supple and the skin radiant. Feeling distinctly unsupple and unradiant Josie returned her attention to the letter, it had been sent from Nick's boss who was requesting her to contact him as soon as she felt able to. Although the letter was filled with condolences she felt there was an undercurrent, a deeper message that somehow she couldn't quite decrypt. It unnerved her, it felt as though there was a sinister beckoning – had Nick been fleeing the country after having embezzled the company's money, or had he been handing designs and patents over to rival competitors; was that why he had died? Had the company organised his killing to avoid an embarrassing situation; no that definitely sounded too far fetched. This was Miller & Moss, an advertising agency, not something out of the Sopranos; she slammed the lid on the incredulous thoughts. The feeling of normality that Tara had briefly fostered yesterday had been lost leaving uncertainty and fear to creep in to the dark spaces that grief made. "Well there's no point sitting here worrying" she heard her sister say in her school-marm voice, practical and unemotional. "Might as well make the call and find out what it's all about." Taking the plunge she picked up the phone and dialled the number.

When she had made the meeting with Neil Rank's secretary she hadn't considered the issue of what to wear. She had planned to throw on her favourite black trousers with a pale pink Ralph Lauren shirt and she'd be off. So how could it be, the woman who had to have a separate room for her clothes, still couldn't find anything to wear even after half an hour. It's all very well being able to admire your new thin body in the privacy of the bathroom with a frisson of guilty pleasure, but quite another when you're trying to dress to see your dead husband's boss. Her outfit looked as though it was designed for another woman, which it was; a happy married woman, not a gaunt grieving widow. Where the trousers had emphasised her femininity now they hung loosely from her giving the impression she was wearing charity cast-offs. Sighing she pulled off the carefully tailored trousers and threw them onto the bed with the other discarded clothes. Finally in exasperation she came across a black pencil skirt at the back of the rail. It had been an impulse buy during the sales at Georgio Armani, a skirt that was designed to look as though you had been sewn into it, with a high wide waistband that clung across the body with two slits at the back to allow the wearer to walk. She'd never actually worn it before, always feeling the seams were a little too stretched for decency, now she stepped into it and fastening the zip turned to look at herself in the mirror. The cut was as flattering as it could be, turning her gauntness into a lithe fashion statement. Slipping into a pair of jaunty suede pink kitten heels that matched her shirt she looked a cross between a well-heeled Italian and a 1950's film star. Putting on her large Jackie Onassis sun glasses she now felt prepared for battle, whatever Miller & Moss had to throw at her she was definitely ready. Let them beware if they were expecting a simpering girl; this lady meant business.

The taxi driver was openly appreciative of her new look, even letting her off 60 pence when it turned out she was short of money. 'I must go to a cash point' she instructed herself realising that this was the first time in over a month that she had ventured out of the flat; she needed to start getting back to normal. She would definitely buy some food as she went home instead of living off delivered pizzas and Indian takeaways. Stepping out of the taxi she found herself staring up at the imposing entrance of Miller & Moss, the offices where Nick had spent most of his working life as a graphic designer. Josie had always loved visiting Nick here. The imposing sterile exterior of glass rose up from the pavement, towering above you, and the only relief was a discrete sign reading "Miller & Moss" placed at such an angle so as not to disrupt the eye from the silver building. When she had questioned Nick about how clients found them if the signage was so discrete he had chuckled ironically responding that only clients who could afford them came to the offices – and their drivers knew where everything was.

The cold calm exterior belied the energetic and dynamic core; as soon as you entered the offices your senses were assailed by a myriad of colours and sounds. The buzz of the creative teams was set against the chatter of account directors with their clients discussing pitches, arranging lunches and signing deals. The air hung heavy with success and large bonuses, a modern day royal court. It was as though you were entering into the bloodstream of the organisation. There was a constant movement as individuals flitted between the designers, the copy writers and the account managers. And yet somehow out of all this apparent confusion and mayhem came order. The amount of times they had been watching TV or out with friends when Nick would casually point at an advert or a billboard and say 'that's one of ours'. Some were beautiful, some were witty and some were just too clever for her to understand without an explanation from someone else. Her favourite had been the Allium perfume advert for L'Oreal; a black and white advert showing a woman reclining off a rock, her white cotton dress caught by the breeze, its hem dancing, and her hair cascading into the water below in such a way that it was difficult to see where the rippling locks ended and the crashing waves began. The whole feeling of the image was one of utter serenity against a turbulent backdrop.

Pushing open the heavy glass door Josie was aware of the under-lash stares of the two receptionists as they took in her clothes, trying to work out if she was a potential client or a wannabe model.
"I'm here to see Neil Rank." She said by way of introduction to the youngest, trying not to stare at the tiny silver bolt punctured into her left eyebrow.
"Who thall I thay ith here?" She lisped as another silver bolt, this time in her tongue, clicked against the roof of mouth and clinked on her front teeth.
"Josie Carrington." There was a slight intake of breath, accentuated by the oral accessory, as the name registered with them, followed by an embarrassed silence of not knowing what to say to the wife of an ex-colleague. The silence was eventually broken by a buzzer and the receptionist, glad of the interruption, said "Mr Rank will see you now."
Neil's office was a monument to cutting edge design; the desk was a swathe of crystal clear glass that sat upon chrome legs, making his laptop and phone look as though they were hovering mid air. The flooring was dark cherry wood, picking up the wooden legs of the square linen covered sofas; their angular lines rising majestically in contrast to the busy wall coverings of coffee with cream concentric

circles. His desk chair was a copy of the Jurgen chair, a chocolate brown classic.

"Josie!" Neil Rank put out a comforting hand and kissed her gently on the cheek. "How are you?" His voice sounded concerned; it then turned to embarrassed admiration, realising it was in poor taste to compliment a grieving widow, but he couldn't help himself. "You're looking good." He murmured against her ear. Josie's confidence took a tiny soar, may be this meeting wouldn't be too bad; taking the initiative she sat down on one of the sand coloured sofas, feeling the rough linen fabric prickling the back of her legs.

"Thank you Neil; you're not looking too bad yourself." He ran his hand self consciously through his blond hair, which no matter how often it was cut always insisted on doing its own thing. The warm caramel tones of his skin showed his love of outdoor pursuits; saved from a ruddy weathered look by the rigid regime of male grooming he followed under the strict gaze of his girlfriend Claudia. His principal passion was sailing; the thrill of pitting himself against the elements on a boundless sea with just a sailing dinghy with which to do battle. Outside of the office he would be found slopping round in deck shoes and cotton sailing shirt discussing weather forecasts and the benefits of spinnakers over main brace for the difference in winning a race, much to the chagrin of the long suffering Claudia who was definite a life-long land-lover.

"I didn't mean you had to come in so soon." He joined her on the opposite sofa that were strategically positioned so one could talk as well as admire the vista of London that stretched out beneath them, a smaller Lilliputian world almost.

"I'd forgotten the views," she said half to herself, standing up momentarily to appreciate the stunning panorama. Neil watched her, mesmerised by her heels and delicate legs beneath a skirt which looked as though it formed a second sleek fitting skin. She had obviously lost weight, but he couldn't remember her looking so alluring. He watched her sit back down and was about to restart the conversation when his secretary appeared through the door. A fifty year old matron figure who scared the new designers half to death and was the only one who could organise Neil's life both socially and at work.

"Josie." She stalked over and unabashed gave her a hug. "Neil said you were coming in today. I couldn't believe it, it's far too soon for you."

"Mary, how lovely to see you. No I'm fine honestly." How many times had she reassured people since Nick's death? Early on she had learnt no one really wanted to know you still felt so awful that even seeing a happy couple on TV could make you cry; so she resorted to the habitual line of 'I'm fine'. "Besides I have to try and start getting out. I'm not really suited to being completely alone all the time."

Mary patted Josie's thin hand with her own liver-spotted one.
"Well don't let him be too hard on you. If he is just let me know." She instructed Josie conspiratorially.
"I am here." Neil objected "And I am a fully paid up member of the modern-man-with-feelings club."
"Hah!" Marry said as she turned to leave.
"Any chance of a coffee?" Neil enquired to the retreating back.
"Yes I know; yours is a cappuccino and Josie's is a latte."
"See what I have to put up with." Neil complained in mock disgust as they settled down companionably again. "Insolent staff with no respect for me."
"You wouldn't have it any other way; and now could you put me out of my misery and let me know why I had to come in today. I don't think I can take much more of the suspense."

As she lay in bed that night she reflected on the day; it was a strange turn of events in the end. It had been comforting to see Neil again; a strong masculine presence who gave a small degree of solidity to the fragmented disorder she was currently living.

"I can't believe Nick has actually gone." He'd admitted as they had sipped their coffee. "I still expect him to turn up 5 minutes late with some fantastic excuse."
"I know what you mean." Josie agreed "I wait for his mad phone calls to explain why he's working late even though I've cooked his favourite meal." There was a quiet reflective moment as both looked out across the sprawling metropolis seeing not buildings but memories of distant times.
"So what was the letter for?" Her question broke into the silence. Running his hand through his hair leaving it even more ruffled, he looked thoughtful. Josie noticed the blue of his shirt matched the piercing blue of his eyes.

"It's business things." He sounded slightly embarrassed at having to raise the subject so soon after Nick's death. "And I wouldn't have bothered you with them, except our Vice President is flying in from the States this week and we need to have our paperwork in order."

Josie nodded to show empathetic understanding while trying to work out what Neil was talking about; it still seemed a complete mystery.

"I know it's not a terribly nice thing to talk about," he continued "And I appreciate now isn't a good time for you, what with the funeral and sorting out Nick's affairs. But the thing is when any employee leaves we have to collect any company assets that may have been given out at the time of employment." There was a tiny embarrassed pause. "I need to get back his laptop and the phone, and all the designs he was working on. We've been fobbing the client off on why there has been a delay, but we do need something to show them. I also need you to go through some paperwork." he indicated a manila folder that was lying on the coffee table on top of Sailing Weekly and Marketing Monthly. He looked at her, concern and worry creasing his brow.

"Neil don't worry, I understand it's just business; that you're only trying to help. Of course you can have everything back, if I had thought about it I would have brought it with me. But you know how it is, I'm not thinking straight at the moment." She squeezed his hand, feeling the callous on his palm that had formed from the sailing despite the rigorous applications of hand-cream. A flicker of frisson shot through her, and she pulled away confused, she had always seen Neil as Nick's boss, she had never considered him anything else, so what was happening? "What's the paperwork?" She asked quickly, trying to appear unperturbed by her wayward feelings.

"Oh simply Nick's death-in-service leaflets. You know the company pays out on the death of an employee if they have been with Miller & Moss for more than five years. Well because of Nick's length of service you get three times his annual salary. You were aware of this weren't you?" He asked as a blank expression settled on Josie's face.

Josie shook her head. "Neil, we were married for two years; I'm only thirty one; how was I to know I'd need to prepare myself for widowhood so early on?"

"But you know about the loan he took out?" Neil was anxious about the way the conversation was turning out; the confident widow act was obviously starting to crack. Feeling she was suddenly in unknown territory she looked at him warily.

"What loan?" She asked slowly.

"The company offers low rate loans to employees for things like travel cards, deposits on houses, professional courses that kind of thing."

"What would Nick want with a loan?"

"For the deposit on the flat you were buying."

"But we weren't buying a flat. He always thought a mortgage was too much of a commitment." She paused. "We couldn't afford to buy anyway since I'm not working."

"So how are you coping now?" He gently pressed.

"Ok."

"I mean financially; presumably you've got Nick's life insurance coming through to help with the bills if you're not earning." The sentence in its utter simplicity pounded in her ears. The words sounded like the death knoll of bells. Tears came unbidden and pricked at her eyes.

"I'm sorry." She whispered. "It sounds stupid but I've no idea. I hadn't even thought about it before I came here." He leant across and took her hands in his, pushing away thoughts of kissing away the tiny iridescent tear drops that lay on her pale cheeks.

"Hey I'm the one who should be sorry. I didn't mean to upset you by talking about all this." She gazed down at his firm manly hands as they covered her own, noticing how clean and neat his nails looked.

"I didn't know what our finances were like before Nick died, I've no idea what we have now." She stopped and corrected herself. "What I have now."

"Listen, would it help if we talked about things some other time away from the office? If you want some help I could come over one evening and give you a hand to sort things out if you want." She looked at him, her brown eyes glistening with unspent tears and numbly nodded her head.

"Well that's settled then; of course I don't mind. That's what friends are for. Now try and dry your tears," he passed her a clean handkerchief to wipe away the mascara. Taking it she caught a faint whiff of Ralph Lauren's Polo. "I'll go and check that no-one's around; we can't let Mary see you, or she'll skin me alive for upsetting you!"

And that was how the afternoon had ended. A promise to help sift through the papers and get her life into perspective; her thoughts drifted back to the jolt she had felt touching his hand. She'd better keep her sentiments under strict control, the last thing she needed was an emotional attachment at the moment.

The thick stone walls of the convent radiated silence as the inhabitants glided noiselessly down the corridor from early morning mass towards the refectory. The building was a gothic style courtyard built by a Victorian philanthropist who thought that the way to secure a place in heaven, was to create a little bit of God's work here on earth. It was unusual in the design, being designed to hold a small order of nuns who worked in the village helping the sick and elderly. There was no private chapel instead the nuns used the local parish church, which had ensured they were truly part of the community, and had reduced the original building bill. The church sat to one side, adjoined to the convent gardens by way of a discrete palisade gate set into a deep dry stone wall that ran around the edge of the garden, decorated here and there with sprigs of scented wild roses and rambling honeysuckle.

After a simple but fulfilling breakfast of porridge and bread the nuns quietly dispersed, each off to do their daily chores. As Mother Mary Joseph and Sister Benedict entered the small dormitory of rooms they looked after, their eyes ran down the parallel lines of beds, smiling greetings to the elderly women propped up on the stiff starched pillows. Sister Benedict walked over to the patient on the left.
"Good morning Nellie." Her voice had a slight Irish lilt left over from her early childhood years. "And how are you this morning?"
"As well as can be expected" was the sanguine response. Sister Benedict used her basic nursing skills to check the patient as they talked about the weather and of flowers.
"It was time Sister Stephen was planting those freesias she potted." Nellie pointed out.
"I'll let her know." The nun assured her.
"And tell her to try putting egg shells down to get rid of the slugs. It's far better than that modern stuff people use nowadays."
"Perhaps you should go down and give her a helping hand, I'm sure she would appreciate it." Sister Benedict suggested as she had done each morning since Nellie Craythorne had been admitted four weeks ago. Nellie's crippled hand patted the delicate skin of the Sister's.
"May be I will after I've had a little rest. These bones of mine seem to get so tired these days."

"Well you stay put and keep an eye on Sister Stephen from the window." The long elegant sash window next to the bed looked out onto a carefully nurtured garden bursting with colourful flora. "I'm sure she will be up to see you after morning prayers for her usual chat."

And making sure her charge was as comfortable as possible she took the dirty linen and caught up with Mother Mary Joseph as they made their way to the laundry.

"How was Nellie this morning?" The older nun enquired.

"Not one word of complaint, but I think she is really starting to notice the pain."

"We'll ask Dr Goodier to have another look at her when he calls in; see if he can increase her medication. There's no sense in her suffering."

As they walked across the cobbled courtyard the weak winter sun directed a warm glow across the gap. Instinctively, like flowers, they lifted their heads to feel the sun on their faces. Sister Benedict remarked:

"At least it's a nice day for Annie's funeral. She would have liked that."

Both their thoughts roamed back six months when Annie, a wiry framed woman, had been brought into their care at the convent by Dr Goodier. "She's nowhere else to go, and she hasn't got any family." He explained. "What else could I do? She can't look after herself and she needs proper attention. Social services are offering to do meals on wheels once a day and to arrange for a community nurse to pop in, but she needs more than that."

Annie had been a quiet dignified patient; her lack of complaint although her body was riddled with cancer obviously came from a life time of rigid self-control. It was only right at the end when her medication had caused her to be only partially conscious that the self-control had slipped.

"Where's my baby?" She had cried out. "I can't find my baby boy. Where is he? Why have you taken him?" Her voice pitiful with desperation. And as she had thrust about in her bed the two nuns had taken turns to try and calm her so that she would be able to succumb to a peaceful sleep.

"I wonder if she lost a baby?" mused Sister Benedict reflecting on the woman's heart felt cries.
"That would probably explain it," Agreed Mother Mary Joseph as they watched the sleeping body of the now silent woman, her life slowly slipping away like mist disappearing at dawn; recognising Annie was probably now at peace with the world.

The chapel bell began to chime, interrupting the talk of funeral arrangements.
"Oops we'd better hurry." Mother Mary Joseph said gathering the hem of her habit so that she could walk a little quicker without tripping over it. "We don't want to be late for morning prayers." And the two figures hurried off into the distance; two retreating specks whose wimples were being tugged playfully by the spring breeze.

Josie's flat was in the East End of London. It was a warehouse in the middle of the shipping district, with views over the Thames and across to Southwark. In a previous life the building had been a warehouse, used by an East Indies merchant to import and store large bolts of silk from the exotic Far East. Over the years it had fallen into disrepair, gone was the busy hustle and bustle of the merchant's company and the oriental sailors tripping in and out of the building, along the quay side and milling around the pub at the opposite end of the street sliding away, leaving behind an air of destitution. The trade people were replaced with down-and-outs seeking protection from the elements and pigeons roosting in the rafters and broken windows. Then the regeneration of the East End began, and property developers with a weathered speculative eye on the market developed the area and where once there had been poverty, it had been replaced with expensive professional executive flats.
"Left or right?" Neil stood in Josie's doorway; he'd obviously come straight from the office as he was still in his Italian linen suit, creased from the day's business.
"Left." Josie said smiling.
"What a good choice." Neil complimented her as he produced a bottle of red Shiraz from behind his back.

"And if I had said right?" He drew out his other hand showing the brown paper bag from a Chinese takeaway.
"I took a chance that you hadn't eaten and so I went via Chinese Charlie's. I've no idea what you like, so I just got loads of everything."
"Wonderful – come in," she led him into the kitchen. "I keep forgetting about food at the moment." Neil watched her as she walked about, busily pulling dinner bowls out. She had always had a feminine figure, with a little roundness in all the right places; but this new Josie had a latent sexuality where the other had a naivety. The slender figure was lithe, moving like a new born gazelle, unused to the new body. She handed him a corkscrew and let him do the honours as she continued to hunt round for two matching glasses. She and Nick had never been particularly organised, often breaking things, so that what they were left with were a mis-match of survivors and hand-me-downs. Selecting two out of the cupboard that seemed vaguely similar she watched as Neil deftly poured the ruby red wine.
"If you can take these through to the sitting room, I'll bring the food." She carried on searching for matching dinner bowls, chopsticks and a dried up bottle of what the label proclaimed to be soy sauce. "Considering we used to live on take-aways I'm surprised I can't find everything." She apologised through the archway; before appearing a couple of minutes later bearing their feast.
"I thought we could eat in here and then go through the paperwork if you're still up to helping me with it. I've been going through everything, but nothing is in any order, and I can't make any sense of it."
"Well let's eat and then we'll get down to business."
They settled down on the floor around the coffee table, amicably tucking into the delicious myriad of oriental dishes; the tangy chilli beef, the succulent cashew chicken and the piquant texture of the Peking Duck. Neil envisaged how it must look to an outsider, perching on floor cushions, feeding each other with morsels, pointing at each other with their chop sticks to reinforce a point as they chatted. He thought of Claudia and how she would have insisted on sitting formally at the table, not that they ever bought a take away, and he'd never have been allowed to sort out papers in the sitting room. "Darling you just never know who might pop

round." Which was true. The constant stream of friends and callers sometimes drove Neil to distraction. Occasionally all he wanted to do after work was to veg out in front of the TV with a beer. As though reading his thoughts Josie asked "How is Claudia?"

"She's fine – just starting a new job actually as editor of Bling and Boudoir." Claudia was a polished journalist with burnished copper hair and titanium for a backbone. Josie always felt inadequate when she was in Claudia's company, not helped by being 4" shorter and 5" wider.

"Goodness sounds very impressive."

"Well you know Claudia – she does impressive better than most."

"So will I be able to get a free copy now, I love reading it? She'll get to meet Lawrence Llewyeln-dooda, he's always being featured."

"Is he the one who is always talking about houses made out of straw bales?"

"Nah – that's the other one."

Although Josie didn't eat much, she savoured each mouthful, filling up in record time. Looking at the table still bearing half the dinner she felt a pang of remorse, but she couldn't eat another bite. He topped up both their glasses and then pointing to the snow storm of papers that lay scattered round the floor and suggested "Perhaps we had better make a start on these."

"Good thinking." Josie scrambled to her feet, standing up suddenly feeling a little light headed. She took another gulp of wine before very slightly swaying towards the largest pile in the middle. "These are all our bank statements; and then over there are the visa bills, behind me is everything to do with the flat, anything else I shoved over there, and this," she bent down to pick up a solitary piece of paper, steadying herself as she did so "is Nick's will." She brandished it at him like some kind of Medieval Ages amulet.

"Thank god he's got a will." Neil thought relieved. "At least that means he's got something worthwhile to leave her." And taking it from Josie he went to read it; puzzled he turned it over then returned to the front again. "But it's blank." He was perplexed.

"I know – he never believed he would die." She gave a small sniffle as she felt the onslaught of tears again. "Sorry," she apologised. "I keep crying over everything."

"Now why don't you sit down there." He propelled her to the nearest sofa and handed her a refilled glass of wine. "And I'll take a quick look at these." And grabbing the first pile of paper began to try and make sense of the jumbled numbers Nick had left behind, never expecting them to be seen by strangers. The time wore on, and he continued to labour over the piles, jotting down numbers on a pad and cross-checking the figures. The sounds out on the street below began to die away as the roads became deserted, and Neil continued to study the piles, trying to understand just how badly off Nick had left Josie.

Josie was only faintly aware of the dull ache in her crooked neck; the deep thudding inside her head precluded anything else. Her cheek felt numb against the arm of the sofa, and her skin had the imprint of the herringbone pattern of the fabric. Slowly she prised open her eyes and then shut them suddenly as the sunlight bore into them with an intensity so extreme a thousand lights bounced around inside her brain. Gingerly she tried sitting up, trying to recollect last night. The telephone ring screeched into her thoughts; with a good deal of effort she leant across and picked up the receiver.
"'Orning." Even her voice box had become gummed up in the night.
"Josie?" Tara questioned not recognising the voice. "Is that you?"
"I think so, but I can't be certain at the moment."
"What's wrong, you sound awful?"
"Humiliation, hangover and headache, and not necessarily in that order."
"Goodness – why the humiliation?"
"I slept with Neil." There was a total silence at the end of line, making Josie wonder if Tara had hung up until she heard the sound of something being dropped and breaking on the floor and a smothered 'bugger'.
"You did what?" Tara asked in amazement.
"Neil came round last night to help me look at some paperwork, and he bought round some food and wine. Anyway I proceeded to drink almost the whole bottle by myself as he waded through the figures."
"Mmm very kind of him – now tell me the details." Tara said eager for an update on the gossip.
"Well I can't remember much; but I have a hazy recollection of lecturing him that it was about time he got married, then weeping on his shoulder before passing out as he tried to explain my finances to me."
"Ohh." The disappointment at the lack of scandal bubbled momentarily to the surface before consideration for her friend

returned swiftly. "Well at least you didn't do anything you really regretted."
"I know." Agreed Josie, but that's small comfort she thought when last night I would have been happy to do something without any regrets. "But what should I do now?"
"From the sound of you have a strong black coffee and lengthy shower."
"No I mean with Neil."
"Just give him a call and say you're sorry. He must have seen you drunk before."
"Never." Josie said primly. "I was always very well behaved at Nick's work parties."
"Well I've seen you at your worst, and I've never known you to do anything too outrageous."
"Thanks for the vote of confidence, but I feel too embarrassed to speak to him." In fact embarrassed was the understatement of the decade; it was positively toe-curlingly awful just thinking about getting drunk in front of your dead husband's boss.
"Do you want me to come round; I can cancel my tennis lesson if you want."
"No I'm fine." Goodness was this going to become her catchphrase?
"I'll call you tomorrow." Saying goodbye she put the phone down and surveyed the neatly arranged piles of paper and the coffee table, cleared of last night's dining debris. Puzzled she walked into the kitchen and switching on the kettle (she definitely needed an extra strong caffeine intake) she noticed the clean dishes carefully stacked by the sink. On top in bold elaborate handwriting Neil had left a note "Don't know where these live. Give me a call." The fact he had been thoughtful as well as helpful just made things worst; she sipped her coffee and tried to think what she should do.

"You filled out that accident report yet Bill?" A rotund figure asked as he flicked through various files.
"It should be over there with the others." The younger policeman indicated to the ageing filing tray which was right in front of the older chap. "Don't tell me you've forgotten your glasses again Jimmy?"
"Less of that cheek – if they didn't keep changing these forms I wouldn't have no trouble finding them." He huffed to himself. "Never joined to be a pen pusher, wanted to catch the criminals and

keep the streets safe. Instead I'm stuck in here filling everything out in triplicate."

"It weren't like this in the old days." Bill said under his breath as he carried on working.

"It weren't like this in the old days;" Jimmy continued caught up in his old rhetoric. "Look at this for an example." He dangled one of the traffic reports between his pudgy forefinger and thumb. "Young lad driving along the Forster Way, no other traffic around and he still manages to hit a tree."

"What was that?" Bill asked having phased out the conversation until the words "Forster Way" caught his attention.

"Don't you youngsters listen? I was talking about how someone can hit a tree when there's nothing about." Bill took the report and read it through; somehow it seemed familiar. Flicking through his thoughts he recalled visiting Josie to break the news. She had been the curvy blonde wife, or rather widow, who had listened quietly as he had outlined the incident of the previous evening and explained the need for her to do a formal identification of the body. He read the report from the officer at the scene.

"The driver was heading due west along the Forster Way. There was no indication of any other traffic in either direction."

Wait a minute – that hadn't been the message he'd been given; he remembered the constable who had called him to speak to the widow saying: "Car was involved in a traffic accident; terrible crash; no-one survived. Visibility awful. Call came in to us from the scene." He read on. "There had been heavy rain all evening and there were several large pools of water lying on the road. Visibility must have been severely limited. It appears the driver, unfamiliar with the lane, had either hit a pool of water or swerved to avoid something, causing him to crash into a tree on the opposite side of the road head on. The crash occurred before the Drayton Beauchamp turning by the telegraph pole. The driver died instantly."

For some reason Bill felt a chill run through him; surely it wouldn't matter that the facts had become a little muddled, nothing could bring that woman's husband back. Hastily he shoved the form back into Jimmy's hovering hand and abruptly walked out leaving Jimmy, for once, speechless.

"How much do you owe this time?" Henry asked.

"Hundred and fifty."

Henry shook his head in disbelief as long as he'd known his cousin, Adam had always been in hock for something.

"I take it you actually mean 'one hundred and fifty thousand'?" He asked trying to emphasis the vastness of the gambling debt but knowing that Adam would never succumb to any shame. 'It's what I do' he would say when he had first started to confide in Henry when the debts were a bit larger than usual. 'Some people work, some people drink, I enjoy a flutter.'

Although to give Adam his due he did look a little uncomfortable at the sum. The problem with Adam was he had been born too good-looking. Men and women alike seemed attracted to his sun god looks and devil-may-care attitude, while other people would move about a room Adam would fill the space with a radiance that acted like a magnet. So far he had actually avoided any real discomfort in settling his debts; he had always got another godmother or ancient aunt to help him out 'just until I get myself sorted' he would say with a laugh and a kiss on the cheek, determined to keep his word, until the lure of the cards would tempt him once again.

They were sitting in Henry's living room after dinner sipping a rather fine example of Glenmorangie. Their feet were stretched out towards the glowing fire as they lounged in their leather club chairs just as their fathers had companionably done before them.

"Any plans?" Henry enquired tentatively.

"Not a bean of an idea." Adam said cheerfully.

"What did you gamble on to lose so much? It's fairly steep even by your standards." Adam looked at his cousin during the accusation but decided to rise above it.

"I was meeting a couple of chums in town for a spot of dinner when I came across a charming fellow – turned out he shared the same turf accountant, before he was imprisoned for fraud, anyway he was saying that he knew that there was a small card game on at his club and did I want to go. Well I thought it would be awfully rude of me not to go; so we went."

Henry could see it happening; like a child being offered the keys to Hamleys.

"Well I've never been much good at poker, but I kept thinking my luck would change. Trouble is it didn't."
"So you ended up blowing a hundred and fifty K." He gave a low whistle. "And what happens if you can't pay?"
"A gentleman always pays." Adam said haughtily. "Besides which he threatened to shoot me with a Perdy next pheasant season if I didn't."

As he lay awake Henry tried to decide whether it was the second ill-advised whiskey; Adam's debts, for which illogically Henry felt responsible for; or the lumpy bed that was keeping him awake. True it was the very bed both his mother and her mother had given birth in; but sometimes family heirlooms weren't all they were cracked up to be. Wriggling around in a desperate attempt to get comfortable his thoughts returned to Adam. Although they were cousins they'd been so close in age to almost be twin brothers, not that they were alike, like their fathers before them they were the Roman Twins Romulus and Remus – one was steady and sensible whilst the other was a free spirit. Uncle Alex had been a wine and woman type of man, marrying Lady Jane De Vomty and proceeded to spend both her money and his on bottles of vintage Bollinger and expensive trinkets for the latest infatuation. Bizarrely Lady Jane had never seemed to mind his misdemeanours. "Well those poor women aren't one of us darling." He'd overheard her telling his mother "And what else do the poor dears have in their dull little lives? Besides he always buys me the most exquisite jewellery to say sorry." It was true Lady Jane's collection had been infamous throughout the county, she had known how to bling with class. What a pity Adam had pawned it over the years to settle his debts.
They had been a very different couple to his own parents. His father, being a younger son, had always known that his only inheritance would be an outdated title and a dubious Gainsborough, the rest was tied up in ancient trusts for the first born. So he had studied law and set up as a country solicitor back in the village, where he met his wife at a local Conservative function, and invested his money into bricks and mortar; leaving Henry with a mortgage free house and a strict self-discipline on saving. Some may think his life had in fact become a re-run of his father's; as he'd gone to university to study law. He had stayed on in London after he'd qualified working in chambers while he enjoyed carefree salad

days. It was only after his parents' deaths that he had decided to make the change, taking over his father's practice and golf membership, whilst studiously avoiding the other duties of local conservatives fund raising and reading the lesson at church. He may be following in his father's footsteps but he wasn't quite ready to step into his slippers.

As he viewed the early glow of the dawn Henry gave up all hope of getting much sleep. Slipping out of bed he quickly pulled on a pair of worn Levis and a thick Guernsey sweater to keep out the chill and whistling to himself went downstairs. As he walked into the kitchen a pair of chocolate drop eyes looked up in surprise, stiffly the old Labrador made her way out of her basket and over to her master silently wishing for an early morning stroll. He stooped down to pat her. "Fancy a quick walk old thing?" He enquired lifting the latch on the back door and they stepped out into the cold crisp dawn.

They walked across frosted fields, their feet leaving fairy trails behind them, the man's staying straight never deviating. the hound's rushing from one side to another as exciting new smells were discovered. The quiet enveloped the pair in an amicable silence each wrapped up in their own thoughts. Their breath hung heavily in the air, puffs of wispy cotton that lingered momentarily before dissolving away. On and on they tramped, walking in a large circle so that as the new sun rose higher in the sky the warmth moved position around their body warming as it circled round.

As they reached home the sun was peeking over the top of the roof between the chimneys, casting a warm glow on the golden stone so that it seemed infused with a terracotta wash. The house never failed to lift Henry's spirits, its graceful Georgian symmetry combined with the long elegant windows gave it a welcoming benevolent personality. Heading round to the back, past the old stable block that now housed an ancient Mercedes estate they re-entered the house ready for a hearty breakfast. For a man living alone Henry could conjure up a mean breakfast. It was the only cooking he had ever really mastered, and so he took great pride in perfecting the talent. As he settled in to his poached eggs, bacon and mushrooms (well, it was a workday) he contemplated the rest of the day wondering what it would hold.

As it turned out it was a fairly average day; two clients enquired about divorce handlings (luckily unrelated), one of his father's old clients made an appointment on behalf of her daughter and he was asked to draw up a will for an elderly lady. Nothing unusual, but then again when did a country solicitor ever get involved in anything unusual?

Chapter 2

Marylebone High Street was buzzing, everywhere Josie looked there were people living out their every day lives in front of her. Yummy Mummys wielded designer prams as the must-have accessory of the season. Love struck couples mooched along gazing at the flats in the letting agents' windows dreaming longingly of places of their own. Older couples pottered along enjoying the time out, reminiscing about other days out in other high streets. Students on their way to lectures juggled conversations on their mobiles while ordering grande lattes to go, and in the midst Josie walked along almost as an ethereal spirit who wasn't part of this world but merely a spectator.

For the first time in her life Josie had felt a small concern over her future. It wasn't something she'd ever had to worry about before, after university she found her history of art degree didn't really provide any real support to her career. In fact she had taken a job in a small design agency as a temporary fill in. That had somehow stretched out for five years when she and Nick had got married and then learnt that there was a risk of redundancy. Neither of them minded – they had been planning to have a family, so why wait? And so Josie had settled down to becoming a housewife and looked forward to having to decorate a nursery.

When Josie had left university and realised that she had no obvious job skills, little money and even less career direction she hadn't been worried. In true youthful style she had believed something would turn up, which it had. Now that she had been catapulted back into the same scenario it felt curiously depressing. Although it was a familiar situation the fact she was eight years older with nothing really to show for that time seemed to sap her energy. It was as though a blanket of lethargy had been thrown over her and she couldn't see out beyond it. Her unconscious meanderings came to a halt and looking round her she smiled recognising an old favourite haunt. Her eyes greedily ran over the tempting cascades of colour that shone and sparkled in the window. Coils of luscious ribbon lay carefully intertwined, offset with voluptuous pouting silk roses. Pushing open the door she stepped inside the Aladdin's cave of VV Rouleaux, pausing momentarily to drink in the inviting textures and

hues. Slowly she walked around the showroom, running her finger along the silky lengths of satin ribbons, through the crystal beaded fringes and across the feathery boas. The choice and the amount bombarded her senses and her mind immediately flew to what she could do with the turquoise ribbon and where she could put the stiff fabric lilies. On impulse she picked up two rolls of pink ribbon, one plain satin and the other a small gingham, and several silver butterflies whose gauze wings rippled stiffly in the breeze. She took them over to the old wooden counter to pay, queuing behind two well heeled ladies who were obviously up from the Home Counties for the day. "What on earth are you going to do with that?" she heard one of them ask as her friend took ten metres of leopard skin ribbon. "Thought I might use it instead of name tags on Charlie's underwear; she'd be far too embarrassed that way to ever take it off in front of anyone." They laughed obviously at the shared joke as they made their way out of the shop.
"Can I help you Madam?" The tiny Vietnamese shop assistant stood demurely peeking above the till.
"Two metres of these two and the butterflies please."
"Oh how gorgeous – they're one of our best sellers this season. What are you planning to use them for?" And suddenly Josie's imagination broke free from the grey shackles of depression and fired up out of its cage. Ideas tumbled out, cascading over each other in an attempt to get a poll position. Creations flitted in front of her eyes as combinations came together only to be replaced by other even more exotic concoctions.
"I have to admit I'm not sure yet." She said and clutching her ruby red bag she walked back purposefully out into the street.

Now it was deciding what to do with them; her mind was still in overdrive as she pictured ornate hair adornments, accessorising her jeans or creating a stylish window adornment. The trouble was everything seemed a little too extreme; what she wanted was something she could actually use and enjoy – so that it felt there was a purpose to making it. Suddenly inspiration struck and she turned abruptly on her heel, narrowly missing an elderly couple whose reminiscing had turned nasty when they didn't remember the same way. Dashing across the bus stop she jumped onto the 89 and climbing up to the top level watched the passing buildings as the bus trundled its way down to Sloane Square.

Jumping off at the King's Road Josie marvelled at the differences in the microcosms London held within its streets. Here the passers-by had a more urbane look, influenced no doubt by the surrounding galleries, art houses and design boutiques. Carefully crossing the road she began to walk past Habitat and The Pier each one trying to entice her in. She carried on until she reached the imposing double doors of Peter Jones. As she pushed them open she couldn't help but think of her mother who truly believed there was a heaven on earth; and that sat fairly and squarely within the Sloane Square store. She took the escalator up to the first floor to the haberdashery department, the neat rolls of fabric lay fanned across the counters; presenting themselves like appetising petit fours on a plate. This time though there was no casual glancing or longing caresses. Josie strode purposefully past the florals and checks ignoring the linens and damasks. Her eye had already spotted exactly what she was looking for. As she stood in front of the shimmering silks and silky satins she pulled out a roll of silver taffeta, shot through with a cerise pink thread, so that as she held the fabric up to the light it changed colour from silver to pink. Carrying the unwieldy roll up to the cash desk her mind was already formulating the final designs.
"Is that everything Madam?" the sales lady asked politely after she had cut the fabric from the roll and carefully folded it into a small square.
"Yes I think so." Suddenly the designs ran swiftly through her thoughts. "Oh no... I'm going to need thread and needles and ...." She ground to a halt. "I'm not sure what I need actually." The older lady smiled "How about you tell me what you are planning to do with this, and I'll see if I can help?"
"That would be perfect." Josie sighed in relief and she started to sketch out her idea. Half an hour later they had discussed the advantages of hand stitching versus machine stitching and cotton thread over nylon. Walking out of the store with a goody bag of items all carefully chosen with the help of the sales lady who guided Josie past the expensive mistakes and towards the tools of the trade.

Once again, clutching her prized bags, Josie was out on the street. Turning towards the bus stop she started to walk back down the King's Road when a vacant taxi caught her eye. Impulsively waving a hand full of bags and catching his attention she jumped in the back; there was no time to lose.

Josie wasn't sure what time it was when the doorbell rang. Several hours ago she had to turn on the lights as the wintry dusk had fallen. Walking absent mindedly to the door she picked at the small bits of cotton and fabric that clung to the soft fabric of her blue shirt and jeans. How could something so iniquitous as fabric shed so much fluff? Rubbing her forefingers and thumbs together she felt a small layer of glue furl up leaving the skin feel adhesive and sticky. She rubbed her hand down the front of her jeans trying to rid the sensation and opened the door.
"Hi Josie."
"Neil!" Her cheeks scorched scarlet as she saw him lounging against her door frame and her thoughts panicked at how she should respond. She had managed to avoid calling him by blanking out the embarrassing episode. Now she had to deal with it.
"Look no wine." He held up both hands, showing his palms calloused from all of the sailing.
"Oh please;" she began "I feel awful enough as it is."
"I thought you might do when you didn't return any of my calls. But honestly you don't need to. You didn't do anything to feel embarrassed about. I decided that if we were ever to speak to each other again I would have to do the running, and make the effort to track you down."
"That's very kind of you – I think it was the combination of an empty stomach and a broken heart. Anyway come in if you have time. I warn you now that I don't have anything to drink other than tea or coffee. I've taken a vow of absolute abstinence – well until the next time I get offered a glass of Chablis."
"Coffee sounds good." He followed her through to the kitchen and watched as she put the kettle on and reached up into one of the wall cupboards for the cafetiere.
"Can you grab the milk? The fridge is just behind you." She put her hands on his hips as she squeezed past his bending figure to get to the coffee cups. Her face flushed again as another bolt of electricity shot up her arms at the contact with his body. She waited until he was standing back upright and squeezed back past trying not to touch any part of his body, ignoring the smile on his face at her obvious discomfort.

"Milk." He held out the small plastic carton. Stiffly she put everything onto the tray and plunged the top of the cafetiere down forcing the coffee grouts to the bottom of the glass jug.

"Let's go through to the sitting room, there's more space there." Josie suggested lifting the tray and leading the way giving Neil the opportunity to appreciate a glimpse of bare flesh where her jeans, now too big, had slipped down to sit on her hips, leaving an inch of skin between the bottom of the shirt and the top of the jeans.

"This looks a little tidier since I was last here." Neil commented as he sat down of the large squashy sofa; Josie sat down on its twin, trying to keep as much space between them as possible. "What's happened to your new look of the paper piles? I thought you might have started a trend there. I know quite a few students and bachelor pads that would have taken it up."

"Tracey Emin may be able to get people to pay for that look, but I don't think anyone is interested in distinctly mono-coloured red bank statements."

"Ahh but you could have used them as evidence to sue the government for the subversive capitalist machine their democracy has created which had exploited your retail weakness; thus making you a victim of our morally corrupt society."

Josie stared at him "I think you lost me on about the second word."

"So what are you really going to do with them?"

"Well I've hidden them in the cupboard for the time being." Josie admitted. "The more I tried to understand them, the more confused I got. When we should have had some over at the end of the month we didn't – instead we seem to have got in the red even more."

"Do you want me to talk you through where I think you are financially?"

"Goodness that sounds very professional; next you'll be telling me shares can go up as well as down." She paused. "Sorry. I didn't mean to be rude. It's just deep down I want to be an ostrich and not have to do anything about it and hope it will all go away. I'm dreading hearing just how bad it is, because then it will be real, and I can't pretend nothing's wrong then."

"Well don't be too down; nothing is ever that bad." He drew a wad of paper out of his jacket pocket. "Now I reckon you are about £3,000 overdrawn on your current account; I couldn't find anything on a savings account."

"There isn't one, we never had enough to need one I'm afraid."

"Well your outgoings are about £1100 on rent for the flat, £200 on your council tax, then about £150 on your utilities." He read out from his list. "So that's approximately £1500 before you add in food and other bits. So if you're not careful by the end of three months with no job you'll be up to £11000 in debt."

Josie felt a fine sweat break out on her brow at the same time as a tidal wave of nausea hit her diaphragm; she clutched her hands together so whitely that the knuckles stood starkly white against the backdrop of denim in her lap.

""Then you've got the £10,000 loan Nick borrowed from the company."

"So where has the money gone?" Josie demanded.

"I've no idea." Neil confessed. "I searched through all the paperwork and bank records and I can't find any specific mention, I think it was probably spent on just keeping you day-to-day, it doesn't look as though anything is left."

Josie thought guiltily of her wardrobe, and her constant retail trips. Since giving up work she had become increasingly bored and had taken to popping out to the shops for some window shopping. This inevitably ended up with her bringing home several bags of purchases that had caught her eye. She berated herself – why hadn't she questioned where the money was coming from, she should have realised that they could never have afforded the lifestyle on only Nick's income. But that had been the story of her life. She had never given a consideration as to where money had come from, she had never had to. If she was in trouble there was always someone to turn to, either her parents, her current boyfriend or later on Nick. She had never taken responsibility for her spending; why should she – there was always someone there to pick up the pieces. With a sickening realisation of how shallow her outlook had been she turned here attention back to Neil.

"Unfortunately the loan is repayable to the company immediately on Nick's death; company policy I'm afraid."

"How could he do this to me!" The fear had turned to indignation. "How dare he die and leave me to sort all this out." She realised what she was saying was ridiculous but she felt angry and abused.

"In total you owe thirteen thousand pounds," Neil continued unperturbed. "But it will creep up to over twenty thousand if you're not careful."

"Twenty thousand! But I haven't even got an income. What hope have I got of paying it back?" The anger rang out resonantly in her voice. "It's not even as though I can ask anyone to lend it to me – I'm not exactly a solid investment." By this time she had propelled herself up from the sofa and was pacing up and down the cherry wood floor her socks making a soft pthud pthud at each stride.

"That's the debt." Nick continued to consult his list. "Now you do have Nick's life cover."

Josie stopped pacing. "What's that?"

"His death-in-service payment. I told you about when you visited the office if you remember."

"Did you?" She sounded vague "I don't remember. What is it – more money that I owe?"

"Au contraire Mrs Pessimist. It's the company scheme for insuring our employees' lives, so that if something happens their nearest and dearest aren't thrown out onto the streets blaming Miller & Moss for destroying their lives."

"How considerate." Her voice had a hard edge to it, the sarcasm spilled through like acid. He put his hand out and caught her arm, forcing her to sit next down next to him.

"Josie, I know nothing can bring Nick back, but at least this way you're not left with huge debts and no means of being able to survive the next three months without making the situation worse."

She contemplated this and finally said. "I suppose so. So how much is it?" She furtively crossed her fingers and hoped that it would at least cover some of the debt. Maybe her mother would be able to lend her the rest, just till she got herself sorted; but then who was she trying to kid? How was she ever going to get her life sorted out.

"It's three times Nick's salary; so it's sixty six thousand."

"Sixty six thousand!" she gave a low whistle, she had never owned so much money. "Sixty six thousand." She repeated it softly stunned at the amount. "Sixty six thousand." Her voice had became dreamy as she imagined just how much retail therapy that would cover; she would be able to buy that little black dress in Joseph she had had her eye on all season, and she would be able to get Jimmy Choos to match the two Channel outfits she had seen in this month's Vogue.

"Minus your debt." Neil's voice sliced through her thoughts forcing the vision of herself walking out of Harvey Nicks laden with bags and parcels out of her mind.

"Oh yes those debts." She said dismissively.

"Yes those debts." Neil's voice was stern, forcing her attention to stay focused on sorting her finances out.

"Well by the time I have paid off the bank overdraft, the loan, the rent..." she was ticking them off one-by-one on her fingers "and general running costs, that would leave..." Her brow furrowed as she pondered on the mathematical conundrum. "That would leave..." but the answer still eluded her. "How much would that leave?" She finally asked conceding defeat.

"By the end of this month you will have about fifty thousand pounds."

Josie brightened again, fifty thousand - that was still a lot of retail therapy; perhaps things weren't going to be too bad.

"But you have to remember that if you're not earning then that would only last about a year and a half. Maybe two if you were careful." Neil reminded her like a chastising parent. Once again the glistening image of Harvey Nicks was dispelled by a cold shower of reality. The feeling of euphoria had instantly deserted her at the mention of being destitute again. She looked up at his face, her eyes trusting and sad pulling at his conscience.

"What do I do then?"

"Are you asking for my advice?" Neil asked with wry amusement, thinking of the times Claudia had argued with him as he spent yet more money on his 'rust bucket of a boat' her words not his. He couldn't find the exact words to describe the beautiful sleek lines of his racing yacht.

"I'm not sure who else to ask." She admitted. "I don't think my mother or my sister would know, and Tara has literally no idea where her credit card bills go, she still believes in an all year round Father Christmas."

"I'm really not the best person – because I'd probably blow it on a new set of sails. But if you were going to be sensible then maybe you need to start thinking about getting a job to help pay your monthly bills and saving the rest for a rainy day such as buying a flat."

"But what would I do?" It was a rhetorical question that had reverberated around her mind for the past two weeks. "I really don't have any skills. I could try and go back to being an office assistant, but they all want quick typing skills, shorthand and at least

a passing acquaintance with computers. None of which I have, At which point I get stuck. I can't think of anything else I could do."
"Something will come up." He assured her. "I'll ask around if you want, see if anyone knows of anything." She smiled a weary smile at him.
"That's kind of you."
"Not at all;" he glanced at his watch. "I'd better get going. Claudia's invited some of her new colleagues round for drinks tonight so I'll have to be there on parade." He added bitterly.
"Sounds fun." Josie sympathised as they stood up and walked to the front door. "Neil." He turned back and quickly she kissed him on the cheek. "Thank you for all your help. I'm sorry that I'm being so pathetic at the moment."
"You're not." He assured her and raising his hand up to her hair he gently removed a small fragment of ribbon. "I've spent the whole evening wondering whether it was the latest thing in hair fashion."
"Oh! Don't ask! It's a long story." She said as his departing figure chuckled to himself as he walked down the stairs.

Claudia had been surprised by Neil's cheery acceptance of another two guests arriving for drinks. Far from retreating into his normal polite but distant persona he'd actually said "Fine it'll be good to meet Teddy and Babs" before presenting her with a beautiful bouquet of flowers he'd picked up en route from Josie's. Plus he had changed into her favourite shirt and was now happily putting two bottles of his cherished Pouilly Fume into the fridge. If this wasn't a good omen then what was? Only this morning, when she had visited her psychic to find out what the heavens held, she had been told that a monumentuous occurrence was due when Saturn passed through the moon of Jupiter, which happened to be tonight. After years of anguished conversations with married girlfriends all the signs looked like Neil was gearing up to pop the question. Her mind began to wander as she weighed up the possibility of a sun kissed beach wedding (except too much sand was never romantic) versus a Las Vegas special (too tacky and so last year). Of course there was always a romantic dusk ceremony in an Italian monastery high up in the Umbrian hills. Hello may even want to photograph it, well her magazine would never cough up for her wedding photos; she'd have to get Hello to agree to say publicly that they had secretly photographed the loving event, but if she knocked 10% off the fee she was positive they'd never quibble.

She spent the whole evening being the perfect wife-to-be. Taking an interest in Neil's conversations, laughing at all his jokes and looking meaningfully into his eyes when ever the opportunity arose. She was the life of the party, keeping her colleagues entertained with jovial stories and witty little ripostes which showed that she and Neil were a real couple. When the men had trooped off to inspect Teddy's new car, Claudia, Babs and Lucy had stayed in the kitchen admiring the brand new Gaggenia coffee maker that looked as though it would be more at home in an Italian coffee shop.

"You'll have to excuse Teddy for dragging them off like that." Babs apologised "But this car is his new big love, and its far more effective than HRT or bromide for the male menopause."

"You and Neil seem to be getting on well." Lucy commented recalling some of the screaming matches she had overhead at the office. Buoyed up with her news Claudia couldn't keep quiet.

"I think it's that time." She blurted out, her face split by a huge frightening grin.

"What time?" Lucy looked blank.

"You know that time in a relationship when you stop being just a couple and become an 'item'." She stressed the word item and continued to grin innately.

"What?" Lucy continued to look blank, obviously aware she was missing something but unable to work out what it was.

"She's talking about marriage." Babs hurriedly explained, worried the whole evening would be spent on the intrigue and not on the gossip.

"Oh you're getting engaged – has Neil proposed then?"

"Well not actually proposed, but I can just tell he's going to. When you've been together for as long as we have you can just sort of sense these things."

Not wanting facts to get in the way of a good gossip they started to embroider Claudia's suspicions.

"So when do think you'll get married?"

"Well I don't want a long engagement so it would probably be in the summer. It would need to be between printing dates, so that means the second week of the month."

"How lovely, summer weddings are always the best. Where do you think you'll go on honeymoon?"

"May be a safari in Kenya, or go diving in the Maldives. Haven't decided yet. Conde Nast did a really good article on this tiny island off the Maldives where you get your own personal servants and all the meals are carb-free so you don't put an ounce of weight on when you're there."

"It's so exciting! I remember my honeymoon – did I ever tell you about the time Teddy took me out on the boat…" Lucy and Claudia exchange a look with raised eyebrows – how often had they sat through the story in the office.

"Yes, yes. And he presented you with an oyster shell and it had pearl earnings in it." finished off Claudia; goodness didn't people know when to concentrate solely on her wedding plans. "I'm sure Neil will do something equally romantic when he proposes."

"How do you think Neil will do it; down on one knee?"

"Or go all traditional and ask your father for your hand?"

"I don't know, maybe he'll whisk me away to Paris and propose at the top of the Eiffel Tower. That would be so romantic." They paused as they pictured the scene; each mutually appreciating the thought of romance, of Paris and of the gorgeous French men. Their meditations were interrupted as the boys reappeared talking about mpgs and the need for tom-toms. Neil noticed three expectant faces looking at him as he walked through the door with another bottle of wine, but couldn't fathom why they were. He racked his brains, he was positive it wasn't Claudia's birthday, or Valentine's day. Was it an anniversary? Did they even celebrate such things – he couldn't remember. He decided to play it safe and go along with it.

"Everything ok darling?" He asked Claudia hoping for some kind of clue.

"Oh yes." She replied sounding slightly breathless which made Neil think she might be coming down with a cold.

"Oh I picked something up from the shops for you today; it's in my briefcase. I'll go and get it, I think you'll find it interesting. Shall I go and get it?"

"Yes!" Claudia said at the same time as Babs and Lucy said "No!" There was a momentary confusion while Lucy and Babs jumped up and grabbed their respective husband's arm.

"I'm sure Neil has things to talk about to Claudia." Lucy said slyly looking across knowingly to Babs and Claudia.

"Yes," Babs agreed. "These young things need their space; not like us old *married* things."

"Good luck" they whispered as they air kissed goodnight and the four of them scuttled out of the apartment. Neil wandered off to his study, noticing that he'd just catch the end of the big match, and came back with a small paper bag containing a box.

"Is there something you were going to ask?" Claudia enquired from where she had propped herself on the sofa in her most beguiling way, designed to enhance his view of her not insubstantial cleavage.

"There is actually." He shook the box out of the paper bag and handed it to Claudia. "Have you ever tried this for colds. It's supposed to work wonders."

"What?" Claudia sat bolt upright, this wasn't supposed to be the question.

"Well I know how run down you get in winter, and so when I heard someone recommend it I thought of you." He leant forward and flicked the remote control to turn on the TV. "Shame they all had to leave so early, but no doubt you girls will catch up tomorrow."

Too right they would, how would she ever live this one down?

"He's looking at you."
"No he's not."
"Yes he is, and he's walking over this way."
"Tara, that's the waiter."
"Oh is it – I could have sworn it was that lovely banker we bumped into."

It was a Thursday night and Tara had decided that what she and Josie both needed was a girls' night out. After all what was a better pick me up than getting all dressed up; downing a disgusting array of unpronounceable cocktails before dancing the night away to your favourite Abba hits.

They had been at the same bar for two hours and had already tried the Moscow Mule, Red Square and the obligatory Harvey Wallbanger. As they tried to focus on the cocktail menu to decide their next concoction a voice behind them discretely coughed and said. "Excuse me."

Turning round in sync they looked up into a pair of dancing green eyes and a cheeky school boy grin, topped off by wiry ginger hair.

"Yes? Can we help you?" Tara asked trying not to slur her words.

"Actually I'm wondering if I could sit at your table. I'm due to meet a friend but he's just phoned, to be sure, to say he's running late. And rather than look like the sad eijit who has been stood up, as I so often am, I wondered whether there was any chance you'd take pity on a poor lost soul and let me sit with you until George arrives." His Irish lilt was entrancing, and before Josie could utter a word Tara had jumped in with.

"Of course, no problem. But it will cost you two TVRs." Robbie looked perplexed.

"What in the name of all things holy is that?"

"They are drinks." Josie explained helpfully pointing to their cocktail glasses. "Tequila, vodka and red bull. They're actually quite nice." She laughed as Robbie looked at them in mock horror.

"Well at least it'll be your hangover tomorrow and not mine." He walked over to the bar which stood three deep and waited until he could catch the attention of a barman.

"Nice bum." Tara said dreamily, her chin resting on her hand as she watched his posterior.

"Tara!" Josie scolded. "You're a respectable married woman. Whatever would Jeremy say if he knew you were discussing another man's derriere."

"Wouldn't notice unless it was couched in terms of stocks, shares or gilts." She gave a peal of laughter at her own joke. "Anyway nothing wrong with the occasional bit of window shopping as long as you know where you're store card lies."

Josie shook her head, giggling away. They watched as Robbie returned balancing two cocktails with a pint of bitter.

"Thank you ehem… sorry what's your name?"

"Robbie." He stuck out his hand. Drunkenly Tara and Josie pumped his arm saying "very nice to meet you" until he managed to stop them.

"So you really do drink this stuff then. Amazing." The Dublin accent was working its charm on the girls again.

"Don't tell me – where you come from women never drink anything except Guinness."

"Too right – all the women in Clapham drink Guinness." He joked.

They chatted on amicably and Josie was surprised at how she was enjoying herself – even though she had switched to drinking water. "I'm getting old." She'd explained to an astonished but happily pickled Tara. "I just can't drink as much."

When George did finally arrive to join his friend, worried about having left Robbie to wait for an hour, he was a little taken back to find him firmly ensconced with two gorgeous women playing bar games.

"Sorry I'm late – but I couldn't get away. It was the client from hell. I've only just managed to escape." Tara pulled out a chair and patted the seat, almost missing it the first time and only just being saved from the indignantly of sliding off her own chair. "Sit down here – it's my round so what would you like."

"Moscow Mule." Josie demanded

"It'll definitely give you a kick." Robbie added and then all three burst into floods of laughter at the shared joke. Feeling like an awkward outsider George hovered uncertainly.

"Sorry, sorry. Earlier joke." Tara soothed. "What about a pint?"

"Sounds good."

She headed off into the throng, winding here way through the crowds oblivious to everyone else as she went on the search for new drinks.

Where Robbie was the eternally cheeky school boy, George was a firmly chiselled statue. His sheer cheekbones and finely defined features gave him almost a Slavic look. He didn't smile much although he did seem to be enjoying himself as the evening wore on and he began to retell his evening's escapades with dealing with irate client. He silently surveyed the rest of the wine bar like a watchful cat, running his eyes over the crowds. However handsome he was, Josie couldn't see him as fanciable; after all there were occasions when you just wanted to be able to curl up on the sofa in your oldest pjs with your boyfriend and watch films. George didn't seem to give out the air of ever slouching and vegging out. He was so carefully turned out that she guessed even his socks were ironed.

Towards the end of the evening a small area at the end of the bar was cleared and music started playing. Obviously catering for the slightly more mature market there was no Limp Bisket or, thankfully, Westlife; instead there was the firm favourite. And as

the opening chord of "Dancing Queen" rang out, women from all over the room turned and, as if by some mystery magical force, raced to the dance floor. Tara was amongst those who had experienced the primeval calling of Sweden's famous foursome.
"Come on!" she hastily beckoned the others. "Come on let's dance." And through a combination of cajoling, threatening and bribing managed to head up the procession onto the dance floor.
Instantly Robbie and Tara lost their inhibitions, well as many as were left after six cocktails, and started to strut their stuff in tandem across the whole of the dance floor. Josie, who had suddenly sobered up, watched George's impassive face as he swayed awkwardly to the music. Hoping it wouldn't be the 12" version, she danced with a much as enthusiasm as she could muster. When finally the last notes of Dancing Queen changed into Waterloo Josie knew it wasn't just the DJ's choice of music that was making her queasy. George obviously noticed as well, as her complexion paled.
"You ok? You look very pale."
"I think I'll sit this one out." She felt a light sheen of sweat appear on her forehead, not a good combination with foundation and blusher, and her stomach lurched ominously. Fleeing to the ladies toilet she fell into an empty cubicle. Her whole body seemed to be shaking and she was sweating profusely. Dimly aware of the comings and goings of others she tried to concentrate on slowing her breathing – anything to take her mind off the nauseous sensations seeping up her stomach. She hadn't drunk that much, so why was she feeling so rough? Ok, so she still wasn't eating properly but there didn't seem to be any reason why it would affect her like this. She heard the main door opening as a hen party loudly made their way out talking about the lack of equipment that the Bob-the-Builder stripper-gram had been blessed with. In any other circumstances it would have been funny. Outside it went quiet before the tip-tip-tip of high heels on the mosaic floor tiles got louder.
"Josie." Tara's voice called out softly as she worked her way along the line of the cubicles. "Josie; are you here?"
Josie weakly opened the door and looked dishevelled and pitifully up into her friend's concerned face.
"I don't feel very well." She mumbled with a rush of self-pity. "I want to go home." Tara put her arm round her friend's shoulders and wiped her smeared mascara away with a piece of toilet roll.

"Come on, I've got Jeremy out of bed and he's waiting to drive us home."

"I'm sorry." Tears pricked behind her eyes. "I didn't mean to spoil the evening. I don't know what's wrong with me."

"Don't worry love; we'll be home in no time and you're staying with us tonight, so you're not alone."

"Thank you." A watery smile floated to the surface, grateful to be going home to bed.

"How do you feel?" Although it was the next day and Josie had slept solidly for nine hours, her complexion still appeared very pale against her tangled dark hair. "Judging by the look of you though not much better. Here take these." Tara handed her two paracetamols and a glass of cool iced water.

"I don't understand why I feel so bad. I can't even pinpoint what's wrong. It's not like a hangover – more like a bad case of flu."

Tara sat down on the end of the bed and contemplated her friend.

"It's not as though we drank that much, I must just be reacting badly to it."

"Well you have lost a lot of weight since…" Her voice tailed off.

"Since Nick's death? You can say it you know. However horrible a fact it is, we can't hide away pretending it isn't happening. Nick has gone, and there is nothing I can do to get him back."

"Perhaps you should see your doctor, just to get yourself checked out."

"May be." Josie said non-committally, never keen to visit the doctor. "Where's Jeremy?" she asked to divert Tara's attention.

"I sent him out with his golf clubs and forbade him from coming home until this evening."

"You didn't!"

"I thought you might like a lazy day here, and the last thing you would want was Jeremy quizzing you over the state of your index-linked finances."

"He'd never do that!" Protested Josie weakly.

"Mmm maybe not but this way he gets to enjoy his golf without me feeling guilty about getting him out last night."

"Was he very angry?"

"Have you ever known Jeremy to do angry? No as usual he was his cool, calm self, although I nearly had to put the phone down on him when he started to do a financial comparison between ordering a taxi and collecting us himself."

"He didn't!"

"Well perhaps he didn't actually say it, but I could tell the thoughts were actually going through his mind. Anyway what shall we do today?"

"I wouldn't mind getting some clothes from my place. I don't think I can wear those." She indicated the discarded sequinned top and floaty chiffon skirt and tendonitis inducing sandals.

"Let's go over to your place and get you some clothes, then we can wander round the high street boutiques before having a bite to eat and coming back here to watch some chick flick." Tara climbed off the bed and patted down her chinos. "I'll just go and get ready to go out while you get up. Now there's loads of hot water so take a long shower and when you're ready we'll go out." Josie watched her friend walk out and smiled, Tara was the only person Josie knew who would routinely change her clothes three times a day, and put lipstick on just to collect the post from the front mat.

"Home sweet home." Josie said dryly as she put the key in the door and let them both in. "Would you be a dear and make some coffee while I get ready?"

"Have we got time for ground?"

"No! Afraid you're having to slum it with instant today." Josie heard the tutting follow her as she went into her dressing room. Having selected here old favourites of black bootleg Levis and a cerise pink polo shirt she wandered back in to the sitting room.

"Where did you get this?" Tara demanded enviously. "I definitely want one. It's gorgeous." She ran her hand over the shimmering silver fabric that bound the photo album. Along one edge two parallel ribbons lay silkily on top and towards the top of both, slightly off set were two jaunty butterflies.

"Actually I made it." Josie admitted surprised that a woman who had never looked at anything unless it had a very famous brand name attached and an equally large price tag was interested. Tara was silent.

"How?" She finally asked.

"Trial and error really – when I saw the ribbons and the butterflies I started to imagine what I could do with them. I also wanted to do something that I could remember Nick by. So I decided to make the album cover and put all our favourite photos in it." She pulled a face. "I suppose it's a bit sickly sweet."

"No, it's a fabulous idea." Tara turned it over and watched as the silver turned to pink. "Would you make me one?" Tara asked, causing Josie to burst out laughing at the suggestion. "No I'm serious." Tara continued. "It's our wedding anniversary next month and I've been racking my brains to try and think what to buy Jeremy. I mean what do you get the man who has everything."

"You mean everything other than a JC photo album."

"Exactly!"

"What do you want on it? Any thoughts?"

"No idea." Tara admitted happily.

"It's your fifth anniversary isn't it?" She mused to herself "What is the fifth one?"

"Annoying mainly!" Tara said ruefully.

"Some help you are. Anyway I'll find out and we can then decide."

"You are a sweetie. Now if you're finally ready let's go and splash some cash. I've found this new boutique just down East Street. It sells clothes that are simply to die for."

The telephone rang on his desk, making Henry jump with a start. Goodness he'd almost nodded off to sleep there. He'd have to watch it or he would be turning even more into his father. He smiled at the recollection of the carefully diarised 2pm daily appointment with Miles Young – Kent Investor Partnerships that his father regularly scheduled. When he had questioned his mother about the lack of invoicing of this client she had recommended he relooked at the entry. He had looked at it blankly until his mother had enlightened him. "Try looking at the initials." She had suggested; and of course it them became obvious; it had been his father's witty way of writing 'my kip'. "Well he's getting on, dear." She had reminded Henry, "And as we get older we all need a few more appointments with old Miles Young of Kent Investor Partnerships." He brought his attention back to the telephone and lifted the steel grey receiver.

"Henry Beaucher." His voice was a deep with a resonance of solidity like English oak.

"Ahh Mr Beaucher, I trust I am not disturbing you. It's Reverend Mother at the St Francis Convent in Drayton Beauchamp."

He immediately pictured her tiny shrivelled features and beady black olive eyes; he had known her all his life and she had always been old to him. Yet like most nuns she seemed to have an inner calm aura that radiated from her directly conflicting with her aged looks; and those worldly wide eyes that seemed to be able to peer right into one's private soul to see the true person was quite unnerving sometimes, being set into such an innocent face.

"Good afternoon Reverend Mother; how can I help you?"

"It's one of the visitors." She explained. "We've come across a will she made before joining us and wondered if you would be able to act on it. You are normally so helpful in these matters; just like your dear kind father."

Henry had continued to work with the convent since his return; helping to prepare wills for the 'visitors' to the convent's hospice; all of whom knew how precious time was and wanted to sort out their life time collection of paltry savings and small benevolences.

He consulted the large red leather diary on his desk, his finger running through the week's appointments and activities.

"I'm passing your way on Wednesday afternoon, would it be possible to call in to you then about 2.30?"

"That would be most helpful Mr Beaucher. We will look forward to seeing you then."

"Until Wednesday; goodbye."

"God bless Mr Beaucher."

As it happened sorting out the will wasn't the only activity Henry was required to do. He was ushered into the gloomy room Reverend Mother used as a study and place of solace. Dust motes hung languidly on the air and the musty smell of old paper wafted across his nostrils.

"Please take a seat Mr Beaucher." The diminutive figure of the nun indicated an ancient battered leather club chair, while she sat straight backed on a wooden upright seat. "Thank you for coming over at such short notice. We are of course always grateful for your help in these matters."

"It's not a problem." He smoothly assured her. "Now you mentioned a previously written will," he pulled out his notepad from the tan briefcase that stood by the side of his chair, and extracted a fountain pen from the inside pocket of his jacket, carefully unscrewing the lid. "What was the lady's name?" he enquired, pen poised at the ready to take down the copious notes he required.

"Well;" there was a pause and it appeared to Henry that the Reverend Mother seemed uncertain of herself. "Well, her name was Annie Grey; at least that's what she was introduced as, and that was the name she used." Another pause developed causing Henry to prompt the conversation with:

"But you think it may have been something else?"

The Reverend Mother nodded her wimpled head. "It may be the musings of a silly old woman, but there were a couple of things that just didn't fit together." Henry watched her astutely as she produced a small bulk envelope from her desk drawer and handed it to Henry. He had known the Reverend Mother long enough to respect her judgement; if she felt there was a basis for questioning, then there probably was. He turned the envelope over, it was a hard backed envelope, the type you used to send photographs in to keep them flat. On the front in large spidery writing were two words "N Carrington". Quizzically Henry looked at the nun; he couldn't see the mystery in leaving a package for the attention of a friend. The old lady may well have no family left, and so had left her entire possessions to one of her nearest and dearest friends. He couldn't see why it was so interesting.

" As Annie was dying she gave us a package and said it wasn't to be opened until after her death. We try and make all our visitors last few hours with us have as much dignity and peacefulness as possible. But poor Annie didn't die peacefully, Sister Benedict was quite upset by trying to calm Annie; but she was a very self-tortured soul. I only hope that she finds a little peace now. Of course we respected her wishes in respect of the package and didn't open it until after her funeral. "

"And what was in it."

"Not much I'm afraid, this envelope, a post office account for a small amount of money and a short covering letter. I think the drugs must have been taking effect when she wrote it, as it rambles slightly. It asks for God's forgiveness for losing her baby and talks about the loneliness of repentance. Then it goes on begging us to make sure that Mr Carrington receives this package when he arrives, so that she can finally rest in peace."

Henry raised one eye brow.

"Sounds highly dramatic." His voice had a tinge of cynicism embedded in it.

"I don't think it is, just the wishes of a dying lady to make her final peace."

"And has Mr Carrington been in contact to arrange to come and collect the envelope?"

"No; and I have to say that I don't think he will. Annie didn't have any visitors when she was here, nor did she appear to have any letters. We had one person enquiring whether she was in fact staying with us, but nothing ever came of that. My impression was that she was a very lonely saddened woman, who had a tormented past."

"But what makes you think she wasn't Annie Grey; nothing you said suggests that her name isn't that."

The nun leaned across and with her wizened fingers opened the post office savings book. Her index finger highlighted one line.

"Because of that Mr Beaucher." She said pointing to the account name of Annie Carrington. "Because of that."

They walked into the hospice area; an almost comical pair, the petite habited nun and the tall upright solicitor. The light streaming in the Victorian sash windows contrasted strongly with the dimness of the study, and both paused on the threshold allowing their eyes to adjust to the brightness. Quietly they walked across to the lone occupant in the room who was dozing in the afternoon sun.

"Nellie? " the sound of the Reverend Mother's soft voice caused Nellie's eyelashes to flicker and lightly she turned her face towards the two visitors. "How are you feeling today Nellie?"

"A little tired today Reverend Mother to be honest; not one of my good days. Thought I would just try and rest a little." The nun patted the patient's hand tenderly as though reassuring a dear friend that everything was going to be alright.

"Sounds a good idea Nellie, you've got to build up your strength so you can give Sister Stephen some guidance out in the garden. I've lost three of my best rose plants this week to her pruning."

"Shouldn't be pruning roses at this time of year." Nellie was horrified at the idea.

"I know that, and you know that, which is why we need you up and about more than ever. Otherwise it's going to cost me a fortune restocking the flower beds." She moved aside to introduce Henry to the patient.

"Nellie, this is Mr Beaucher. You asked about getting someone to record your last wishes. Mr Beaucher is a solicitor."

Nellie's pale blue eyes stared intently at Henry, and she beckoned him forward. He moved closer and pulled a chair from the side of the bed so that he could sit in her line of vision, without her having to turn her neck awkwardly. The wheels of memory turned over in Nellie's mind as she tried to recollect a fleeting thought; and then suddenly the picture zoomed into focus.

"I know you. You're a friend of Master Adam."

Puzzled, Henry nodded, unable to place the woman lying in front of him in the hospital bed; wondering if they had met in passing at some village fete, or church event.

"Don't remember me do you?" Her voice had a subtle piquancy of the local accent, partially covered by the harsh rasping of her breathing.

"I'm sorry I don't." he admitted.

"Well that's hardly surprising; you were only a young nipper at the time. I was Master Adam's Nanny, up at the big house." Henry stared in amazement as the shrouds of time descended and he realised who she was.

"Not Nanny Hargreaves?" He exclaimed, trying to associate the tall stern Amazon with this frail old woman.

"That's me." She twinkled, her eyes creasing up in the corners causing her face to become even more crowded with wrinkles and lines.

"But Adam still talks about the day you washed his mouth out with carbolic soap because of some risqué comment about ladies' knickers!"

"Impudent young scamp. Soon taught him some manners for polite conversation in mixed company."

"Does he know you're here?"

"Oh yes. He calls in now and again when he gets time and remembers, always brings me my favourite shortcake. Buys it up at some store in London; such a lovely treat. Not that I can really eat it now, can't really eat anything. But it's lovely hearing all his stories and talking about the good old days." Her rasping voice turned into a cough and her whole body seemed racked with convulsions.

"Steady there." The Reverend Mother swiftly moved Nellie more upright and held her until the coughing subsided. "Henry, can you pour a glass of water for Nellie please; there's some on top of that table over there. Now just you rest a moment Nellie, and take a few sips of this." She helped hold the glass to Nellie's pale lips so that she could moisten her throat a little. After Nellie had finished, the Reverend Mother turned to Henry. "We shouldn't tire her too much. I'll get her settled and then perhaps you could start preparing her will?" Henry nodded in agreement, and settled himself back down in the chair; his notepad and fountain pen once again ready for action.

It seemed a strange afternoon Henry mused as he drove the short drive home though the village. Meeting Nanny Hargreaves after all these years made you realise how short life really was. Not that Nanny Hargreaves had featured heavily in his life, he had only met her when his family had visited Adam's; and even then he had been intent on finding his cousin and exploring the huge cavernous rooms within Drayton Hall. Nannie Hargreaves had only been a shadowy figure who had provided tea and jam in the nursery and insisted on them both washing their hands before eating.

His thoughts slipped back to Annie Carrington; and he wondered how he had ended up playing detective for some long forgotten relative of the dead Annie Carrington, it made him feel like Poirot, but without the moustache or the French accent, or was it Belgian? He could never remember. It was a puzzle that he hadn't dealt with before. How was he going to turn detective to find a missing relative? His mind offered no obvious solutions at the moment. There was so little to go on, just where was he supposed to start? The office came into view and his mind switched back to the current day's appointments, away from his wandering meandering thoughts, and focused on the rich divorcee he was due to see in fifteen minutes; this was one meeting that his secretary, Miss Letty, would definitely be invited to chaperone him through.

Chapter 3

"Have you seen this?" Claudia demanded throwing the magazine down in front of Neil as he slowly savoured his Saturday morning espresso. "I can't believe that snake O'Fara would do this to me."
Realising that his relaxing weekend was seriously in danger of being hijacked by the latest spat in the glossy magazine world he diverted his attention from the rich exotic taste of the coffee to the offending article. His eyes skimmed over it, aware of the impatient pacing Claudia behind him; her Jimmy Choo stilettos boring into the cherry wood floor.
"Look!" her red painted nail jabbed at the headline "Interview with Declan O'Fara." "How could he?"
Not making any sense of the situation Neil read the article. It appeared that Declan O'Fara was the newest thing to hit the 'must have' scene. Apparently his rustic designs and back to nature products were adorning every A, B and C listers' homes. His rural stools, which looked little more than giant corkscrews that would leave you with a cushion full of splinters, and his home spun goat wool throws were moulting on every wannabee's sofa. It all seemed fairly ludicrous to Neil; talk about the Emperor's new Georgio Armani. Waiting for a pause in the ranting Neil innocently asked.
"So what's the big deal? Surely you don't want one of his eco-home decorating kits." The thought of the earthy paints based on goat dung and limestone turned Neil's stomach.
"Of course I don't!" Claudia snapped her skin now alabaster white in rage against her gaudy red lip gloss. "I wanted him. Or rather I had him until he went and sold out to Viva. The sneaky rat. Wait until I get hold of him."
"Hold on." Neil raised his voice and his hand to be heard. "I still don't know what you're so upset about."
"What I'm so upset about? I'm running a tin-pot magazine..." Neil thought of its 150,000 readers and wondered if they saw it as a tin-pot magazine. "... that's being beaten by every new arrival on the block - or should I say newspaper stand to be more precise. I've only got eight weeks left to make an impression or I'll be even more old news than last season's hemlines."

"But what's the news? From what I can see it's just some nutter who has stuck a few bits of wood together, very badly, and woven a few goat hair blankets that I bet stink if they get wet."

"But it's cheap chic." Claudia cried out.

"Cheap chic?" Neil was puzzled by the obvious disparity.

"Yes. Cheap Chic. Everything this season is about rekindling all the old skills our forefathers and mothers would have made for their homes years ago. And Declan O'Fara was Bling and Boudoir's big thing for the season. We were going to feature his designs throughout the summer. I'd spent weeks telling him about the potential; about the fame and the glory; and about the exposure it would give his designs. But all he kept bleating on about was whether we would be able to dedicate the first issue to his goat." Neil turned to the first page showing the Editor's Welcome. A plastic version of a woman smiled wildly back out at him. Her hair was obviously moulded in place with so much lacquer that it would have doubled up as a safety helmet if she ever rode a scooter. The make up was flawless and thick, more than just a second skin it formed an armoured protection. To her right her talon-like hand lightly touched the short spiky fur of Flossie the Goat; "to whom," the inscription read below, "this month's issue is dedicated."

"Bitch!" Claudia screamed at the unnatural features of the editor. "Why should Monica bloody-Manning get to have her photo taken with the goat? She didn't spend months drinking his disgusting nettle and bramble tea. It should have been me!"

Neil surveyed her trying to project some rationality into the room.

"Think of it as a lucky escape. I'm not sure I want to go out with a Moulded Monica look alike who has a goat surgically attached to her hand."

"But you just don't understand." Claudia wailed as she dug around for her mobile. "This means war. If we are to keep our readers we have to get something even better than Declan's goat hair throws." She thumped out a number on the phone. "Babs, have you seen it? Have you seen this month's edition of Viva? How are we ever going to get over it?"

Neil heard a string of indeterminable outraged screeching.

"I know." Claudia agreed. "So let's get Lucy and the others and see if we can come up with something that's better than old farty O'Fara. Book our usual table at The Ivy; I know it's expensive but it's absolutely essential for the creative juices to be cultivated. Ok, yes, ok, see you there." She flipped the phone shut.

"Babs is even more outraged than me." She informed Neil. "Apparently she crashed Teddy's new car on the way back from the newsagents. So we simply have to get something better than Viva." She picked up her Mulberry handbag and dropped the phone in to it. "I'm off out – it's now war."

"It's Saturday." Neil protested, thinking of their plans for a quiet lunch out by the river.

"And... and?" She fixed him with an icy glare that had made her so successful as an editor. "Do you think Churchill stopped fighting the war on Saturday?" An image of Claudia in a plum cord boiler suit, smoking a fat cigar flitted across Neil's mind. "If we don't do something for our next issue, it's curtain for us."

"I thought curtains was the sole subject of the magazine." Neil murmured to himself as he resumed reading the paper. She kissed him perfunctorily on the top of his head as she walked towards the door, picking up the offending article as evidence, and slamming the door behind her. Suddenly there was silence. After the turmoil of emotions that had exploded earlier, it seemed like a peaceful oasis. He poured himself another coffee, his first had grown cold through the tantrum, and he settled down to a morning of devoting his attention to Sailing Monthly. Now this was definitely what Saturday was designed for.

On the same Saturday morning 60 miles away, Josie was wondering if it would be easier to kill her mother rather than return downstairs and grimly try to bear all the sympathy Molly seemed desperate to pour upon her. She had been staying for three days so far and the ability to keep playing the role of grieving widow was wearing thin. Not that she didn't still hurt inside; if she had been given the power she would have brought Nick back instantly; but part of her had somehow become resigned to the fact that Nick had gone for ever, and nothing she could do would alter that. The absolute grief and sorrow when she had first learnt about his death had mutated into a hopeless acceptance which didn't alleviate the pain but it did dampen it to become more manageable. She had tried to talk to her mother when she had first arrived and Molly was fussing about her, treating her daughter more like an elderly grieving dowager; but

Molly had diverted the conversation, not wanting to discuss it. All she kept saying was:
"Poor darling." "…oh you are being brave." "Don't keep it all inside – it's not healthy to bottle it up, just talk to me sweetheart." Josie knew that it was her mother's way of coping with losing Nick; they had shared a special bond that sometimes Josie had felt slightly jealous of. Men weren't supposed to like their mother in law were they, it went against the law of nature.

The doorbell went, announcing the arrival of Sarah. Josie knew she couldn't hide upstairs any longer, she just hoped Sarah wouldn't have the same attitude – it would be a shame to have to kill her mother and her sister. As Josie walked into her mother's sitting room Sarah and Molly looked up together, their attention diverted momentarily from Olivia's carrycot.
"Hello there." Sarah said warily; as sisters they had never been particularly close; having different personalities, different sets of friends and different ambitions.
"Hi." The conversation dried up and hunting round for something to say Josie offered to make coffee. Sarah followed her into the kitchen, leaving Molly transfixed with her granddaughter.
"So how's it going?" Sarah asked.
"Ok; well as ok as it can be for a widow." Josie said half-heartedly.
"I actually meant here." Josie was surprised at Sarah's perspicuity, and gave a wry smile.
"Mum's making me out to be a cross between Great Aunt Hilda and some lamenting Italian wailing widow." She filled the coffee percolator with coffee beans, closing her eyes to heighten the enjoyment of the smell. "I know she means well. What happened is really awful, but she doesn't seem to realise that keep saying "Poor Darling"." She mimicked Molly's deep plummy voice. "and "My brave Josie." isn't very helpful. If anything it just keeps reminding me of what's happened."
Sarah laid a sympathetic arm around Josie's shoulder. "She doesn't mean to be annoying; it's just her way. You know what it's like. She'll have seen her friends at the bridge club and they'll have shown so much concern about you in the hope of getting some gossip about how Nick died as he left you to join his five other wives; that she will have been brainwashed into believing you really

are a simpering wreck hardly able to go on with life. He didn't have five other wives did he?"

Josie giggled. "If he did hopefully one of them will be really rich, then I can sponge off her for a bit." They arranged the cups and milk jug on the tray.

Sarah picked up the message. "Things that bad then?"

"Mmm." Josie agreed relaying the tale of how Neil had helped sort out the finances, carefully avoiding any mention of her drunken activities.

"That was kind of him." Sarah had always liked Nick's boss; she wasn't so sure about his girl friend though. Claudia took frightening to a new limit.

"Yes; it also made me start thinking about what I wanted to do with the rest of my life."

"Josie! You make it sound like you're approaching retirement age." Sarah protested.

"Well I'm 31; I've no career, no real job experience other than working in an office and that doesn't pay very well;" She ticked each one off against a separate finger. "I'm a widow with no prospects, no real home and very little money."

"Goodness; it does sound like you're becoming a real grown up after all." Sarah's voice held a slight chink of irony, making Josie look long and hard at her sister. Sarah was the eldest one, always more serious and responsible. She had always known that she wanted to be teacher, and had studied hard to go to university before then going onto teacher training college. It was here that she had met a fellow student, Edward, who Josie had cruelly nicknamed "Steady Eddie", they had both graduated together before starting work as teachers at a local secondary school. They had married several years later, buying a house on a small estate, because a teacher's salary didn't stretch to buying cottages or palaces. They had spent their holidays improving the run down house, building on a workshop for Edward and finally creating a nursery when Olivia was born. After her maternity leave, Sarah had returned to work, discovering that one salary would never be sufficient for all three to live off. For the first time ever Josie's perception shifted slightly, so that instead of seeing Sarah as the boring one who had her life planned out, Sarah became the responsible one who understood you had to live in a reality where things like death and redundancy loomed unwelcome. And it was she, Josie, that was the spoilt child, still expecting someone to look after her, no planning for those inevitable rainy days, just interested in enjoying herself. She turned and stared out of the window. How could she have been so wrong about things?

"I suppose I have been quite thoughtless." She spoke quietly with a mixture of embarrassment and realisation flowing through. "I always thought you got your happy endings. That someday your prince did turn up and whisk you away from the drudgery."

"Not in this life." Sarah concluded mournfully. They both spent a few minutes watching the wind play with the dread locks of the laburnum tree making them dance insanely like a thousand ravers all hearing a different beat to the music. They heard the sound of the percolator finish, and Sarah turned to remove the jug of ebony coffee.

"So have you any ideas on what you might do?"

"Ahh, not really. I have lots of thoughts flying round inside, but none that come together. The two certainties are I need to work and I need a new place to live. The first I don't know what I can do, and the second I don't know where. So it's not exactly coming together as a good plan."

"You can always stay with Ed and me if you want. It may be cosy, but at least neither of us will confuse you with Great Aunt Hilda."

Josie smiled a thanks to her sister.

"And there would only be minimal baby sitting duties." Sarah said sweetly. Josie felt a pang of guilt; since Olivia had been born, she hadn't visited her once, except to see her christened and that was only because of the lure of the free champagne and Nick's insistence.

"Where is she – still with Mum?"

"Yes. Olivia hasn't learnt that a doting grandmother can be even more overbearing in later life than a mother who fusses."

"I didn't mean to complain about her. I know she means well, it's just I need to start getting on with my own life."

"I know. It's probably her way of grieving for Nick. You know how she adored him. She could vent all her motherliness onto him and he would just sit there and lap it up! Asking for seconds of her rhubarb crumble, proudly wearing those ghastly sweaters she knits. He was the perfect son-in-law."

"Yes I suppose so, but if you could have a quiet word it would make it so much easier."

"I will, don't worry. Now let's go and rescue my daughter before her grandmother lectures her on the need for always carrying a clean handkerchief and never burping in public." They laughed at the shared memory of Molly's instructions to them as they were growing up.

They took the coffee back through to the sitting room where Molly was crouching over a gurgling Olivia who was cheerfully chewing a stockinged foot with relish.

"Goodness looks like one of those impossible yoga positions you see on TV." Josie exclaimed, and then, as though mesmerised by the cute smile bent down by her mother.

"Hello you." Josie said slightly self-consciously, uncertain how to talk to a baby. Aware of the honour of being addressed by an adult Olivia let go of her foot and blew a gentle bubble at her aunt. Leaning forward Josie rubbed her finger against her niece's rosy cheek, feeling the downy softness of the baby plumpness. Olivia caught hold of the finger and held on to it, inspecting it like learned historian with a new antiquity.

"Aren't you gorgeous." She twisted round to her sister. "Could I hold her?"

"Of course." Molly picked the little pudding of a baby up and handed it to Josie's out stretched hands. She was surprised at the weight and solidity of her niece; and pulled the baby into her own body, feeling Olivia relax into her arms. A primeval stirring somewhere deep within her stomach fluttered up like a dancing carnival of butterflies, spreading through her body, that she knew she wanted a baby of her own. So absorbed with the intensity of this feeling she missed the exchanged knowing looks swapped between Molly and Sarah. Oblivious she turned back to Sarah and said "You never mentioned just how lovely she is."

"What do you expect – she comes from quality stock!"

"Poor darling." Molly sighed. "You're being so brave about never having children now that you don't have a husband."

Josie and Sarah caught each other's eye.

"Mum," Josie said lightly. "You must have noticed that you don't actually need a husband to have a child."

Molly sniffed. "Maybe, but it isn't the done thing. Nice girls don't have children without a husband."

"Ah but being a nice girl is always so boring." Sarah commented ruefully.

"So tell me what exactly we're doing here." Molly and Josie were trundling down the winding country lanes; the edges were interspersed with naked trees, their autumn leaves had been stripped in the previous season, leaving the spindly limbs defenceless against the bad weather. Above a grey stormy sky lay overhead, the winter wind gusted clouds along, battering their way across the horizon.
"We're going to see my solicitor." Molly explained patiently.
"But why do I need to come along? I haven't got any need for some legal eagle."
"Darling," Molly's voice took on the tone she used with Olivia when she was explaining an important point. "That's not the point. I have to change my will because of Nick's death, and I thought it would be useful if you had a chat with nice Mr Beaucher. He's always been so helpful to me, especially after your father died." Josie ground her teeth but couldn't fault her mother's logic. "Anyway, " Mollie continued. "It's so pretty round here that I thought you would like to have a day out. I love the excuse for being to come and visit."
Josie sat back in her seat and watched the scenery change from the soft velvets of the open fields edged with brocade hedges; occasionally there were glimpses of solid stone farm houses with ancient creepers climbing up the stone outer walls while below hens, their feathers tousled by the wind, scratched at the dusty yards and dogs barked importantly at strange noises. The white and black iron village sign proudly sang out "Drayton Beauchamp" and along the grass verges the golden tips of daffodil and crocuses could be seen shyly peaking above the grass.

As they entered the high street it seemed a picturesque as the ideal English village should be. The mixture of Georgian and Victorian shop fronts showed a local thriving trade with stores offering local delicacies. The pavements were filled with busy shoppers; but unlike London where the bustle only increased one's sense of loneliness people here seemed to know everyone. You could see them nod to acquaintances, greet friends and huddle to hear the latest news. To the right a large open green spread out around a pond where collections of playing toddlers and prams congregated in small dispersed groups, feeding the hungry huddling ducks and playing a clumsy game of tag. The car continued along the high street and up the hill where the houses began to become a little more spaced out, set back in their own grounds. It was obviously where the well-heeled villagers lived; and it was into one of these that Molly turned the car; in between two tall golden stone pillars topped with pineapples. Josie hadn't seen such a beautiful house in a long time – it seemed more suited to the cover of House and Gardens rather than the place to discuss death, wills and bereavements.

"Aren't we going to his office? Or this is it?"

"Oh no, his office is over the other side of the village. Mr Beaucher kindly suggested meeting here." Molly said airily. "His father used to invite your father and I over once a year for social catch up. I think it's a continuation of tradition. You don't mind do you?"

"Why would I?" Josie snapped, something annoyed her about the whole set up. Sarah had obviously spoken to Molly because she had stopped the fussing, and was being much more matter of fact about Josie's situation. And here she was visiting some boring old solicitor in an attempt to try and sort her life out. They got out of the car and walked over to the imposing black front door, its gloss paint catching the last few rays of sunlight. Molly pulled on the rusted bell pull and deep within the innards of the house a dainty bell rang out. A few minutes later there was the sound of an ancient lock being coaxed into action, and then suddenly the door was open and they were being welcomed in by a Hugh Grant look-alike and an inquisitive Labrador.

"Hello, hello." Henry said affably. "Come in, come in. Betsy leave them alone. Sorry about Betsy." He ushered them into the cavernous hall and across the black and white geometrical tiles to the drawing room, trying to keep a hold of Betsy who was vainly attempting to sniff Molly and Josie by way of a greeting. "She loves visitors, but unfortunately doesn't get to see many these days, so she always makes up for it whenever she gets the chance." Josie felt like Alice-in-Wonderland as they entered the graceful proportioned drawing room. On one side a table was set for afternoon tea, complete with silver tea pot, cucumber sandwiches without the crusts and cream scones. Any moment she expected a faithful old retainer to appear and curtsey to them all.

"Take a seat; anywhere you like. Betsy sit down and stop being a pest." He gestured to the seats by the fireplace and timidly Josie made her way over the armchair nearest the roaring log fire, and Betsy silently followed; waiting for Josie to sit down before thrusting her golden head onto Josie's lap in the search for some attention.

"Push her away if she is a nuisance." Henry instructed. "I know not every one likes dogs."

"It's fine." Josie assured him, stroking the satin fur head.

"How do you keep the house so tidy?" Molly asked. "It always looks so immaculate."

Henry smiled wryly "If you saw the rest of the house, and the notes left by my cleaner you wouldn't be quite so complimentary."

"What happened to that nice young lady from the local Conservative Association? I thought you made such a lovely couple."

"Went and married the local MP; she unfortunately didn't like dogs, so she gave me the ultimation of her or Betsy. And as you can see Betsy stayed."

"Poor you. It's like Josie, a widow at 31. It must be so difficult for you youngsters today; it seemed so much simpler in my day; you liked a boy, he would ask your father if he could court you and then you got married."

'Oh no.' Josie thought dropping her eyes and blushing fiercely 'She can't be lining up husband number 2 for me can she?' Molly brazenly carried on.

"Well if you need a partner for the Summer Dance I'm sure Josie would be free, wouldn't you dear?" Josie wondered if she was going to ignite from the intense burning of her cheeks; dragging her eyes up to Molly she silently pleaded with her to stop this conversation, and then onto Henry to see his reaction at the blatant match making.

"Thank you Josie, I'll definitely bear it in mind." Henry said his tone light but slightly mocking, and she realised he had seen right through Molly's ploy and didn't seem to fazed. Relaxing slightly she smiled back conspiratorially, he was obviously too polite to tell Molly he was old enough to find his own woman.

The conversation changed tack and Molly and Henry caught on mutual friends, village activities and good-cause events; half-way through a conversation about charity work which Josie had drifted out of Molly turned and asked. "Did you bring the photos?"

"Sorry?" Josie was startled back into the conversation.

"Henry and I were just talking about the Christmas Carol Concert at the convent. I took some photos for the WI newsletter and I gave the film to Nick to be developed the last time the two of you visited." Molly turned to Henry. "Nick always used to get his professional printing company to develop my photos for me. Always such a lovely quality, you can really see the difference."

Josie bit her lip to hide a smile from forming. True Nick had always kept promising to get them professionally developed; but he inevitably forgot and it always ended up with Josie running down to Pronto-Snaps for a one hour service just before they left to visit Molly.

"So did you bring them?" Molly asked again.

"No; I don't remember even getting them printed. I'll check when I get back." Josie assured her mother.

"Well perhaps you could get a copy for Henry so he can let his clients see them?"

"I'm sure I can."

Henry remembering he should be a more responsible host suggested they make a start on the afternoon tea.

"Oh yes," Molly gushed as Henry carried the small gate-leg table into the centre of them and placed the tray on top of it.

"Molly, would you mind being 'Mother'?" Molly flushed with pleasure and Josie could see Molly getting herself prepared for this as a full time role.

"Such a lovely spread." Molly said as she handed out the delicate white bone china cups and saucers filled with steaming scented tea.

"Mmm." Josie agreed munching on the melt-in-the-mouth sandwiches and eyeing up the crumbly scone halves. "You certainly know how to cook."

Henry guffawed, shaking his head with laughter so that his chestnut brown fringe flopped forward before being pushed back. "I can't claim any credit other than ordering them from Melissa at the local deli. Cooking is definitely not my strong point." Josie half expected him to say something about it being a woman's place to be in the kitchen, but he didn't. In fact he seemed a different person to the one she had initially presumed; from Molly's description and the initial impression she had expected him to a bit of an old doddering buffoon, but it looked like he wore this as a disguise to hide the sharper insightful personality that had glinted through their conversation.

As they finished the feast, the evening had begun to draw in and outside the afternoon dusk smeared the views.

"I suppose we had better get down to business." Henry said finally with a tinge of reluctance to break up the sociable chit-chat. He addressed himself to Molly "Now the items you wanted to discuss..." He stood up and walked across to the door to his study. "The papers are just in here, shall we run through them?" Molly followed him. "Will you be ok in here?" He asked Josie.

"I'll be fine." She said airily, patting the fat pile of last weekend's papers by her side. "I'll just wade my way through these." She watched as they disappeared into the study, their voices becoming fainter until they were indistinguishable murmurings. Picking up one of the glossy supplements she started to flick through it; in the background the slow leisurely tick of the grandfather clock and the occasional crackle of the apple logs on the fire created a restful atmosphere and Josie stretched, feeling relaxed and comfortable. Twenty minutes later the sound of Molly and Henry returning roused her and she smiled in greeting as they entered the room.

"Hope you weren't too bored." Henry's brow was furrowed with concern.

"I was absolutely fine."

"Molly mentioned about your husband, it must be awful." Josie nodded, no longer ready with a stock of answers. "Death is always horrible though." He finished.

"Darling, weren't you going to ask Mr Beaucher some questions?" Molly prompted. Henry looked expectantly at her, his open friendly face willing to be of assistance. Josie glowered at her mother. The cheek of it; this had all been Molly's idea.

"Well, ahem, I don't think there is really anything to discuss." She said lamely. "Nick's affairs weren't exactly in order."

"Have you had anyone else to look at them?" Instantly Henry had slipped into his professional persona.

"A friend did help me unfathom the worst;" she looked across at her mother pointedly "obviously though not professionally."

"So he didn't leave a will?" Henry the solicitor was efficiently summing up the situation.

"No, only a financial mess."

"Would you like me to have a look over everything? Just as a second opinion. I'm up in town next Tuesday if you are free."

"Oh Josie, isn't that kind." Molly interjected firmly guessing her daughter was about to refuse. "It would be wonderful if you could, I would feel so much better if you did." She said to Henry.

"Are you sure?" Henry asked Josie softly not wanting to force himself on what was a delicate situation. Too angry at her mother's interference to speak Josie mutely nodded and tried to fix a smile.

"We mustn't waste any more of your time Mr Beaucher." Now that Molly had secured the next meeting she didn't feel the need to stretch the afternoon out any longer. "The tea was delicious; just like the one your mother used to make."

The three of them walked out to the front door and Henry held it open for them; their goodbyes became muffled by the dusky air and as they got into the car the house became shrouded in a dark mist. Still shaking with rage Josie fumbled with the seat belt and broke a nail. Swearing loudly she threw her bag onto the floor.

"How could you?" She fumed. "You only brought me along today so you could marry me off."

"That's a slight exaggeration my dear." Molly rationally pointed out. "I just thought that the two of you should meet. Plus you know you need to get your affairs sorted out." The truth of Molly's argument didn't help Josie feel any better.

"You shouldn't interfere." She wasn't going to let her mother get off that easily.

"Darling, that's the one prerogative of being a mother, we always get to interfere. Now stop fussing and tell me what you'll wear on Tuesday."

Josie fumbled with her hair and wished she hadn't agreed to this. She should be at home finishing Tara's photo album; not arranging to have dinner with Henry. She smoothed the black skirt down and tried to calm her nerves as the taxi sped through the deserted streets; recalling it was the same outfit she had worn for the meeting with Neil, and that had worked out alright. She'd been fine about it until Tara had called to wish her luck on her date. She'd tried to protest that it was only dinner with a friend; but the disbelieving silence at the other end of the phone only illustrated who Josie was trying to kid. As soon as it had been labelled a date she had started to dread it; it was making it into something it wasn't. Henry wasn't interested in her like that; she was certain that deep down he was the type of man who wanted a woman who would be a staunch member of the WI, Conservative Party and Church Flower Arranging Guild. None of which she had the least interest in.

"'Ere you go love. Laa Maysen doo Flear." The taxi driver called over his shoulder as he pulled up outside the restaurant "Le Maison de Fleur". "That's free pounds firty." In her nervousness she pulled out ten pounds and got out without waiting for change, leaving the driver chuckling to himself about first dates.

Josie stood paralysed; unable to take the four simple steps to the front door; she wasn't sure she was ready for dinner with a man other than Nick. It was all too soon; she berated herself for agreeing, but it had seemed so innocent when Henry had suggested they catch up for dinner while he was in town, that she hadn't hesitated in agreeing instead of sitting alone for another night watching mindless reality tv programmes and ordering pizza. Now that she was here though, dressed up and the air of expectation hanging heavily overhead, the emphasis seemed to have shifted, no longer was it just dinner, it was now becoming a date and that was the one thing she didn't need right now. Instinctively she half turned, about to make a run back home when she heard her name being called.

"Jooosie!" Across the street Henry was trying to catch her attention; briefcase in one hand, umbrella in the other, both being waved frantically. He darted across the street narrowly missing a collision with a cyclist and hurried over to where she stood. "Hi;" he kissed her briefly on the cheek "I'm sorry I'm late I got held up and I was afraid you wouldn't wait." The sound of his voice, and his confident presence reassured Josie, and she relaxed all the pre-date nerves dissipating instantly. He put his hand gently on her arm and steered her towards the door.

"Were you thinking of going?" He asked lightly; and Josie was surprised at his insightfulness.

"Yes." she admitted. "But I'm glad you're here now." They entered the restaurant and the head waiter ushered them to a table over looking the garden. Tiny pin pricks of lights reflected in the window from the floating tea lights on their table; the heavy linen tablecloth rustled as they sat down.

"Menus;" The waiter produced the two chocolate leather brown books with a flourish. "For Madame, and for Sir." They took the weighty tomes and began running their eyes down the select choices.

"I thought you might have cancelled tonight." Henry said, continuing their previous conversation, his head bowed with his gaze on the beef Wellington with turnip puree.

"Mmm; it did feel a bit strange." Josie answered, considering the scallops with chilli on a bed of rocket."

"So what made you decide to come?"

"The options of Big Brother and pepperoni pizza have lost their appeal; plus I thought it would be ..." she dug around for the right word and plumped for "nice."

Her response almost took him by surprise and his head was instantly lifted, watching her as she continued speaking. "Well it was really kind of you to make time to go through all the paperwork. I'm not sure I'd ever make sense of it, but you and Neil were really helpful."

"It was no trouble at all; besides your mother would never have forgiven me if I hadn't at least looked. There's something about having a client who has known you in nappies that manages to intimidate even the strongest of solicitors." He grinned, his eyes sparkling with humour changing subtly from brown to hazel flecks.

"My mother is incorrigible! I couldn't believe her cheek! If I didn't know better I'd bet she had planned the whole charade that Saturday just so she could instigate the meeting."

"She was probably talked into it by the bridge club."

"Oh don't talk to me about them; how sweet respectable old ladies can turn into such sneaky, cunning foxes I'll never understand. They seem to egg each other on." They carried on with the horrors of mothers until the waiter appeared and discretely coughing enquired if they had chosen.

"Heavens, I haven't." Josie always took ages to choose the meal, she had to envisage each one, and then decide whether it would work with the starter and the dessert, and she hadn't even started this.

"Another five minutes." Henry suggested to the waiter who nodded graciously and backed away.

"The food certainly looks good." Henry said. "Have you been here before?"

"No; I've always wanted to come, but somehow Nick and I never got round to coming." They addressed their menus in silence, studying them intently until the waiter reappeared.

"Think I'll have the duck terrine followed by pheasant in port." Henry decided "Josie, have you decided?"

"Goats cheese compote and the skate please." Her taste buds were crying out for the tangy textures of the caper sauce that accompanied the fish.

"And a bottle of the Pouilly Fume." The waiter slid away. The restaurant was starting to get busy with locals appearing at their usual tables, chatting with the staff and noisily greeting friends. The soft violin concerto that had been playing became drowned out by the chatter of voices, and the atmosphere became more energetic.

"This is excellent." Henry remarked as they saw a plate of melt-in-the-mouth filo parcels pass by. They sipped the wine, its cool lemon taste floated round the mouth.

"So any suggestions on what I should do?" Josie enquired, pre-occupied with the topic, picking up the conversation they had started in the flat as Henry had given his professional confirmation that yes things were dire.

"The main thing is start having an income you can live off. The lump sum will soon go if you use it for everyday living."

"Neil said the same." Josie said gloomily. "It's just trying to work out what I'm good at."

"What was your degree in?"

"History of art – not much use to a thirty-something widow. Pity I didn't do bricklaying or hairdressing, at least then I'd have some skills."

Henry put his head on one side and wrinkled his brow. "Can't say I exactly see you in either role."

"Maybe not – but you know what I mean. I've been able to organise an office and enjoy working with people. But I loathe technology and computers are a real no-go."

"But what do you enjoy doing? Have you got a hobby or an interest? You always hear about successful people who have made careers out of their hobbies."

Sadly she shook her head, she had no outside interests, unless you counted shopping, and that would never make any money.

"Well here's to a lost cause." Henry joked lightly as he raised his glass.

"Definitely a lost cause." Josie agreed heartily chinking her glass against his.

"You could always become Betsy's official dog walker." Henry said casually. "If you didn't have anything else on."

"And what sort of hours would that entail?" Josie asked, her lips curving up into a smile.

"Well we could try Saturday, if you are free. You know, treat it as your induction, and see how it went on from there."

"I'll have to ask my recruitment consultant if she feels it adds value to my thrusting career. Of course if it was on behalf of a charity I could put it down on my CV as good works."

"Did I forget to mention that it would be aid of a local charity." He hit his forehead with the heel of his hand. "How could I forget that? So you'll come over?"

"Yes if you like, but strictly on the understanding it's to see Betsy."

"I wouldn't dream it was for any other reason. Don't forget to bring your Wellingtons, you'll definitely need those."

Josie gulped a huge swig of wine and nearly choked; she hadn't worn Wellingtons since she was ten years old, and she didn't think Henry would be too impressed if she turned up wearing green wellies with frog eyes peeping up on the toes. "What actual wellies?" She asked cautiously, realising Saturday wasn't going to be some glamorous date.

"Oh yes – you know the things that the Chelsea farmers keep extremely clean." He eyed her speculatively. "You don't own a pair do you?" He was amazed - everyone owned a pair of wellies. "Ok, don't worry about it." He said thinking fast, producing plan B "What size are you? There'll be someone in the village I can borrow from." Feeling a little relieved that she wouldn't need to find her own she finished off her glass of wine and poured another. After all, a quiet stroll in the country on a Saturday afternoon couldn't be too bad, could it.

Chapter 4

The glorious thing about waking up to find the sun streaming into the room is it gives you such a sense of contentment and wellbeing. Josie lay luxuriating in bed; stretching her toes and arms to their fullest extent. She had finally got to bed about two in the morning, having spent the whole day, and most of the night working on Tara's album. She pictured it lying on the dining room table waiting for her friend to collect it later that morning. She had decided on a bridal theme and had used the ivory silk Tara's wedding dress had been made from for the main cover. On the inside was the deep blue velvet that Tara had chosen for the bridesmaid dresses and Jeremy's waistcoat. Josie remembered the burning indignity she had felt at having to the wear the frilled Little-Bo-Peep style dresses that Jeremy's size 8 sister had insisted upon, knowing that she would outshine Josie, even if she couldn't outshine the bride. While Vikki had been a diminutive pastoral figurine, Josie had been a voluptuous wench, which was not the look she favoured; being all curves and bumps, unable to move without the frills sashaying wildly side to side.

Josie had rummaged round all her keepsakes and hoardings to find the invitation and menu (surreptitiously stolen from the table after the wedding breakfast) to remind her of Tara's wedding theme. Cream card with navy script, and on each corner was a delicately intertwined blue J and T initial surrounded by a sprig of leaves. It had taken Josie ages to try and think how she could incorporate it; and finally she had struck on the idea of creating her own rubber stamp, which meant that now in every corner on every page was a delicately entwined J and T. On the front she had used the same basic design, but had embroidered the initials, rather than a flat stamp, in glossy lustrous silk so that it gave the front texture and depth. The delicate stems she had embroidered, but the leaves she had cut out from the velvet and appliquéd on, decorating each with a tiny seed pearl along the spine so that it glittered and glistened in the light like dew on real leaves.

Around the bed were packing boxes and piles of books and shoes; since her meeting with Henry she had realised she needed to either rent somewhere cheaper or start looking for her own house.

Strangely the idea had given a fluttering sensation of excitement, rather than feeling bereft, it actually felt like the start of an adventure. Ok, so the only house she could afford was one of the new bunny boxes on the wrong side of town, but the thought of setting up her own house was thrilling, it meant she was finally graduating to maturity. Stepping over the piles Josie pulled her dressing gown on; snuggling into the comfortable sensation of familiarity. She padded into the kitchen and put the kettle on and found her herbal tea bags. For some reason she had gone off drinking coffee first thing in the morning, and now enjoyed the pleasant incense of camomile and ginger. Perching on the kitchen stool and looking out of the window she contemplated what the day held – after Tara had collected her album she would catch the train out to Drayton Beauchamp to meet up with Henry and Betsy; and then what? How on earth did one dress for an unknown activity that somehow involved Wellingtons. She hoped that it meant just a gentle walk through the woods before supper at some wine bar. Somehow Henry didn't give that impression though. Was it worth taking the risk and wearing her Versace jeans; probably not. She sipped the team infusion and enjoyed the subtly taste; she knew she needed to get moving in order to be ready when Tara arrived, but she needed a few more minutes to relax and prepare herself before starting to get ready. Suddenly life was becoming quite hectic.

"Tell me, tell me!" Tara pleaded as soon as the front door was open. "I want to hear everything, and I mean absolutely everything." She headed into the kitchen waving a smart paper bag in one hand. "I've got bribes as well; so you had better give in; there's no way I'm moving until I hear all about the evening with Henry."
"Ok." Josie surrendered. "Providing they are double helpings of New York cheesecake."
"Of course; what else would I bring; I had to go to Carluccios especially for them." Tara said delightedly, realising her bargaining talents were working. With reverence they took the extra large slabs of rich carrot cake topped with the creamy whipped icing out of the bag and onto the plates; unable to resist Tara dipped a well manicured French polished nail into the topping and like a naughty child liked her finger with satisfaction. "Mmm, Carluccio definitely makes the most heavenly carrot cake. It is official. This really is better than sex." They started to tuck into the slices, savouring the

light bouncy cake with the firmer, sweeter icing. Both silent as they relished the calorific delicacy, broken only by tiny escaping groans of ecstasy. "So tell me everything." Tara demanded as she wiped the crumbs away from her last mouthful. "Jeremy has stopped speaking to me; he said as I couldn't talk about anything else it wasn't worth him trying to hold a conversation with me." She took a sip of coffee to cleanse her palette. "Well of course I couldn't; this is the most exciting thing to happen for ages. I mean you had your first date!"

"There's not much to tell you. He came over last week and spent an hour or so very politely condemning my finances, and Nick's contingency planning. Which is nothing I didn't already know. Then I think he felt so guilty about being the bearer of bad tidings, and mindful that I probably couldn't afford to eat this week he promptly offered to take me out for a meal."

"Yes I know all that, skip forward to the date." Tara was engrossed with the story.

"We had a very nice meal." Josie said mock-helpfully.

"Forget the meal, did he see you home; did you invite him in for a coffee?"

"Actually," Josie admitted a little shame-faced at her actions. "I had a cab ordered for the end of the evening."

"Josie you really are the limit. How is the poor bloke supposed to feel if you have a taxi on tap? Why on earth did you do that?"

"Well I thought that if it was a really awful evening and it turned out to be a real nightmare, or a total bore then I could claim my mother was ill and needed me, and let me get away quickly."

"Oh, so no coffee invites then?" Tara sounded disappointed.

"No. Sorry to have no real gossip." The excitement and anticipation seemed to ebb out of Tara.

"Oh well, as long as you had a lovely evening, that's all that really matters. You did have a good evening didn't you?"

"Oh yes; especially if you count the goodnight kiss which definitely lasted longer than it should; and the fact he has invited me out today."

The flame of anticipation was instantly reignited within Tara.

"Ohmigosh – you actually had a kiss?" Josie nodded. "And it was good?" Josie nodded again with a smug look all over her face. "Oh wow. And you are seeing him today? Where are you going somewhere romantic?"

"I'm going over to Drayton Beauchamp; we're walking Betsy."
"Who is Betsy?"
"His labrador; at least I hope it's walking the dog. He said I needed wellies." She explained.
"Wellies! Why would you need those?"
"I've no idea; which makes deciding what to wear infinitely more difficult. Can you believe it, I've no idea what to wear. But whatever I choose it is not going to say 'sexy'."
"Men! Don't they know the basic rules of first dates includes letting the woman know exactly where they are being taken so that she knows which outfit to wear."
"I don't think Henry's exactly the type to have read any rule books, other than De Bretts. It's strange, sometimes I think he is more like a typical hooray henry, and then he totally surprises me with his insightfulness and thoughtfulness."
"What time are you supposed to be meeting him?"
"I've got to catch the twelve fifty train, that gets me in at one forty. Henry is meeting me at the station."
"I've got the car today, I'll give you a lift to the station if you want, to save you getting a taxi. They are a nightmare to find sometimes." Thanks, that would be helpful." She tidied away their plates and mugs. "Now do you want to see the photo album?"
"Oh yes definitely. Did I tell you Jeremy has been dropping heavy hints that it is our anniversary on Monday? He thinks I've forgotten because I haven't been pestering him for ideas on presents this year. It's been such a giggle really."
"Bless him." Josie said fondly imagining Jeremy's anxious concern.
"At least he still remembers that's a fairly major achievement for a man. Nick never did, and we were only married two years." Laughing they walked into the sitting room and over to the dining room table where the photo album sat proudly on a fluttery pile of crisp white tissue paper already to be wrapped.
"Here you go." Josie motioned to it. Tara stopped chuckling, her laugher dying in her mouth as she looked at the album, transfixed momentarily before stepping forward and staring at the beautiful cover. Turning to Josie she said slowly.
"You made this?"
"Yes." She began to apologise. "Look Tara I hope it's ok, if you don't like it don't worry. It's probably a bit too home made looking

and shabby for you. Please don't be polite. You don't have to worry about my feelings."

"Not at all." Tara stretched her manicured nails across and ran her fingertips over the silky fabric and the intricate embroidered design of the J and T intertwined on the front. "It's amazing." She said breathily. "It's really good, I can't believe you actually made it. How did you remember what our wedding design was?"

"I didn't, but I did keep all the invites and the menu so I pulled them out for some ideas." She opened the album to let Tara see inside. "And I lined it with the blue velvet." Tara gasped and then hid her flushing cheeks in her hands. "Oh no, those awful velvet Little Bo-Peep dresses! I'm surprised you stayed my friend after I put you in all those frills. I can't believe I forced you in to it."

"I have to admit it was a bit testing."

"Blame Vikki and my mother-in-law. They persuaded me it was all the rage in fashionable society weddings. If I hadn't been so afraid of the old dragon I might have stood up to her a bit." Tara flicked through the pages of the album. "How did you get the pages personalised?"

"I made a stamp and then used liquid gold leaf to print it on each page."

"Josie, this is seriously good. You definitely have a talent for this." Josie flushed with pleasure.

"I enjoyed making it. Shall I wrap it for you?" Tara nodded, her thoughts momentarily distracted. Josie turned her back to Tara and started to intricately fold the layers of tissue paper around the album, forming a smart parcel around which she tied a thin velvet ribbon finishing it off with a long tailed bow. Idly Tara picked up a folded pink gingham blanket from off the table, opening it up she saw it had six pockets sewn on the front, each was edged in felt, and contained a different soft fabric animal. She held it up, examining it closely.

"Did you make this as well?"

"Yes, I thought Sarah might like it for Olivia."

"How long did it take to make?"

"Not that long once I had come up with the idea and the basic designs."

"And you enjoy making these?"

"Yes, it's exciting coming up with the original designs, and then seeing them come alive as I make them. It's, well, quite satisfying. Like creating something from scratch."

Tara opened her chocolate brown Todd's handbag and pulled out her filo-fax; she was the only person Josie knew who needed such a large address book for her contacts. Undoing the neat leather fastening, she pulled a thick white card out and pausing as she weighed something up, she tapped the invite against her teeth. Then coming to a decision she held it out to Josie. Intrigued Josie took it and read through the invite advertising the Knightsbridge Ladies Social Morning for the next month.

"What is this for? I don't really go in for ladies who lunch; I think it is more aimed at the Chelsea Chicks than me."

"One of the wives of Jeremy's partners holds these social mornings. It's an excuse for her friends to buy lots of expensive items while not going out to the shops, and of securing their photos in Chic and Viva."

"And what has this got to do with me? I still don't understand."

"Why don't you take a stand at one of her mornings; you could make some more of these and sell them. It might not be a huge money earner, but it might be a start. What do you think of the idea?"

"Tara, I think you are a genius! Are you sure you think these are good enough to sell though. I wouldn't want to embarrass myself."

"Of course they are good enough; I can't believe you haven't done this before. When I get home I'll give Gigi a call and get it sorted. I can't see why there would be a problem. It'll be so exciting, your first new job."

Ideas started fizzing through Josie's imagination.

"I could do some suede covered journals, and maybe a baby changing mat; perhaps with a matching baby bag. What do you think?"

"I think it's lots of hard work, and as long as you don't ask me to help, then you'll be fine." Tara said laughing, glad her friend seemed to be enthusiastic about something after being so low. "Now how much do I owe you for the album?"

Josie flapped her hand, still thinking of new designs. "Nothing, I enjoyed making it."

"Josie," Tara's voice was firm. "I didn't ask you to make it as a favour. This was a business arrangement."

"But the fabric was only four pounds, and the album was about twenty pounds. Twenty four pounds?" Her voice was uncertain as she suggested such a high price.

"Love, if you are going to make a living from this then you have to learn to charge properly. I don't know how long it took you to make this, nor how much it cost to buy all the different bits; but if I was buying this in a shop then I wouldn't expect to get much change from a hundred pounds." She pulled out her purse and plucked out five crisp twenty pound notes. "So here you go. And make sure you start keeping proper records, otherwise Jeremy will only start nagging you! No arguing, just take it. And we're short of time, so go and grab your things, otherwise you'll be late for your date with Prince Charming, and that's not what you want to do on a date."

While Josie was nervously counting down the minutes until she would arrive at Drayton Beauchamp station, Henry was finishing off a pint of the local ale at The King's Head. He'd arranged to meet Adam for lunch and they had finished off the chunky steak and kidney pie, carrots and thick gravy which Tina, the pub owner, had freshly prepared for that lunchtime. Contentedly they leant back in the worn wooden chairs watching the darts team trying to practice in between the visiting tourists who kept popping in to see if a table had come free yet in the busy bar.

"So who's the young lady?" Adam asked as he drank his pint.

"The daughter of a client. She was widowed earlier this year and her mother got me helping her sort out her affairs."

"Aha! So you are stalking a rich young widow then."

"Hardly; having seen her finances it is definitely not her money that I'm interested in."

"So I can't tap her for money to pay off my debts then?"

"You can try, but I think you'd have more luck approaching Church Mice Inc. So you still owe the money then?" Henry had hoped the lack of conversation about the gambling debt had meant Adam had managed to find the funds to pay if off.

"Oh yes." Adam said cheerily. "They've been quite understanding so far; but I'm not sure their patience is going to hold out much longer."

"Aren't you worried?"

"Henry – they are a couple of investment bankers. They are not exactly the sort to set the heavies on me if that's what you were imagining." Much to his chagrin Henry's ears flushed red, admitting he had envisaged Italian style mobsters waiting for Adam down dark alleyways to remind him of the debts. Adam hooted with laughter.

"Honestly Henry you are the limit. I'll have to tell Nanny Hargreaves when I see her next. You watch too much TV, you need to get out a bit more."

"I forgot to tell you I met her last week; she recognised me straight away. I had no idea who she was. I meant to let you know."

"She's an amazing lady, never forgets a name or a face. Poor old thing is really suffering at the moment. She is having a rough time."

"What's wrong with her? I didn't like to ask when I was there."

"The big old C. Apparently it's spread everywhere. She is absolutely riddled with it." Henry shivered despite the warmth coming from the roaring log fire.

"How awful."

"It is rather." Adam agreed. "But she doesn't say a word. Never complains. Not like Nanny Bloom."

"Old Bloomers – goodness I'd forgotten all about her. Didn't she end up with her own private nurse she had so many ailments?"

"Not quite, but she did keep trying to get a free consultation with the Mater's doctor every time he visited. I don't think she and Pa worked out whether old Bloomers was really ill or just had a huge crush on the Doc!" They laughed at the shared childhood memory; transported back to the days of short trousers, playing conkers and long holidays from prep school. Henry took a final swig of beer and placed the glass firmly on the table. "Well that's me done. How about you – another pint?"

Adam shook his head. "I've got a date with a lady too you know. Only mine's a bit older. I'm off to visit Nanny Hargreaves, and if I turn up smelling like a brewery she'll probably take the carbolic soap to me again. You know it turns my stomach just smelling Pears soap in Boots."

"I'll settle up here – my treat." Henry offered graciously, pushing his chair back, standing up and walking over to the bar where Tina was chatting to a couple of regulars. He didn't notice the female visitors take another look at the local attraction as he walked past, in his casual levis and thick cable knit sweater.

"Hello my darlin'." Tina said accompanied by a stream of tinkling as the gold bangles she wore on either arm slipped down. "'Ow was the food?"
"Delicious as ever. You certainly know how to make a man happy." Henry complimented her smoothly.
Tina winked one huge mascaraed eyelash. "I've 'ad no complaints." She boasted. Tina was known throughout the village as having a big heart and an even bigger chest measurement. She enjoyed the male attention she got both in the bar and in her bed, but as she was only too happy to point out to all her un-happily married friends, a good book and a bar of chocolate gave twice the pleasure for a lot less hassle. She had casually dropped a few hints to Henry about getting together, but despite going out for drinks a couple of times it had never materialised into anything. Not that Tina really minded, after all it's probably better not to sleep with the solicitor who's handling your divorce case.
Tina totted up the bill mentally. "That will be ten pounds fifty darlin'. Unless of course you want to settle up by leaving me with that gorgeous cousin of yours." Tina inclined her head towards Adam, who Henry noticed was chatting to two of the female visiting tourists who had been looking for a table earlier.
"Sounds a very tempting deal, but I think you'd be demanding a refund by the end of the day." Henry joked as he handed over the money.
"Nah, worth every penny. It's not every day you get to bag royalty."
"Mmm; I don't think he's actually related to the Queen..." Everyone knew Tina was a true monarchist.
"Shame; I could just see him in that fur and crown get up."
"Tina, you're outrageous."
She gave his arm a friendly pat. "I know darlin', it's wot keeps me so young." And cackling with laughter she turned away to another local. "Bert – wot's it to be? A pint of the usual?"
Henry waited for Adam to extract himself from the cosy trio.
"Are you sure you and your friend don't want to join us? The brunette said coyly.
"We'd love to." Adam lied smoothly. "But we've got to go; his wife and children are waiting at home for him." He flitted his hand at the beer mat that she was holding. "But give me a call if you're

ever in the area; I definitely don't have a wife." He gave them a dazzling smile and followed Henry out of the crowded pub.

"What was that all about?" Henry asked. "Since when did you give out your number to strange women?"

"She was hardly strange. Perhaps a little desperate – but not strange."

"You know what I mean."

"Since Tina gave me this." He held up the latest mobile phone, a tiny matchbox sized gadget.

"Tina? How is she involved in all this?" Henry's heart sunk a little, it was never straight forward with Adam.

"Well she and I were talking about business and the lack of it during the week, and we decided to go into partnership. I arrange to meet all the women back in the pub and that way Tina improves her takings and I get free drinks."

Henry shook his head. "But you hate having to make polite small talk."

"Oh we've already thought of all that. What I do is arrange to meet them during the week one evening and then just give them a call to say I'm held up. That way they'll spend more while they are waiting and Tina can let them down gently about how I'm the local Casanova, strings of broken hearts all over the county, you get the picture." Adam looked pleased with himself. "And that was the first one; maybe I should turn up seeing as it's the first one. Except she's just going through a messy divorce and I don't think I can cope with a desperate woman at the moment." Henry raised an eyebrow, Adam's commitment-phobia was even greater than Tina's.

"I can't wait to see what happens." Henry said wryly as he walked over to where Betsy stood, tail wagging.

"Perhaps you could get Tina to relax the ban on dogs in the pub. Betsy hates being left out here all alone."

"She does not." Adam contradicted. "She loves it, not only does she get all the attention as people keep arriving; she also gets fed by all the children who feel sorry for her stuck outside." He stroked the soft golden furry head. "In fact she'll probably need the walk to the station just to wear off all the chips and scampi she's been fed this afternoon."

"Well she's certainly going to get some exercise today, it's the Little Acorns' Jamboree this afternoon."

"You're never taking Josie to that." Adam said horrified.
"It won't be that bad." Henry assured him.
It was Adam's turn to shudder. "I still have the scars from the toasting fork." Adam protested. "Don't tell me you're dragging Betsy along as well."
"Of course – after all I'll need some protection."
"Oh yes," They looked at Betsy happily wagging her tail at strangers trying to make friends. "She makes such a good guard dog!"

"Come through, come through." Henry's voice echoed in the hallway resonating off the black and white geometric marble floor. Josie felt a sense of déjà vu coming back into the house, but instead of being ushered into the elegant drawing room they went through to the kitchen. Glancing round Josie saw a cavernous room fitted out with several huge Welsh dressers packed with an assortment of china, a long refractory table that could easily seat ten, and a cream Aga.
"Wow; this is massive. My whole flat would fit in here." Henry looked slightly abashed, he had never considered it anything other than a normal kitchen; he watched as Josie wandered over to the window above the porcelain butler sink and looked out over the park like gardens. "Is this really all yours? There aren't several other families living here as well are there?"
Henry shook his head "It's just me."
It had seemed strange to Josie but there didn't seem to be any awkwardness between them. He'd met her from the train and after giving a chaste kiss on her cheek had taken her hand and led her out to where he had parked his car outside the station, and brought her back to the house explaining they would need to get ready. They had chatted about their week and it had been easy and relaxed.
"So what exactly are we doing this afternoon?" She enquired when he returned with a large glossy bag in one hand.
"Erm, well it's the… it's the Little Acorns Jamboree."
"The what? What on earth is the Little Corns Jam-whatisit?"
Refusing to meet her eye he studied the toe of his shoe and tried to adopt a casual attitude. "Well it's nothing special really. It's just once a year all the children in Drayton Beauchamp get together to have a camp day. You know the sort of thing; burnt sausages over the campfire, getting soaked in the rain and overexcited toddlers.

Anyway some cunning parents realise it is the ideal opportunity to rope in the rest of the village to help look after the apples of their eye."

"Yikes – you never said there were children involved." Josie felt she had only just mastered babies, children were a completely new thing. "Erm what do we have to do exactly?"

"Nothing much really;" Henry said airily. "Just help to keep them entertained for a bit, you know the sort of thing; it's just giving a helping hand that's all."

Josie looked down at her beloved Versace jeans and Whistles cashmere jumper; it wasn't exactly children friendly wear.

"You might need these though." He offered her the large lustrous green bag with cord handles. Intrigued she took the bag, pulling out a large rectangle box. "Go on open it." Henry urged as she held the box with anticipation. He watched as first intrigue, then understanding, then amusement showed across her face.

"They are fabulous!" She enthused, leaning across and kissing him firmly on the lips, causing him to redden slightly. Taking the cerise pink gingham Wellingtons with tiny pink roses by the top out of the box she pulled them on. "Where on earth did you find them? I haven't seen any like these before. I thought they only came in boring green or blue."

"One of my clients organises the county show; he knew someone who just set up a company specialising in trendy wellies. So I gave them a call and they posted them down to me. I had to take some advice on the design; I have to admit I was at a loss to know what you would like."

Josie gave a little jig, pointing her toes out and admiring them from all angles. "I can't wait to show Tara, she will be sooo jealous." Henry was amused at her enthusiasm, as well as privately glad he'd taken Tina's advice. He'd been planning to just buy the traditional green Wellingtons but Tina had baulked at his suggestion. 'Take my advice darlin'," she'd said while pouring out a large glass of wine for them both after they had been discussing the latest saga of her divorce. 'She sounds more like a city chick than a country casual. Make it big, make it bold, but definitely don't make it green'.

"And did you bring a waterproof coat?"

"Erm, only this little jacket." She indicated the Agnes B tweed box jacket she'd hung over the back of one of the chairs.

"I think you are going to need something a little more... robust. Don't worry I'm sure I'll be able to find something. There are normally loads of old jackets left by visitors over the years." He disappeared into the depths of the boot room, returning with a lady's Barbour jacket. "I know it's seen better days, but it's ideal to keep for visitors to borrow. Try it on; I think it should be about your size."

She shrugged herself into the heavy coat, breathing in the smell of wax and dogs as she did so. It felt heavy and warming, strangely protective; she twirled round in front of him, fashioning it for his benefit. "Goodness if Tara could see me now she would have a fit. Are you sure I'm going to need all this?" She asked pulling at the sleeves of the coat and pointing her pink gingham toes.

"Oh yes – the more protection you have the better with the Little Acorns." He glanced up at the old enamel faced kitchen clock and saw it was coming up to half-past two. "We'd better make tracks so we're not late. Betsy! Come on we're going." He called the dog in from outside and attached the lead onto her worn leather collar.

"Are you ready?" He checked with Josie.

"Ready as I'll ever be." She tried to fix a grin on her face. "Let's go and jamboree."

They walked through the fields across to the large open common area that Josie recognised as the village green she and Molly had driven past when they had first visited Henry. In the background the high street was bustling with locals and tourists. In the centre of the green a nomadic camp had appeared around a large unlit bonfire; the pile of branches and twigs rising up dominating the scene. The smell of barbequing food and the sounds of shouting and whoops floated across the spring afternoon air. What looked like hundreds, but was probably in reality only about 30 children, were running round, shouting to each other. On closer inspection Josie realised they were playing some form of tag.

"This way," Henry directed her over to where a group of adults were congregating round the primitive kitchen, with a gentle hand on the small of her back. As they approached a blonde woman, looking very chic in Paul Costello weekend, waved across at them and hurried over.

"Henry, how lovely you could make it." She kissed him on either cheek as he murmured his hellos. "Toby's just on sausage duty and

Max is somewhere in the crowd." The blonde woman turned to Josie. "Hi I'm Caroline; Henry said he'd managed to convince you to join us. You really are awfully brave. I'd have run a mile if it wasn't that Max was here."

"Oh I'm looking forward to it." Josie lied airily.

"Well come and meet the others; Henry go over and see if Toby needs rescuing yet. You know how awful he is at cooking; I think he needs some moral support." Henry gave a questioning look as though checking with Josie that it was ok to leave her alone; that she didn't feel abandoned. With a small inclination of her head she mouthed "Go on; I'll be fine." He set off towards the group of men huddling round the barbeque, greeting them with a slap on the back, and a rowdy hello; taking the offered outstretched can of beer.

"White or red?" Caroline asked as they walked round the trestle table, borrowed from the village hall, laden with wine. "The white is a very nice Chardonnay, but you might prefer a warming red in this weather."

"Yes, definitely the red." Josie agreed watching as Caroline poured two huge goblets of red wine for them.

"So how long have you known Henry for?" Caroline asked as she handed over one of the glasses and chinked companionably with Josie.

"Not long at all. He's my mother's solicitor. She got it into her head that it would be sensible to ask Henry to look over my things. I've recently been widowed you see. My mother was trying to be helpful – you know how they are."

"You poor thing." Josie's heart sank at the pity she could see in Caroline's face; it was the usual story when anyone heard about Nick's death, they immediately started to feel sorry for her, casting her as the pitiful widow. "I know exactly what it's like."

"You do?" Josie was perplexed.

"Oh yes, my mother fixed me up with Toby." Josie tittered realising she'd misread Caroline's concern. "We never stand a chance against them you know."

"But it obviously worked out for the two of you."

"Yes, but it took another twenty five years before he proposed. My mother and his mother went to school together and they had always agreed what a wonderful idea it would be if their children got married, so you see I had no chance of escape. They had us betrothed right from nursery." They were interrupted by a gaggle of adrenaline-fuelled hyper-excited children running over.

"Is there anything to eat yet?" One of the boys at the front asked, puffing his fringe off his sweaty forehead. "We're starving!"

"Max you only had biscuits about an hour ago. Honestly, you can't really be hungry."

"But we are." They chorused, looking up with pleading eyes. "We're really starving."

"Well if you go and see your father he may have managed to cook something by now."

"Oh no, he isn't in charge of the cooking is he?" Max looked concerned fully aware of his father's limited ability on the culinary front.

Don't worry he's got Uncle Henry with him, so you should be getting something edible. Just don't eat too much if you're going to be running round or you'll all be ill." But the cautioning was lost on them as they headed off in search of food.

In their wake several other mothers appeared, and although they seemed knackered by the careful administrations, they were all turned out in natty puffa jackets, tan leather boots and chestnut brown cords. Josie felt like an ugly duckling in her outfit; very conscious of the slightly too large Barbour jacket against her denim jeans; a mismatch of country and city that clashed.

"Drink?" Caroline offered, holding a bottle up.

"Gin, straight from the bottle, forget the tonic and ice." One gasped. "Why do we do it again? This is sheer torture."

"Because the Little Acorns is part of the history of the village." The others chorused repeating the words that appeared every year on the posters; the words that get drummed in to each child as they join in each year.

"It's a shame the Little Acorns just grow up into skulking teenager oaks that wouldn't be the seen dead camping on the green." The other newcomer said.

"Josie this is Suki and Helena; mothers of Octavia, Thomas, Lizbet and Alexia."

"Hi." Josie said shyly, feeling particularly excluded through the lack of a husband or children.

"So Henry persuaded you to help out." Suki, the taller red head seemed impressed.

"Ohh! Ohh! Look!" Helena's curly hair bounced wildly as she pointed at Josie's feet, jiggling in excitement. "Aren't they just heavenly."

"Where did you get them from? They look so much more fun than the boring green ones Charlie bought me."

"Henry brought them for me." Josie confided. "I didn't own a pair before today." The three women turned to look at her in surprise, seriously impressed. Josie must have Henry well trained if he was buying her trendy boots already. Each thought back on the duty free perfume, chocolate and M&S cardigans that were routinely bought for birthdays and occasionally anniversaries, when remembered. Each of which was either given to the church jumble, eaten in a fit of pique or swapped for children's school uniform items.

"Well they'll be just the ticket for this afternoon." Caroline commented thinking of the activities planned. "Now we had better go and check the children are actually being fed something vaguely edible; or it will be 1999 all over again." The women pulled faces.

"I hope not – there's only so much vomit you can cope with in a tent." Suki said shuddering.

Caroline slipped a friendly arm through Josie's as they retraced their steps to where the men and their offspring were crowding round trying to eat the charred fingers of burnt sausages that Toby had carefully prepared.

"Get Henry to bring you over to ours for dinner next time; that way you can enjoy the food and not worry about being ill the next day. If I were you I would stick to the wine and avoid the food." There was a wail from one of the small boys as Betsy tucked into his hot dog from off the grass. "I'd better go and sort it out." Caroline said with a sigh "David what do you expect to happen if you leave your plate on the floor, of course Betsy is going to eat it." She called out to the youngster as she walked over and dried his tears before finding him another sausage. "Betsy, naughty girl." But Caroline's scolding words fell onto deaf ears, all Betsy was interested in was finding her next prize.

Henry detached himself from the group of men and walked over to where Josie stood slightly alone.

"Everything ok?" His face looked concerned, guilty at having deserted her amongst strangers.

"Yes of course. Everyone seems nice; Caroline was being really friendly."

"She is;" Henry enthused. "You'd never know that her father owned half of Fleet Street." Josie was amazed, Caroline seemed far too down to earth. "The family own Shaker Publication; you know the ones that print Bling & Boudoir. "

"Wow." Josie's eyes opened even further in astonishment. "But they are seriously rich." She said hardly able to get the words out.

"Yeap, her old man's rated in the top ten for this year's rich list."

"But she's so nice."

"I know. Doesn't it make you sick. If she wasn't so nice I could hate her." They leant into each other and shared a momentary chuckle. Josie breathed in the woody scented cologne from Henry and felt slightly light headed.

"Are you two ready?" Toby shouted across to them. "It's time for the offing, and we need you two to start it."

"Henry;" Josie's voice was muffled against his sweater and his neck. "What exactly are we doing?" She watched as his cheeks slowly infused pink.

"Didn't I mention it before?" He leant across and spoke slowly into her ear, causing a thousand shivers to run up and down her spine. "We are doing the Little Acorn paper chase."

"The what?"

"You know; someone runs off pretending to be the hare and leaves a trail of paper behind them for the hounds to follow."

"And we're expected to run around dropping little bits of paper?"

"Oh no; we're looking after the hounds – it's far more exciting. When Adam and I were little we used to always be the winners at catching the hare. Although we would get a sound beating from Nanny Bloom afterwards for ripping our socks and getting grass stains on our trousers." Josie watched Henry's face animate up as he recollected the childhood memories; and then gave his hand a quick squeeze.

"We'd better get going then." They hurried over, hand in hand, to where all the children were lining up ready for the off.

"Uncle Henry; Uncle Hennreee!" Max waved his hands in the air desperately trying to attract their attention. "Come and run with us; we want you to run with us." Even Betsy got caught up in excitement and started to bark eagerly. Josie saw a faint trail of paper stretching out to the east of the common into the woodland and onto the open fields beyond.

"Is everyone ready?" Toby bellowed trying to be heard above the loud incessant chatter, his brightly coloured start flag fluttering in the crisp spring breeze making firecracker like snaps as it twisted and turned. "Let's start." His flag dropped dramatically and the crowd of exuberant children swarmed off in hot pursuit of the inviting paper trail. Josie and Henry were forced apart by the crowd; Henry ended up at the front motivating the eager leaders; urging them on. Josie already feeling warm faced had dropped to the back where some of the younger girls were already questioning how much further would it be.

It was several hours later that the mirage of base camp came into site; its appearance being welcomed by the stragglers who had bravely stayed the course, knowing they had no chance of ever catching the hare but still gamely taking part. Henry and the boys had hurtled round the trail; tearing through bushes and hedges that stood in their path; storming through the streams and puddles they encountered, so that by the time they returned victorious they resembled a crowd of wild creatures, splattered with mud, clothes torn, adorned with leaves and burrs, hair tousled and feet soaking wet. But their spirits were still as high as ever and they relived their adventures and tales of bravery to their mothers, fathers and any other audience foolish enough to listen.

Josie and the girls had taken a more sedate approach, and because they had taken less wrong turns and false trails than the boys they arrived back soon after. Two of the smaller girls held hands tightly with Josie, as though trying to garner strength from her. Josie had been startled at how much fun it had been; they had sung all the chants the girls knew several times over, did a round of singing London's Burning; and told her which of the boys they fancied, what they were going to be when the grew up and the time had simply slipped away. Where the boys had charged through hedges, they had found the styles, and where the testosterone fuelled leaders had wildly splashed combo style through the streams, they had gently picked their way across, using the larger rocks as stepping stones. Some of the older girls had found some early flowering daisies, and Josie had shown them how to make dainty daisy necklaces and head bands to wear. So as they trudged across the green to the camp site their faces were glowing with health and they looked as neat and tidy as they had set off. They chatted animatedly amongst themselves before spying the cakes and orange squash which they then swooped upon; swapping stories with the boys and showing their floral jewellery to their proud mothers.

"I wish I had a girl." Caroline said wistfully to Josie as she handed her another large glass of wine. "You should have seen the state of Max when he got back. His Racing Green trousers are completely ruined. I thought Henry and Betsy would be a calming influence – but it sounds like he just egged them on even more. I guess I should have known better."

"I think it is something to do with reverting to childhood. Men can't seem to help themselves."

"Tell me about it. Toby's now decided he's going to camp out with the boys tonight. Which means like every other year, tomorrow he will be complaining bitterly of a stiff neck and having lumbago from being cold and uncomfortable all night, and expect me to lay on the sympathy and remedies." Josie smiled in empathy. They were joined by Helena.

"I've just seen Lizbet and Alexia; I can't believe they're still clean. It's the first time ever."

"Don't rub it in." Caroline implored.

"And they really enjoyed it; which is another first. Normally its tears and tantrums." She looked admiringly at Josie. "You are obviously a natural with children you must have your own?"

Josie glowed warmly with the compliment but admitted.

"No I don't have any. They were all very well behaved; I didn't really do anything."

"Well let me know if you ever fancy doing any baby sitting. I've never seen my two so content." In the distance they heard Toby announce supper to a chorus of disappointment and a few burst into tears.

"Oh dear, I'd better go and rescue him." Regret tingeing Caroline's voice. "I think we'll be retiring to the pub for the adult food; so we'll be ok." She reassured Helena and Josie. "Once the terrible tearaways have finished their suppers we can make our escape. I hope Tina's got a huge G&T ready for us. After today I reckon we all deserve it!"

The exhausted figures started to make their across the green in the evening dusk; the ground felt soft and squidgy underfoot from the early evening dew; and the air was filled with the autumn smell of bonfires, and behind them glowing warmly was the central pyre the children had built, crackling and snapping as the flames licked greedily away at the sappy wood. The children were now slowly retiring to their tents, tired by the day's exertions; the boys were playing half-heartedly on portable play stations and telling improbable ghost stories to frighten themselves as the gloomy darkness engulfed them. The girls were experimenting with 'borrowed' make up; daubing their cheeks with spots of rouge and lining their eyes with cyan blue; talking about favourite pop-stars and gorgeous actors. The next shift had appeared a short while before, relieving the day parents who were now heading towards The King's Head.

Henry and Josie were making small talk; shattered after the energetic activities of the day. Even Betsy seemed subdued after the excitement; plodding slowly by the side of Josie, began to show signs of her age. The three figures reached the edge of the green and began to walk along the high street which Josie had only ever seen from the seat of the car. The stone Georgian shop fronts were turned to a pale gold by the street lights, illuminating the signs over the doors and casting the windows into deep cavernous shadows. Josie's step slowed as she stopped to look in each one. The first one was the butchers; the painted wooden animals showing the different cuts, and in the back ground she could just make out the dark blue stripped apron and the dull glint of the knives and axes. Next door was the greengrocer, arrays of fruit and vegetables, some native, some exotic lay piled high in inviting displays with large hand written price labels stuck on the baskets. Beyond that was the bakery, the delicatessen and several boutique clothes shops that seemed to cater for the trendy village mothers. A small bookshop sat next to the coffee shop; an antique furniture restorer and the ubiquitous gift shops, which judging by the Drayton Beauchamp tea towels, post cards and boxes of chocolates decorated with scenes from the village were designed for the visiting hoards of tourists. Between the coffee shop and the antique restorer she noticed the filmy windows of another shop. It seemed grime encrusted with age; a look of neglect and deprivation that was out of place with the rest of the sumptuously rich village. She put her face to the glass to see better, shielding out the street lights with her hands; the glass felt cold and damp against her skin as she peered into the darkness. Her eyes slowly became accustomed to the dark, and she could make out the outline of what looked like a few rolls of fabric lying on top of an oversized table and propped up against the walls. At the back was a Victorian cast iron fireplace, stuffed with old newspapers that spilled out across the hearth and over the floor; a tiny door at the back obviously led off to another room, and by this.... a body hung from the roof, lifeless and limp, swaying slightly in the breeze. Hearing Josie give a scream, Henry hurried back, retracing his steps so that he was standing by her looking into the window at where her startled gaze was held by some mysterious object.

"What's wrong?" There was real concern in his voice as scanned the old shop to try to see the cause of her horror. With a shaking hand she pointed.

"It's in there; there's a dead person hanging from the ceiling." Her stomach was churning over and over; and she half turned away not wanting to see it any more.

Henry looked through the window, scanning the room intently for the mutilated figure; finally his eyes alighted on it, and he gave a chortle. Putting a comforting arm around her shoulders he turned her to face the window.

"Take another look in there. It's not a dead body I promise you; it's just one of those old fashioned tailors' dummies." Timidly Josie raised her eyes and looked again, this time her eyes saw the torso was in fact on a wooden base, standing on a small table. Relief flooded through her, and her racing heart began to calm a little.

"Oops; how could I have been so silly?" She murmured reassured that it wasn't anything as dramatic as a murdered corpse. Henry laughed at her predicament and gave her a long comforting hug "This used to be the gentleman's outfitters; it belonged to old Jack Hargreaves. After he died it looks like it was just shut up. I'd forgotten it was even here; it's so easy to walk past it and just miss it."

They both looked up at the building with its pealing paint on the windows and missing roof tiles, looking neglected and uncared for.

"What a shame no-one looks after it." Josie pictured how it could look with a touch of paint and a thorough clean.

"I think there were plans to turn it into a house, but no-one really wants to be living right on the street during tourist season with all those nosy busy-bodies peering into your front room. There's no way into the back garden either from here, so it isn't ideal." Henry pointed to the neighbouring shops abutting either side.

"It would be a shame to change it – I bet it would make a wonderful shop." Josie sounded dreamy.

"Don't tell me you're thinking of opening up a shop!"

"Of course not! But it doesn't stop me thinking it's an ideal location for someone who does want a shop."

"I bet it gets snapped up by a Starbucks or a Pizza Express." Henry said gloomily recognising the tide of change that generally happened to small picturesque towns.

"Oh no." The thought filled her with horror, the new owners would ruin the simple elegance of the oak floor boards and panelled walls, trying to turn it into a pseudo Italian trattoria with terracotta paint work, olive trees by the door and heavy cast iron furniture inside. "Who owns it now?"

Henry shrugged "No idea, Probably one of Jack's many relatives I guess."

Eyes gleaming, she turned back to face him. "Why don't you buy it?"

"Josie what would I do with it? I already have an office, and I don't know anything about running shops."

"I suppose not; daft idea really."

"Not one of your brightest I have to admit." He took her hands and felt their icy chill. "Heavens you're frozen, you need warming up. Let's get going; the others will be wondering where we are." Off they set towards the cheerfully beckoning King's Head and the rousing thought of roaring fires and warming red wine.

Chapter 5

"You never call me; you never come to see me; you don't even bother returning any of my emails!" Neil said with mock anguish in his voice. Josie giggled.
"How lovely to hear from you; I've just been going silently mad trying to choose between checks and stripes."
"I would always go for cheques, or cash if possible."
"Not that kind of cheque dummy, the square kind."
"Am I missing part of this conversation?" He sounded confused.
"Oh don't worry – I'll tell you all abut it when we catch up next." She soothed. "There's just so much to update you on." The past few months had been so busy, with everything that was going on, that Josie couldn't quite believe she was the same person.
"So you've started making a few plans then?"
"Yes, I've definitely decided to give up the flat. As lovely as it is I can't afford it on my own, and I don't want to share it with anyone, it wouldn't be the same after having been here with Nick. So I'm moving back to my mother's house in 6 weeks."
"Erm, and that's good?" He asked hesitantly
"We'll probably end up strangling each other, but at least that will encourage me to keep looking for a place of my own. Plus I've got my mini-project on the go."
"Your what?"
"I'll tell you when I see you – it's far too long and complex to go into now." Her mind drifted back to the weeks of planning and designing that had been happening. Now it was just the awful anticipatory countdown of the D-Day as Tara kept calling it. "Anyway, why did you call? Not that it isn't lovely to hear from you. But a busy executive like you," She pictured him in his office, sprawled out on one of the armchairs overlooking the view, feet propped up on the coffee table, "Doesn't usually make social calls at..." she checked her watch "two fifty five on a Thursday afternoon."
"Correction. This busy executive does when he is ordered by his incredibly bossy PA." Josie heard an outraged exclamation in the background and a firm voice saying something she couldn't catch to Neil. "Actually Mary says 'Hi'. The real reason for calling is that it is the work's picnic on Saturday the 20th and we wondered if you were free."

"Yes, I've nothing planned." Her mind flitted back to the other picnics and days out that Miller & Moss had organised for their staff. The combined advantage of being incredibly creative and having very famous clients meant the parties were always held in extraordinary places. She and Nick had been to a tea party with the chimps in the London Zoo; they had cooked their own lunch at The Ivy and invented their own gin cocktails at Vinopolis. "Where is it this time?"

"Hyde Park. We're really having a picnic this year; no I mean it." It had been a long running joke that every year the staff were invited to the staff day-out picnic but they never actually had one.

"Neil, you say that ever year! What time is it kicking off?"

"How about I pick you up, Cinders, about 1.30, that should give us enough time to get over to Hyde Park."

"I'll be waiting. Do I have to wear anything special?" She thought of the circus day when they had been all dressed up as clowns, trapeze artists and strong men. Neil, of course, had been the Ring Master, resplendent in black and scarlet with a huge droopy moustache that kept falling off every time he drank his pint.

"No, just wear you want, everything you need will be there."

"Sounds intriguing, I can't wait."

"It is, and if Mary wasn't stood beside me and still listening in I'd tell you all about it." Again Josie heard an indignant squawk from the far end.

"She says I've got to go and do some real work instead of gossiping with you all day, so I'll see you on the 20th and we can catch up then."

"Ok and give my love to Mary." She put the phone down, and thinking about the picnic walked back to the piles of fabric laid out on the dining room table. Neil had always made her smile, his ridiculous sense of humour and the way he made Mary out to be the boss, well may be secretively she was, she'd give him that one. She tried to think what the staff day would be. May be they would do horse riding down Rotten Row? Hopefully it wouldn't be swimming in the Serpentine, as much as she loved watching the ducks and geese sedately float across the slime green water, she didn't want to become too intimately acquainted with it. The telephone rang again before she had moved a couple of yards. Presuming it was Neil phoning back with another last minute instruction she answered with:

"Don't tell me, we're going green and planting trees." She waited to hear Neil's response; only it wasn't Neil.

"Josie, have you taken to drinking at lunchtime?" Tara demanded. "I know it may be tough at the moment, but drinking isn't going to help."

"I'm not drunk." Josie protested; embarrassed at assuming Neil would be calling her back. "I'd just finished speaking with Neil and I thought it was him phoning back."

Tara's antenna twitched, the delectable Neil phoning Josie during the day might mean some new gossip.

"So what did the hunk want?"

"I wish you wouldn't call him that." Josie scolded, and then because she was bursting to tell someone about the 20th instantly forgave her and launched into a lengthy recount of the picnic invitation.

"So why do you think he asked you?" Tara said archly, rationalising that now that Nick was dead Josie didn't actually have any connection with Miller & Moss.

"Probably because Mary told him to; she was standing with him when he called."

"No other reason?"

"What other reason could there be?"

"And is it just him picking you up, or him and Claudia."

"Just him... well he didn't say about Claudia, but I'm sure..." She stopped, confused about what that actually meant.

"Aha, so he is ditching Claudia for you."

"No he isn't. He's been living with Claudia for goodness knows how long. I think he is definitely off the potential partner market. Claudia is probably having to go straight to the picnic from somewhere else, and Neil is just picking me up so I don't have to go there alone."

"How boring! Well if you are not going to give me any interesting love life gossip then the least you can do is tell me how the sewing is going." Since Tara had put Josie forward for the Knightsbridge Ladies Social Morning she had been taken an avid interest in the progress, clucking round Josie like an old mother hen. Strangely Josie had found it really helpful; Tara had an instinctive eye for what the ladies who lunched would consider was hot, and what was not. So out were the pearls, chiffon and tweeds, 'too last season darling', and in were taffeta silks and organza roses; suede fabric and jaunty diamante detailing. They had spent mornings traipsing all over London finding stockists Josie had come across on the internet. Tara had even roped Jeremy in to give her a crash course in running a business. He had helped Josie to work out how to keep costs down when she was designing her memento boxes, photo albums and journal covers. 'Remember to take in all your costs.' He'd instructed her one evening as the three of them sat having some supper. "It's not just the cost of buying the fabric and the fancy bits. You have to build in how much it costs to get to the shops, and the cost of postage to get things delivered."

"But that's going to make everything so expensive, no-one will want to buy them." Josie wailed as she saw the figures mounting up. Jeremy had pulled out a large calculator from his brief case and wielded it officially, coming into his element as a keen business man.

"How much does item cost to make?"

Josie shrugged her shoulders. "Depending what it is between fifteen and thirty pounds."

"And how often have you been to the shops to buy things?"

"Oh absolutely loads." She said proudly. "Ohh." Her face fell. "That isn't a good answer is it?" She said noticing Jeremy shake his head and then tap vigorously away on the calculator keys.

"And how many things do you think you will sell at this ladies soiree?"

"Erm, between twenty and thirty?" Josie suggested her voice was timid, worried she wasn't giving the right answer. Jeremy tapped away on the calculator again, paused, then tapped in a few more numbers.

"I predict that at this rate you'll be making about five pounds profit on each item." He watched her smile fade away.

"That's not very much is it." The thought of all the work and effort she put in; it didn't seem a great return. She finished her glass of wine with a huge gulp and held it out to Tara for a large refill. "I don't think it's got much of a future for me. I'll never be able to earn much from doing this."

"Ahh, but there's a few secrets that you need to learn." Jeremy said looking conspiratorially across to Tara, who smiled knowingly back at her husband.

"The first thing is to limit the outgoings. You've done the research on who has what, so try and buy things from the same supplier. Normally it's a fixed postage charge, so that way you don't spend more on postage than you do on the individual items you are buying."

"Ok, that makes sense – but surely it would be even better if I went to pick everything up. That way I'd save on the postage as well." She felt pleased with her idea, she could get into this cost cutting exercise just as easily as Jeremy could.

"Not necessarily; you have to compare the costs. If postage is working out about £5.75 for most of your deliveries, then how much is the travel and the time it takes you. You have to compare the two."

"Because," Tara chipped in, "Every hour you spend collecting things is an hour you've lost to make something." Jeremy nodded approvingly at his wife.

"I'm never going to learn all this." Josie grumbled looking across at the two of them, enthusiastic support gleaming from their faces.

"Of course you will." Jeremy said matter of factly; unable to believe anyone wouldn't be born without the basic business skills firmly embedded. "Just keep one eye on the costs and work out what your customers want. That's all there is to it."

"Right. It's a lot trickier than I thought. I was just going to design a few things and make them. I didn't intend going for world domination."

"If you're going to do anything it's worth getting the best return you can." Jeremy reminded her. "After all why bother if it isn't going to help you financially? You might as well stick to secretarial duties within a dull nine-to-five job."

Josie didn't reply, although unable to find fault with the logic, it all seemed a far cry from the original plan. But they were right, she did need to start thinking about how she was going to earn some money properly – and soon.

"Have I come to the wrong place?" Neil asked doing a double take in the sitting room.

"I would say sit down, but I honestly don't think there's any spare space." Josie admitted.

"I can believe that. What's in all these boxes?" Everywhere he looked there were cardboard boxes, all different shapes and sizes.

"Well all the boxes over there are the moving boxes; all the boxes beyond that are my new deliveries, and all these boxes," she pointed to the ones nearest her "Are my finished stock."

"Hold on; moving, deliveries and stock? We don't speak for a few weeks and suddenly you've become the cardboard box queen."

"I know, it does all feel rather sudden. But I've started to try and plan what I'm going to do."

"This is all my fault isn't it." Neil said suddenly, remembering their discussions over money when he had helped Josie to sort through Nick's things.

"No, you just helped me recognise what I already knew. That I needed to start taking control of things."

"So tell me about your plans then." Neil said eagerly as he leant back against one of the boxes, flicking his fringe back, only to have it fall forward again. "What's been happening."

"Where do I start?" Josie mused casting round for the best place to begin. Neil carried on watching her as she gathered together her handbag and purse ready to go out, he noticed she had started to fill out a little, her clothes no longer hung off her, her hair looked glossy and she had lost the pasty paleness and now seemed to radiate energy and vitality. "Well it all started with this." She walked over to the coffee table and picked up the original pewter grey photo album, handing to him. He turned it over appreciatively, recognising the craftsmanship and skill. "I had made it as something to keep photos of Nick and me in as a sort of keepsake. Then Tara, do you remember her? Well she asked me to make one for her wedding anniversary. Which I did, and she thought it was good enough to sell to other people. So she organised for me to take a stall at the Knightsbridge Ladies Social Morning," she saw his eyebrows rise in disbelief. "No honestly it really does exist. So I've got a stall booked at their next forthcoming get together, and so since organising that I've been busy designing and sewing things to sell."

"What sort of things?" He sounded intrigued, he had never seen Josie as the creative type before. She led him over to the boxes by the coffee table.

"All sorts of things. In here are notebooks and journals covered in suede with silk ribbon page markers." She ran her fingers lightly over the cerise pinks and apple greens in the box, enjoying the smooth downy sensation of the fabric against her skin.

"In this one there's matching photo frames, and that one by you is a mixture of memento boxes and linen bags."

"And you've made them all yourself? That's pretty impressive. I had no idea you were so talented; how did you learn to sew?"

"Neither did I, I was useless when I did needlework at school. All I remember doing is stabbing myself countless times with the needle and bleeding everywhere. But I've really enjoyed doing this. The sewing is all quite straight forward, the hardest part is coming up with the original designs."

"So when's the nit-twit's ladies circle?"

Josie giggled. "The Knightsbridge Ladies Social Morning you mean - it's next Thursday."

"And are you ready?"

"I'm not sure. I don't know how many people go to it, and I've no idea what they will want to buy, so I've just made a few bits to see what people will like."

"So is this the new career? JC designed boxes and books for Knightsbridge women?"

"Hardly, but I did think if I had anything left over I might try going to a few car boot sales and markets. I know it isn't really a proper job, but I love doing it."

"So how is the proper job hunt going?"

She groaned. "Apparently no-one is in need of an office manager who can't use a computer properly, doesn't take shorthand and who wants more than the minimum wage!" She appealed with open arms. "I ask you, what is the world coming to when the untalented are so brutally cast aside from the jobs they are so unsuited to?" Neil tried to stop a smile from twitching at his lips as he watched her dramatic outburst. Leaning forward he gave her an impulsive hug.

"Don't give up hope. Something will turn up; it always does."

"That's what my mother says."

"A very sensible woman your mother."

"Ha! You wouldn't say that if she had tried to set you up on a blind date." Knowing Molly's all absorbing concern for Josie's welfare it wasn't difficult to imagine her hunting down son-in-law number 2 material to look after Josie.

"Tell me everything. What has she done this time."

"She took me under false pretences to see her solicitor and then practically forced the poor chap to see me again."

"And did he?" Neil's voice sounded strained as he imagined some portly balding man only too willing to take a younger attractive

woman out, but Josie was in full indignant flow and didn't notice his tone.
"Yes he did, he was quite sweet about it really. We get on fine actually, which makes it even more infuriating. How could my mother have guessed? She hardly knows Henry at all."
Neil tried to ignore the feeling of recoil that was spiralling downwards inside him; concern that Molly's enthusiastic match making would coincide with Josie's rebound. After all Nick had only died earlier that year; wasn't it too soon for her to be seeing someone else.
"Are you, erm, is it... serious?" He had difficulty finding his voice, his tongue suddenly seemed too large to use.
"Oh no." Josie said breezily. "We're just friends really. We meet up if he's coming into town, or I sometimes go down there." She went on to tell him about the Little Acorns Jamboree and their occasional snatched suppers, but he could tell from the changes in her that it was obviously more serious than she realised. He wasn't sure what to say, he didn't want to seem unfriendly but his mind had gone a complete blank, any topic of conversation had deserted him. Josie saved him from having to speak though, slotting her arm through his and picking up her keys she chattered on about Drayton Beauchamp and Henry's house, oblivious to his unhappy silence.

Hyde Park stretched out before them a rich emerald velvet that ruched and dipped as far as the eye could see. Imperial trees held court amongst the glorious settings as unchanged as they were in the days of Henry VIII. High up in the sky birds circled over head, gliding, calling chirpily to each other as they swooped on flies and dived on insects. The warm gentle breeze rustled the opening buds and shoots as newly formed leaves started to unfurl. Even the sun beamed down on the old regal site with fond benevolence. Standing with your back to Park Lane the pastoral vista seemed more akin to the gentle Buckinghamshire hills than the hustle and bustle of London. The park retained its timelessness appeal, no matter when you visited it always held the same calm welcome. Except today; today there was a different aura. An excited buzz reverberated around the trees and shrubs emanating from the newcomers. It looked like the park had been picked up and dropped back into the 1920s. Around the Serpentine jauntily striped tents had been erected in rose pink and baby blue. Old wooden steamer chairs with plumped up cushions were arranged by the side of the water, inviting ladies to sit back and enjoy the park's attractions in a more sedate fashion. A band stand had been purposefully built to one side, resplendent in scarlet and gold, and on it fifteen musicians, ornate in military uniforms, sat playing a medley of suitably nostalgic music. On the Serpentine the ducks watched in trepidation as the first of the punts struck off across the water, cutting through it gracefully leaving a trail of ripples behind. The blazored oarsmen pushed the pole in with an effortless ease and the small boat shot forward across the glassy surface. An indignant Canadian goose squawked loudly at the invaders as it had to paddle quickly out of the line of the punt, flapping its wings and hissing its displeasure at the invasion of the lake.

Neil and Josie stood by the thick red rope that cordoned off the area from the general public and took in the scene.
"I told you this year it really would be a picnic. After all the years of never getting round to it, we thought it was high time we actually did hold one."
Josie shot him an approving look. "It's fabulous. How did you even think of coming up with the idea. It's just brilliant."
"We were doing some work for a new car launch, and the clients wanted to position it as a car of grace and beauty, something that was designed to impress, but also to enjoy. We started thinking about the 1920s when cars were coming into vogue and based the whole marketing plan around the concept of luxury that was a fashion statement as well. It was while we were doing some of the initial research that I came across photographs of the afternoon tea parties they used to hold in Hyde Park, and I just thought it would be great fun to have one of our own here."
"Oh it is," Josie agreed thinking how elegant everyone else looked, the ladies in their pastel stripped dresses and golden yellow straw hats. The men in rowing whites, peacock coloured blazers and boaters with matching ribbons perched jauntily on their heads. She suddenly became aware of the disparately of her modern clothes with everyone else's. She tugged at Neil's sleeve and whispered awkwardly. "I think we look a little out of it."
"Fear not." He joked "Your own personal fairy godmother is over there." He pointed to two of the striped tents; the one on the left proudly bore the sign "Gentlemen's Outfitters." The one on the

right was "Dressmakers to the Gentry". Intrigued she watched Neil greet a couple of colleagues as he entered the Gentlemen's Outfitters ready to be transformed into an Edwardian dandy. Walking across the soft springy grass to the ladies equivalent she was greeted by two corkscrew permed blue rinses, who were never going to see fifty again.

"'Ello ducks." They cheerily welcomed, tugging at the tape measures round their necks. "Now what's it to be Lady Brockenhurst, Forsythe Saga or Bloomsbury Group?" They looked her up and down, made her turn round several times so they could gauge her from all angles.

"What do you fink Vi?" Vi popped her head to one side, just like a started bird.

"You know what Nelly, I reckon a flapper. We've got that dove grey chiffon dress, and somewhere we should have the matching shoes."

"And there's the long pearls we used for last week's Elizabeth I costume as well." They went into raptures as they started sorting through the racks of clothes hanging up inside the tent. Triumphantly they returned; the layers of chiffon gently rustling on the hanger, the heeled shoes with two button and hook clasps covered in a grey kid leather together with the obligatory white silk tights that every self-respecting Charleston dancing girl of the 20s would have worn with pride.

"Come along luv, let's see how this all looks." They ushered here over to a large changing room, and while she carefully undressed from her modern day persona she could hear the two women twittering away animatedly. She stepped into the dress, the satin lining caressing her body as she pulled it up, cool and silky against her skin. It fitted well; the bodice was a little tight, but luckily the dropped waistline and gathered knee length skirt drew the eye away. She balanced in the shoes and pulled the loops over the tiny pearl buttons to fasten them. There was no mirror to check her reflection in, so completely unaware of how she looked she drew back the curtain and stepped outside.

"Well would you look at that." Nelly commented in approval. "Could 'ave been made to fit you that could. Don't she look a picture Vi." She help up the pearls and a limp looking feather. "We've just these bits and then you're all done." She fastened the long creamy pearls round Josie's neck and adjusted them at the front, clipping them discretely to the bodice of the dress so they wouldn't swing around too much. Then she took the silver headband with the feather and placed it across Josie's forehead. "I feel like a cross between Hiawatha and Bonny Langford." She thought "Goodness knows what I really look like."

Once Nelly had finished arranging the head dress, Vi produced a pair of matching elbow length long satin gloves and reverently they wiggled Josie's hands and arms into them.

"Reckon that's you done luv." Nelly said as the pair of them stepped back to get a better view of their hard work.

"Now make sure you're back before midnight else not only will you turn into a pumpkin, but you'll also owe another day's hire on that." They cackled with laughter at their old familiar joke, never tiring of saying it, and watched as Josie nervously made her way out of the tent.

'Now what?' She thought in a panic.

Recalling the afternoon afterwards she didn't know why she had worried. Between Neil, Mary and Nick's old work friends she hadn't been left alone at all. She had always had a willing partner to take her punting, or bring her a selection of the crustless cucumber sandwiches on a silver platter. She only had to mention how delicious the strawberries looked, and a bowl magically appeared; and dancing to the band as they played Glen Miller and the Charleston she had dance partners lining up. She had been dreading the picnic, having to come by herself without Nick, worried about the memories and emotions it might stir up; but it hadn't. It was as though she had taken on the persona of her clothes, a young carefree debutante, light heartedly laughing her way through the festivities, flitting from one partner to another. The afternoon had been wonderful; she enjoyed herself as Thoroughly Modern Millie; the only slight reservation had been Neil. He had been as kind and considerate as usual, but somehow he seemed to be more reserved and less chatty. He didn't participate in the jovial childish banter of the group. May be it was because he was at work Josie mused, but that had never been the case before. He had always been the proverbial life and soul of every party, matching people's quick wit with own, verbally jousting jokes with anyone. So what had changed? Why had he suddenly withdrawn into himself. Perhaps he was tired, and felt lumbered with having to baby-sit one of his ex-employees' wife. Feeling uncomfortable at that thought she felt a rush of despair, railing at Nick mentally. "Why did you have to go and die like that? Why couldn't you just have come to my mother's as you always did?" But the silence swirled round her and no answer floated down to comfort.

"So how did the picnic go?" Henry asked as they chatted on their now nightly phone call, although to Josie his voice sounded slightly strained.
"It was all fine. I don't know what I was so worried about. Everyone was so friendly."
"That's good." Henry said, although his tone said the exact opposite. Josie wondered if he was feeling slightly jealous. Surely not – there wasn't anyone likely to approach her, but she did subtly drop in.
"Oh yes, Neil was sweet, but a bit quiet, I think he was missing Claudia."
"Oh he's got a girlfriend then."
"Practically a fiancée." Josie elaborated and she felt Henry relax slightly down the line.
"And how are the preparations going for the big day?" Henry asked moving the subject onto less contentious topics. "Are your fingers worn to the bone from all the sewing? Or have you spent all day in A&E having to get them unstuck?" He gently joked.
"Honestly! I have one small mishap gluing some sequins onto a box and you mention it all the time. Anyone could have been distracted at the crucial gluing moment and forget to apply the sequins."
"I agree, but they wouldn't then walk around for the next few days with a sequin attached to them. Most people would have gone to see a Doctor and have it removed."
"Well I didn't have time that day, I was busy trying to get everything finished so I could go and source some price tag labels. Plus it wasn't a couple of days, it was just the one and as soon as we had finished dinner I got rid of it once I got home."
"Ok, ok." Henry said soothingly, conceding defeat. "How did the price tag hunt go in the end? Have you managed to find anything yet?"
"Not really; I'm having a real brain block at the moment. I keep looking at all the paper labels, but they just don't look right. They

either look too cheap. Or they look like they belong in an office. I just can't find the right thing."

"Don't worry about it." Henry pacified "You will. All of a sudden you'll either see the right thing, or it will come to you in the middle of the night."

"I hope so, I haven't got long left." She thought of the few days left and her check list of things to do was getting longer rather than shorter.

"And how are you getting everything there. I've been having visions of you struggling with the boxes on the tube. I would come and help but one of my clients is due in court, and I don't think I can rearrange the whole judicial schedule to be able to help."

"Don't be silly, of course you can't. Jeremy and Tara are helping, which is awfully sweet of them. Especially as Jeremy has had to take the day off work, which he never does normally, in fact I think the last time he did it was only to get married to Tara. Anyway they are going to help me and take everything in their car then help carry boxes and set up." She explained. "And bring everything home again if it doesn't sell." She said despair and anxiety tingeing her voice.

"It will. I'm sure it will all go swimmingly well. And if it doesn't you can always come and work for me if you want. Betsy has declared you a first class dog minder."

"That's sweet – actually if it is a failure I may have to take you up on that. I think dog walking will be all I'm fit for."

There was a slight pause and then Henry tentatively suggested.

"Look, why don't we invite Tara and Jeremy over for dinner one Saturday night? We could use it as a 'thank you' for helping you with the Knightsbridge Ladies. And I've never met your friends. It would be good to meet them. We could get Caroline and Toby over as well, make it more of a party."

A warm glow enveloped her, he was inviting her friends to meet him. He actually wanted to do something as a couple. "That sounds a great idea. Especially if Caroline can make it, it would nice to see her and Toby again."

Her mind started to race, she would be able to show Tara the house, casually opening doors onto the stunning rooms and watching as her friend would start to drool and demand Jeremy to move out to the country so she could have one as well. Then a sudden downpour of reality hit her.

"Would I have to cook? Because if I'm truthful, I don't think anyone would willingly accept an invitation when I'm cooking. I almost poisoned Tara once by leaving the plastic cover on a pizza I grilled. It was only the problem I had cutting it, and the awful smell of melted plastic that saved us."

"Don't worry, we could get Melissa from the deli to rustle something up which we can just heat up if you want?" He suggested.

"You are wonderful." Josie sighed with relief at the thought of not having to go into battle with Delia or Gordon.

"So all my clients say," Henry said modestly, "The only trouble is they are all over 60, and I swear none of them have their own teeth."

She phoned Tara straight away, well it wasn't everyday you got to invite your best friend to such a gorgeous house. After all it was only just after ten o'clock, and within polite society that was still early; and hey, this was important.

"Tara, are you and Jeremy free for dinner in a couple of weeks?"

"I think so love, Jeremy's having to take some clients out on the golf course during the morning, but we'll be free from about six. Are we going out to a restaurant?"

"Not quite – the dinner was Henry's idea, in fact it's his invitation really. We'd like to invite you two over to his house in Drayton Beauchamp."

"You mean we get to meet Handsome Henry? Oooh yes, definitely count us in." Tara was dying to meet the new man in Josie's life, but fate had somehow kept them apart so far. "Ahem, I'm not being critical, but dinner usually involves cooking. Does Henry know about your culinary tussles." Tara tried to be as diplomatic as possible, but visions of plastic impregnated pizza refused to go away.

"Oh yes," Josie said breezily. "We're getting one of the ladies in the village to help. I'll only have to read heating instructions, I won't be doing any of the actual cooking so everyone should be safe."

Tara was amused, girlfriend to a pseudo Lord-of-the-Manor was obviously suiting Josie. "So tell me everything." She pulled her feet up under her on the deep armchair and settled in for a girlie chat. Jeremy recognising the scenario retreated off to bed.

"Well Henry just came up with the idea tonight." Josie enthused. "Wasn't that sweet of him! And you will simply love his house; it's one of those gorgeous Georgian beauties that are simply to die for. And we're going to use the dining room rather than the kitchen so we can have candles and all that sort of thing. We're also inviting some of his friends, Caroline and Toby. I told you about them; they're the friends I met at the Little Acorn Jamboree."

"It sounds like it will be a good evening. What do you think you'll wear."

"I thought maybe something chic but sophisticated. As its our first official dinner party together I thought I should do little black number rather than trendy singleton."

"What about that new dress you bought last month. It would look stunning with some big chunky jewellery."

"I'm not sure…"

"Oh it would be perfect. Definitely has the look of the hostess in control."

"Actually I can't fit into it. I'm going to start dieting next week. I can't believe I'm putting on so much weight." Josie said sadly.

"You did lose a lot of weight after Nick died. It's probably just your body getting back to normal." Tara consoled. "You certainly don't look fat."

"But I feel fat." Josie wailed down the phone. "It's not fair why couldn't I stay skinny."

"It's probably something to do with the number of chocolate brownies and carrot cake you've had over the last couple of weeks." Tara said delicately.

"I haven't had that many." She protested vehemently.

"Ok what did you have today?"

"Not that much. I didn't fancy anything first thing, so I didn't have any breakfast. Then because I missed that I had a couple of biscuits with my morning coffee. For lunch I just had some left over pasta and garlic bread from yesterday. Then I didn't have anything until dinner; oh except I popped out for some fabric and was starving so I have small chocolate brownie at Carluccios. That was it, I had a small steak and kidney pie for dinner and nothing else, apart from may be a biscuit while I was chatting to Henry." Guiltily she looked down at the almost finished packet of hobnobs which had only been opened that morning.

"That would probably explain it then." Tara said laughing. "Don't worry its probably just the stress of getting ready for D-Day. I bet you'll lose all it in no time afterwards."
"I wouldn't count on it." Josie thought gloomily as she ate the last hobnob.

"Darlings! How simply super to see you." A stick thin woman strutted across the stone tiled floor in 6" heels looking as though she had just stepped out of a Dolce and Garbana show room. Her twiggy fingers were so bejewelled with rings she could hardly bend them, and her hair was so moulded into place with hair spray it almost grazed Tara's check when they air kissed.
"Come in; we're just setting up in the Bamboo Room." Tara and Josie exchanged incredulous looks.
"What's a Bamboo Room?" Josie hissed.
"No idea." Tara hissed back "But it's obviously the in-thing."
They walked through the maze of marble floored corridors until they reached the room where six tables had been set up at one end. The whole room was decorated in a Far Eastern theme. The walls were covered in a highly stylised Chinese prints showing Coolie hatted men crossing ornate bridges. The furniture, fireplace and even the curtain poles all seemed to have been made from slender bamboo cane, obviously hence the name. Josie almost expected to see a giant panda to wander out from behind one of the tables and start gnawing on one of the chair legs.
"What do you think of the room?" Their hostess gushed not waiting for a response. "Of course I had to have my feng shui guru check it out first, and it took absolutely yonks to be able to organise his flights from Hong Kong. Poor Mr Wu, he has so many problems with his legs I just couldn't let him fly anything other than business class." She spotted two of the caterer's waitresses trying to balance plates of tiny pastries on top of two huge oriental china jars.
"Don't touch those;" she shrieked shrilly. "Don't you recognise them as Ming?" She hurried away still castigating the unfortunate girls in her high pitched voice.
"I suppose I'd better get the boxes from the car so I can start setting up." Josie said looking around at the other tables. They had obviously done this before, their tables had a professional look about them. One had sparkly jewellery, complete with a glass head and shoulders and reclining hand to show off the wears. Another

was brightly coloured children's clothing, and a small highly polished wooden mannequin dressed in tee-shirt, dungarees and cap sat jauntily on the edge of the table. Beside her a woman with a few object d'art items stood arranging the toile porcelain lamp bases and matching waste paper bins to form an almost art like layout.

Josie hurried out to where Jeremy was unpacking the car. "So you managed to escape Gigi's clutches then?"

"Just about; she was telling two of the helpers off as I left." She lent down to pick up two of the boxes Jeremy had already unloaded when she felt a sudden pain in her side. Instinctively she let out a small cry.

Jeremy spun round. "Are you ok?"

Josie straightened up slowly, the pain subsided. "Must have moved awkwardly." She said embarrassed. "I'm obviously getting old."

"You take those two up and I'll bring the rest. No don't argue, that way you can set everything up as you want. I think we'll probably have lost Tara to Gigi who will want someone by her side when the others arrive so it looks like it's already going well." Josie giggled, it was just like a real life episode of Desperate Housewives.

She placed the final journal in place and stood back to critically appraise her stall. Although she had thought about the layout she hadn't practised it, so when she laid everything out with the tall things at the back, and the smaller things at the front it just looked like a church fete tombola stall, an upmarket one, but still a tombola stall. The lady on the object d'art stand smiled to herself as she watched Josie's crestfallen face. "Is this your first time?" she politely enquired. Josie nodded glumly. 'And probably my last' she thought.

"Hi I'm Sally." She stretched out her hand.

"Josie." They shook hands. "This is hopeless." Josie said indicating the stand. "I can't believe how awful it looks."

"Everyone gets that happen the first time. It's just a question of practice and finding out what suits your things." She paused to run a finger along the suedes and satins appreciatively, enjoying the textural sensation. "Which are all gorgeous by the way. Now have you got any boxes spare; how about the ones you brought everything in. We could use those, and have you got anything we could cover them in to hide them?" Josie shook her head. "Don't worry," Sally continued, "I bet the caterers will have something.

Wait here." And with that she hurried off to where the smell of fresh coffee was coming from. Triumphantly she returned a few minutes later carrying several small table cloths. "Here we go." She held them up to show Josie. "Now if we use one on this side we can put one of those photo frames on it and the albums in front, and then on that side we can create two tiers and have the boxes and make up bags over these." Josie followed Sally's instructions and the two of them quickly re-arranged the stall.

"That looks so much better." Josie complimented as they finished.

"Mmm, it just needs one last touch, have you got any of those butterflies or flowers spare?"

"No, I didn't think of bringing anything extra."

Sally tapped her forefinger nail against her forehead deep in thought.

"I know." She said inspiration striking suddenly; she walked over to the large elaborate flower arrangements in front of the bamboo fireplace and plucked out a deep pink scented rose. Josie looked around in horror, expecting Gigi to come screeching in at any moment to demand the flower be replaced immediately. Sally pulled the petals off gently so as not to rip or bruise them and sprinkled them over the top of the white cloth and then using some of her pins attached some of the petals to the front of the table cloth so that it gave the illusion of the petals gently floating down.

"Amazing; I'd never have thought of that." Josie was in awe of how Sally had transformed the stand.

"I'd seen a wedding cake stand do something similar." She admitted "And I've always wanted to try it out. It does look quite good doesn't it." She seemed astonished her idea had worked in practice.

"I love your price tags by the way. How on earth did you come up with the idea of using laurel leaves?"

"It was one of those things; I'd been trying to find labels for ages and everything was too expensive. So I thought about making something different out of paper, so I used the leaf as a template, but they looked horrendous, too heavy and cumbersome. Then I tried writing on the leaf, and luckily it worked." She was about to ask Sally about her stand when the doors were flung open and Gigi entered followed by a throng of Stepford clones, each as skinny, well dressed and highly manicured as Gigi herself.

The next two hours became a blur to Josie as she alternated between trying to blend into the wallpaper as the ladies who lunched stalked about the room completely ignoring the stalls, loudly talking to each other and exchanging 'horror stories' of how much everything cost these days, just so that they could show off their new purchases. Then to being an attentive assistant to the same ladies as they started to buy odd items from the stalls.

By the time things were coming to an end and she had told the eighth person which colours no-one else had bought Josie began to relax and enjoy herself. She was stunned at the casual way the women had peeled off £50 notes from their purse with scant attention. She had expected people to be put off by the prices, but they didn't seem to be an issue. They were more interested in making sure no-one bought the same as them. As the last few women air kissed Gigi goodbye and left a sense of calm and sanity descended into the room, filling it with a quiet peacefulness after the hustle and rush. The stall holders, now off duty, walked over to where the coffee, champagne and pastries had been served, and joining the two helping staff sat down to savour the left over coffee ad pastries as a well-earned treat.

"Do you want another one?" one of the waitresses offered a plate of tiny exquisite chocolate éclairs round.

"I'd love to be self-controlled enough to refuse, but I can't." Josie took one of the delicate fingers and felt the choux pastry melt into the cream and chocolate. She turned to Sally. "I just can't stop eating." She apologised.

"May be you're pregnant." Sally joked.

"Not likely." Josie dropped her voice. "My husband died earlier this year."

Sally looked stricken. "Me and my big mouth, if anyone's going to say the wrong thing it's always me."

Josie patted her arm "You weren't to know. Anyway tell me how you got involved in this. I meant to ask you earlier but it all kicked off before I could."

"I run a small interior design shop on the Kings Road. Gigi is one of my customers. She suggested it might be worthwhile coming along to get new customers. It's a good way of networking and letting people know about the shop. Anytime someone buys something from here I pop a brochure in the bag. Sometimes they phone, sometimes they don't. It all depends on who's here and who's redecorating at the time." Again Josie felt inadequate. She hadn't thought of putting anything into the bags, she hadn't even thought of bags, Sally had kindly lent her a stock; thinking of this Josie asked. "How much do I owe you for the bags. I can't believe I never thought of that. I don't know what I'd have done if you hadn't come to the rescue."

"Oh don't worry about it." Sally assured her. "It's extra advertising for me after all."

"No I insist; you've really been so much of a help. If you won't let me pay you, at least have something off the stall."

Sally's eyes lit up; she'd had her eye on the apple green silk make up bag all morning. "Well if you're sure, I'd love this." She picked up the make up bag. "At least I won't be ashamed of my aging make up in this." She glanced at her watch. "Heavens I'm going to have to scoot. Do you have a card?" Sensing Josie's re-descent into inadequacy again she quickly continued. "Don't worry, here's mine. Give me a call next week, I've had an idea." In a daze Josie took the card and started to pack up the things that were left on the stall. Thank goodness she wasn't taking all of the stock home with her; she couldn't wait to get back to the flat and count the money. A flicker of excitement stirred within her stomach; today had been a success.

Chapter 6

Claudia wasn't a fool; she had fought her way up the magazine career ladder, coped with the poor pay, long hours and blatant sexual inequality. She held her own on the bitchiness and backstabbing front, and her Jimmy Choos were firmly planted on the toes of any rivals. But she was at a loss to know what was happening to her relationship with Neil. A couple of months ago they were discussing hiring a yacht with Teddy and Babs to sail around Martinique and now they weren't even spending the weekend together. On Monday night he'd muttered something about maybe having to work over the weekend; then he said the weather wasn't very good, and he really needed to go down and check the mooring for his sailing dinghy down in Chichester. And now he was spending the weekend down there so he could make any repairs that were necessarily. She couldn't work out what was going on. All week he'd gone quiet, it was as if he were in pain. Something was obviously troubling him, she just couldn't work out what. It wasn't as though she could get angry at him. He hadn't been rude to her or snappy; if anything he was over polite, as though she was an important guest at a party, making sure she was happy with everything, consulting her on the smallest thing. She ran a finger over the black and white studio photograph of them, taken soon after they had got together, showing them calmly staring back at her. She had to find out what was wrong, it was driving her mad. A knock at the door brought her out of her intense thoughts. "Yes." She barked as a timid editorial assistant gingerly poked her head round the door, deeply wishing she hadn't been the one who had pulled the short straw to give Claudia the proof pages. "It's the mock ups for our Readers At Home feature." The assistant stammered "I thought you might want to see it before we go to print." Claudia pulled on her Calvin Klein glasses and peered at the proofs, flicking through the pages before stopping suddenly in horror. Holding the offending page up. "Why do we have a bald woman in our magazine? We are supposed to be an aspiring read, who wants to aspire to be bald?" She demanded her voice slicing through the air like a wielded samurai sword.
"But she has just got over cancer." The assistant was close to tears, ready to grab her P45 and run. "That's why we chose her, because of the brave fight she's put up for her life and still decorating her

home. She'd been secretly fighting it for two years before she told her family. She didn't want them to worry."

"What was that? Cancer?" Suddenly everything seemed to be falling into place. Neil must be dying of something and he didn't want her worried. How typical of him. She could picture the scene now, Neil lying wanly against the white starched hospital pillows, bravely ignoring the pain, intent only on letting her know that he loved her, that he'd always loved her and only her. How she was the most marvellous woman he'd ever known. He'd turn to the George Clooney Doctor and instruct him to make sure everything he owned in the world would go to his beloved Claudia, and she would be sitting prettily by Neil's bedside, the epitome of the loving partner. Tenderly caring for his every need; trying to persuade him to rest, not to get agitated about her and how she would survive; pressing him to have a sip of water to help his dry parched lips. She would have to invest in waterproof mascara of course. Well she wouldn't want Neil to remember her with panda eyes as he slipped away from her; and while she was at it, she had better buy some of those dainty white handkerchiefs that were de rigour at every scene of desolation. After all she was sure she would shed a few tears; she'd have to if she was playing the devoted lover.

Her mind methodically flicked through all the people she knew wondering who she could call on to find out more. She dismissed her sister who, although she had coped with Claudia's brother-in-law being rushed into hospital with a suspected appendicitis but that had turned out to be a golfing injury, would simply make a huge hoo-ha and have all the attention on her. No that would never do. She thought about Father O'Reilly, the local priest at the family home, but she'd never liked the fact his cassock always smelt of moth balls, and he insisted on wearing cycle clips even when he wasn't cycling. Oh who could she turn to? She needed someone who would be able to be a font of knowledge, but keep in the background and not commandeer the drama. Her thoughts floated to Neil's employee Nick; he'd left his wife a widow earlier this year hadn't he? What was her name... Janey? ...Jackie? No it wasn't that. She could picture her ok, with her rosy cherub face looks and what men referred to as a 'womanly' figure, but which she just called plump. What was her name? She knew it would come to her in a moment. She could go and see her, find out what the symptoms

of a dying partner were. After all if Neil was ill she had a right to know. Josie... that was it; she knew it would come to her. Well no time like the present, she might as well go over and find out from Josie what she needed to start preparing. How long did cancer last? Would she need more than one season's collection of mourning clothes? Picking up her Mulberry handbag she abruptly pushed her chair back; the sound grating on the assistant's nerves like nails down a blackboard. She wasn't sure how much more silent loathing she could take from Claudia. This awful silence had gone on so long that her vocal cords had completely frozen with fear. She watched as Claudia, now oblivious to her, made her way to the door. "Excuse me..." Her voice was high pitched and squeaky as though she was inhaling helium. Claudia turned, looking blankly at the assistant for a moment before pulling herself together.
"Yes, what is it?"
"I just wondered what you want to do with these?" By this time her knees had passed the stage of knocking and were simply morphing into sponge. Claudia grabbed her Mont Blanc pen and scrawled her initials against the first page.
"There you go, they are signed off. Now I'm going out." And with that she had gone.

The post fell on to the mat with a dull thud, the usual collection of brown envelopes and unwanted circulars. Picking them up Josie took them into the kitchen while she waited for the tea to brew. Looking through them she saw the last few bills for the fabric had arrived, which meant she could work out how much profit she'd made from the Knightsbridge ladies. Strangely the thought of working out her costs and calculating the income was appealing, she had loathed maths when she was at school, trying to remember equations, Pythagoras theory and fractions had been impossible to fathom. She had become lost in a maze of figures and signs which seemed to cloud her mind like a heavy winter mist. But doing her accounts on a very simple spreadsheet, by some miracle, made sense. It must be something to do with understanding where the figures came from, combined with Jeremy talking her slowly though all the steps, again and again until it became second nature to her; 'First fill out all your costs with making the items, then any additional expenditure ie new sewing machine, travel, advertising that kind of thing. On the other side write in all your sales. Then we minus the spend from the income and it shows how much money you've made.' He made it sound easy; and she was duly filling in the figures as the bills came in. Although she knew she hadn't sold quite as many things as she had hoped, the one thing she had definitely learnt was that the Knightsbridge Ladies would never buy the same as someone else. So while she thought how clever she was being in having three or four items of the same design, actually she had only sold one of each. She put the suppliers' bills to one side, ready to take through to the dining room table where the rest of her accounts sat patiently waiting for processing. The circulars were consigned to the bin, leaving one Forever Friends envelope. Recognising her sister's writing she tore it open.

Dear Josie it read
Thank you for the gorgeous cot quilt and play mat for Olivia. She absolutely loves them. Todd, one of her nursery friends, came to visit yesterday and they spent the whole time squabbling over who would be able to put the tiny rabbits and toy soldiers in the pockets. It definitely kept them occupied though! In fact Clare, Todd's mum, was wondering if you would be able to make her one, as it kept Todd so quiet.
Have you decided when you are leaving the flat yet? You know that you can always come and stay here with us. It would be lovely to have you staying.
I hear from Mum that you are seeing Henry Beaucher quite a lot, hope everything is going well. I can't really remember him, but Mum's told the Bridge Club that he he's ideal material – what ever that means!
I'd better go and start marking Year 4's history homework before dinner. Edward and Olivia both say 'hello' and hopefully see you soon.
Love
Sarah

The tenderness of thinking about Sarah and Olivia were tempered by Molly's comments of 'idea material'. Not satisfied with setting her up, she was obviously trying to add fuel to the marriage speculation fire as well. She thought about Henry, he was so different to Nick. Where Nick was carefree and impulsive, Henry was steady and thoughtful. While Nick would get caught up in a project and simply forget about everything else, including Josie, Henry always seemed attentive. Nick was the archetypal lad's lad, always ready to party and start another madcap scheme. Henry was a genuine gentleman, he was as kind and considerate as any man you could hope for, and yet there seemed to be something holding her back. She hadn't spoken to anyone about it, she didn't want people to judge Henry badly when it was all her. She reasoned it might be too soon after Nick's death to be totally involved with someone, and the thought of having to be intimate with anyone just sent her running. She didn't want to show her body to anyone at the moment, with a huge effort she made the tea and walked away from the biscuit cupboard, conscious of how much she was craving one of the chocolate digestives.

She was looking at the items left over from the sale trying to decide what to do with it all, when the doorbell rang. Wondering who it could be, since she was meeting Tara later for dinner, she peeped through the spyhole. Pulling away quickly she was surprised to see Claudia standing outside, impatiently tapping her Jimmy Choo clad foot. Opening the door she looked expectantly round for Neil, after all she only vaguely knew Claudia through Neil.
"Hi." She said uncertainly, then as Claudia offered no explanation for her visit suggested. "Would you like to come in?" Claudia followed her through; she seemed to be lost in a world of her own. "Do you want tea of coffee? I'm afraid it's only PG Tips and instant on offer today."
"Coffee would be fine."
Josie left her in the sitting room and went into the kitchen, returning with Claudia's coffee.
"So how are you? How's the new job?" Josie asked in a falsely cheery voice uncertain how much small talk she'd be able to make and still puzzling over why Claudia was now seated in her sitting room. Claudia sat with her manicured French polished nails cupped around the mug of coffee.
"I think Neil's dying of cancer." She blurted out suddenly. Josie sat upright. The force of the sentence acting as a body blow.
"Why, has he been to see someone?" Josie couldn't believe it.
"He's been so quiet this week, it's just not like him; and he's stopped talking to me about the future. We were supposed to be going on holiday, and now he says he can't be sure if he'll be able

to make it." Noisily she burst into tears, all the worry finally getting to her. Josie panicked, what should she do? She hardly knew Claudia; should she try the 'keep a stiff upper lip - we're British after all' attitude, or should she do a Tricia and encourage her to tell all, not to bottle her feelings up but to let them all out. Tentatively she took hold of one of Claudia's hands and squeezed it trying to comfort the sobbing woman.

"When did he tell you about it?" Josie asked softly

"He hasn't." Sobbed Claudia. "That's the worst part, he's keeping it all to himself."

"Well what makes you think it's cancer? Has he lost of lot of weight, or complaining about pains?" She racked her brains, how had Neil looked at the picnic, she thought he looked fine, a picture of health in fact. There hadn't been anything wrong except he'd gone quiet. He hadn't been his usual jovial self. But surely that didn't mean he was ill?

"Has he been to a doctor?" Josie enquired slowly in between Claudia's wracking sobs.

"No I don't think so."

"Then why do you think he's got cancer?"

Something didn't seem quite right – was it Claudia grabbing the wrong end of something, or was he really dying.

"Because he's so distant; he's been so different this week. He's been fussing around, making sure I'm ok, but he hasn't actually talked to me for a week."

"You mean he's treating you like an elderly guest?" Claudia nodded. "He was the same on Saturday," Josie confided. "Quiet and withdrawn. He didn't smile once."

"I knew it, see he is dying of cancer." Claudia got ready for another bout of tears.

"Hardly," Josie said without thinking "It's more likely to be another woman." As soon as the words were out Josie wished she could take them back as she watched Claudia reel from their blow.

"What!" she thundered. Josie wilted under Claudia's stony gaze.

"Well the fussing bit shows he's feeling guilty of something, and the quiet bit is obviously his way of dealing with two women."

"You really think Neil's got another woman?"

"Heavens how would I know? I just meant that the signs were similar to what other women have said. But I can't really see Neil being unfaithful. He just doesn't see the type."

Claudia nodded slowly, thinking it over thoughtfully; one hand wiping away mascara smudged tears. "That's one of the things I've always loved about him. He's always been honest. So why is he doing this?"

"I don't know why? Maybe he's worried about work. Is there anything unusual happening?"

"Well he said something about a pitch they were having to prepare for the new L'Oreal account." She tried a weak smile. "Perhaps it's that?" She suggested hopefully to Josie, her eyes begging her to believe it.

"Yes that's probably it." Josie agreed with insincere heartiness. "Why don't you ask him tonight? Help to clear the air between you. He probably just needs a little encouragement." Goodness, I sound like an agony aunt, Josie thought, next I'll be suggesting they take a mini break to help them get away from everything.

"Sorry about turning up like this." Claudia was feeling a tiny bit foolish, suddenly turning up and blubbing.

"That's no problem, but why me? I'm sure you you've got closer friends who would have been there for you."

"Well you're the only person I know who's actually lost someone. I wanted to know what sort of signs I should be looking out for, and what I needed to get ready."

"Claudia," Josie tried to break the news gently "Nick died in a car crash. I didn't have any warning signs. No premonitions or ghostly visitations, and I certainly didn't have an preparation. One minute I was a married woman, the next I'd become a bemused widow trying to work out why me. It is something I'd never want any of my friends to go through. It is just like a living hell. Time may help you come to terms with the loss, but the slaughter of your dreams is awful. Believe me, you don't want anything to happen to Neil."

"Of course I don't." Claudia agreed sniffily.

"So talk to him, and I bet it will be something as simple as work."

"I hope you are right. I'm not sure what I'd do without him." The conversation came to a sliding halt, neither woman considered the other to be real friend, the confidences exchanged were as far as it went.

"Another coffee?" Josie asked trying to break the silence.

"No thanks, I suppose I'd better get back to work, otherwise the magazine will never get to print."

"So how is the new job going? Neil said you were doing really well."

"Did he," she dimpled with pleasure. "Bless him. Yes it's really interesting, although we're trying to find something for this month's hot to trot section." She briefly explained about Monica Manning's treachery in luring away Declan O'Hara and his goat.

"Do you want me to see if any of my suppliers know of anyone similar?" Josie asked once Claudia had finished.

"What suppliers?"

It was Josie's turn to launch into the story about the Knightsbridge Ladies Social Circle, and how she had started designing and making things for the event. She showed Claudia the items she had left over. Claudia listened first out of politeness and then with a growing sense of excitement. "Are you telling me you sold hand-made items at Gigi Gillespies?" Claudia was open mouthed in admiration.

"Yes it was last Thursday."

"And you haven't had anyone else approach you?" Claudia held her breath, willing that Monica Bloody Manning hadn't once again beaten her to the scoop of the month.

"I've no idea what you're talking about."

"You haven't had any other magazines approaching you."

"Why would they? It's hardly earth shattering news, I've made a few bags and a few boxes."

"Yes." Claudia raised a metaphorical jubilant clenched fist in the air. This was her big scoop that would put Bling & Boudoir on the map.

"Josie," she said hurriedly "Promise me you won't speak to anyone else about your designs. I want Bling & Boudoir to have first refusal on this."

"Of course if you like. But I've no idea what is so exciting about the things I've made."

"Cheap Chic darling, its real cheap chic."

"And that's good?" Coming from Claudia you could never be certain.

"It's this season's gold dust. The theme is everyday things that you could make for yourself, but the reality is thousands of very bored housewives don't want the effort of actually making the things; they just want to buy it from someone else." She started to pace up and down the room as she calmly gathered her thoughts.

"Right I'll need to get Legal over here to go through the contracts. I'll need one of the editorial team to come and interview you so we can get the full story. Then we'll need to photograph the items. We'll probably need to do that in the studio, we haven't got much time if we want to hit this issue. Right, if I get the lawyer over here we can do the preliminaries and then we can sort out timings for the photo shoots." Turning on her heel to face Josie her face was illuminated with pleasure and anticipation.

"Josie, you're going to help me be a star." She said triumphantly.

Chapter 7

It seemed strange to be holding a dinner party, and not having to do anything, True in the old days Nick would have invariably invited friends over for supper and after arguing over who would cook, they would agree on getting a take away. The meals had always been boozy, laid back affairs that had been fun and noisy, and fairly drunken. Tonight was a different ball game through, it was as though she was eating with the grown ups for the first time. Gone were the take away menus and mis-matching bowls, and in was the three course meal prepared by the local deli of salmon on a bed of rocket, chicken coq-au-vin with baby turnips, carrots and dauphinoise potatoes followed by caramel covered profiteroles. The mahogany dining table was going to be fully dressed by the waiting staff with crisp white linen and gleaming silver cutlery and accompaniments.

"I thought it would be too stressful for you to try and organise everything from London." Henry had said when she asked about preparations. "So I've got some Melissa to organise some help." Josie had gone quiet. She had been looking forward to playing at houses and getting it ready for the evening. "I've done the wrong thing haven't I?" Henry lamented as the pause had lengthened. "I just wanted us to enjoy our first dinner party, without either of us having to worry about the cooking or getting things ready." A wave of gratitude that he thought that much of their 'public' appearance swept over her; he was being so thoughtful.

"No, I'm just silly. It's lovely of you to have gone to all that trouble to organise it."

"And I thought you might want to stay the night as well, so we could spend Sunday together." There was another short pause as Josie's brain screamed 'Yikes'; it was all going a bit too fast.

"Josie?" She thought of all the effort he'd put in to planning to their first dinner party, and her inside seemed to glow with a sudden warmth.

"Yes I'm here. Yes, I'd love to stay over." Heavens, now she would have to think about what to wear on Sunday, as well as dig out some slinky night attire other than the baggy tee-shirt she normally slept in.

"It's not too soon for you is it?" He asked with concern.

"No of course not." She lied "I'm looking forward to it." And deep down she was; it felt like she was finally making headway in rebuilding her life. "Is there anything I need to bring?"
"No, I don't think so. Come over Saturday afternoon and we'll have a leisurely time before the evening. Now go to bed, you're sounding really tired."
"I am, it must be all the excitement of the past few weeks."
"Well make sure you get rested, I want you to enjoy Saturday."
"So do I, I can't wait."
They said their goodbyes and Josie made her way to bed. She hadn't felt this tired in ages. It didn't matter how early she went to bed she still seemed to feel tired the next morning; she hoped she wasn't going down with anything, her head felt slightly groggy and her limbs felt heavy. Flopping into bed she struggled down and drifted off to sleep thinking about Saturday.

Josie finished sealing the last box, all her possessions were now stored away in the tea crates ready for the removal people to take down to Molly's next week. It would be strange going home after all this time, and she had no doubt Molly would end up driving her mad, but it was still home and it was just what she needed right now. She wondered how Claudia and Neil were getting on; whether they had talked through the differences, she didn't really believe he was seeing an other woman, but then how could you tell? Her thoughts flitted to Nick, what had he been doing on the night he had been killed, where had he been going? Now that she had come to terms with his death she seemed to have more unanswered questions than answers. She swung between feeling angry at him for dying and sad because she didn't know why. But this evening was her chance to prove she was moving on with her life, that she was starting to make headway. Slowly, but surely, she was building her future; she smiled at the recollection of Claudia's visit, the whirl and twirl of activity as she had first signed the contract of exclusivity and then spent all the time ferrying items across to the photographic studio for them to be arranged, rearranged, lit correctly and then finally photographed. 'I could take some pictures with my camera, if you want and let you have the film.' She had suggested to Claudia; who had looked positively affronted at the proposition. And after what she had experienced she now realised why. Having spent four whole hours watching the photographer

'introduce' himself to the products in order to pick up their vibes; before clapping his ringed hands so that it sounded like two spoons being clashed together, to get the attention of Shane, who he called his little helper; but who in reality just a younger version of himself, did she began to have an insight into the creative mindset. They launched into deep and meaningful discussions about the backdrop, the layout of the set, the lighting and the props, interspersed with cries of 'Oh no, darling that is so passé.' 'We're not trying to appeal to the lower economics I can assure you.' And ''God you can be so catty at times'. Josie felt she had entered a surreal parallel universe. Finally after two huffs, one slap and a good deal of making up they were finally ready. The theme they had chosen was a country cottage and they decided to shoot each piece around that theme; so her journals and make up bags were hung up on a makeshift rope washing line; her memento boxes and photo albums sat amongst a discarded family picnic and several soft cushions sat plumped up in a swaying hammock. "Won't they look a bit strange having that plain white background?" she had innocently asked. Derek and his little helper looked at each other, clasped a ringed hand to their mouths to hide the disbelieving grins.
"Bless her, did you hear that!"
"As if we'd have plain backgrounds!"
"Ohh I know, are you going to tell her or shall I?"
"Oh you tell her Derek."
"Someone tell me." Josie pleaded grimly half to herself "Or I'll be forced to challenge you to handbags at dawn."
"What happens is that we shoot against a neutral backdrop so we can add in a garden scene, or a vista of old apple trees."
"Where would we find a cottage garden blooming at this time of year anyway." They howled with laughter at the thought. And so the days continued; Josie brought in her different items and Derek and Shane spent long paint-drying hours photographing away. The monotony was only broken by the occasional arrival of Claudia's editorial assistant who stopped only to speak to Derek in a low hushed voice. She only hoped that the photos would be worth it, well it would give Molly something to talk about at her Bridge Club if a couple of her things were featured in the magazine. Maybe she would even get her name mentioned, that would definitely give Molly enough food for gossip for several months and put Daphne Hawkes in her place. She could just hear her 'Did I tell you that

Josephine was featured in Bling & Boudoir. Yes, you really must get a copy." In fact single handedly Molly could probably double the circulation rate of Bling & Boudoir.

Pushing the box out of the way Josie began to consider what she would need for the weekend. Her holdall already bulged from all of the clothes, make up and shoes she had packed just in case. Goodness knows what Henry would make of it all, he'd probably think she was moving in. Looking through her wardrobe she looked longingly at her favourite ballet pumps and Paul Costello slacks, but sense told her that two pairs of trousers already packed would be more than enough. Anyway she wouldn't want to crumple the new satin camisole and matching shorts she'd bought. It had felt strange buying them, she'd never bothered with Nick, and yet she felt with Henry she ought to make an effort. She hoped it would be a good luck talisman for tonight; she wasn't sure what she was most nervous of; acting the hostess or being the lover. It seemed so long since she'd been either that she was beginning to feel nervously apprehensive. Supposing the whole evening was a disaster; supposing nobody talked or even worst started arguing; supposing Henry didn't like her body; or she forgot how to do everything. The thoughts pounded through her brain like an steam train; over and over; over and over; on and on making everything seem worse and worse. Her mobile rang suddenly making her jump.
"Hello?"
"Josie, it's Henry. I'm just making sure you're still ok for this evening." His voice sounded so kind and reassuring that her worries melted away unheeded. "It's just something's come up and I can't pick you up from the station; but Adam, my cousin, will be there. He'll bring you over to the house and I'll see you there."
"Oh, ok." Her voice sounded small, like a young child.
"I did try and reschedule, but I couldn't. I promise I won't be too long; just make yourself at home. I've told Adam to take good care of you; he can't wait to meet you."
"Yes, it'll be good to meet him as well."
"What time is your train?"
"Two forty four."
"I'd better let you go then so you don't miss it. See you later."
"Bye."

She clicked the mobile phone off and picked up her bags; all set for the big adventure.

"How did you know it was me?" Josie asked as they got into Adam's battered old landrover.
"I didn't; I just kept going up to all the young attractive women getting off the train and offered them a lift home." He explained.
"You didn't!" Josie was taken back by his audacity, she stared at him before seeing his face break into a sudden wicked grin.
"Got you! Of course I didn't."
"So how did you know?" She persisted.
"Henry told me to look out for a blonde woman struggling under the weight of her bags because she wouldn't be able to decide what to wear." Josie reddened.
"Was it that obvious?"
"Three bags and a suit carrier for one dinner – yep even by most standards that's probably over the top."
"But you just never know…" Josie started to try and explain but what was the point. As a fully signed up member of the male species Adam was never going to understand the finely tuned intricacies of a woman and her wardrobe. "So where is Henry? Called away to the bedside of a dying millionaire who wants to leave all his money to the local cat home?"
"Nothing so exciting; he needed to get the Vicar's signature for some Parish Council papers and it was the only time he could get there." They drove along the road leading up to the house, bumping and jumping as the landrover found every pot hole and every bump.
"Don't worry though; he has left me with very strict instructions on how to keep you occupied while he is away."
Josie raised a suspicious eyebrow.
"No; not like that!" He protested. They pulled into the driveway.
"Isn't it gorgeous." Josie said wistfully as the came into view framed by the tall stone gateway pillars. Its stone walls were glowing golden in the lowering sun. Adam looked at it; he'd never really considered its architectural qualities before. To him it had always been just Henry's family home; it couldn't compete with Drayton Hall for size or grandeur – now that was a house. There were complete wings given over to servants whose only purpose in life was to look after the inhabitants, making sure they life flowed smoothly without any discomfort. The parties his parents had

thrown were etched into his memories; guests invited locally from the village and from London so that the eclectic mix added spark to the party fire.

"Mmm, I suppose it is quite nice." He said politely, causing Josie to try and hide her wry smile, Henry had pointed Adam's house out to her during one of their walks. It had been a magnificent building, a huge Regency style mansion that had wings off each side and stable blocks behind, but somehow it was too large and too grand to be a real home.

They walked round to the backdoor, their feet scrunching on the gravel and Adam let them into the kitchen. Betsy, aroused by the sound of the car was standing patiently waiting, her tail wagging expectantly. She gently pushed her golden head against Adam and then Josie by way of greeting trying her best to put on a hard-done by face in the hope they would be tricked into feeding her, but neither seemed to take the hint and she returned disappointed to her basket.

"Now, first things first." Adam said as he read the list of instructions Henry had left with him. "Champagne!" He went over to the large American fridge that stood incongruously amongst the Edwardian kitchen units, and pulled out the chilling bottle of Bollinger. He poured them both a glass of fizzing creamy bubbles and handed one to Josie. "Cheers." They clinked glasses and savoured the smooth taste of their first sip. "Next instruction is for you to go and check you're happy with the dining room, in fact Henry's exact words are 'make sure you have what you want'!"

'How typical of Henry to be so considerate, wanting her to feel included' Josie thought as they went through to the dining room.

"Now I'll leave you to potter around while I take your things up stairs. Of course with the amount you brought it may take several trips." He said wickedly.

"Go!" Josie said laughingly pointing to the door "Some of us have work to do." He left whistling some indistinguishable tune to himself leaving her to survey the room. The mahogany dining table had been covered with a deep red cloth; matching the walls, at one end stood two piles of napkins, one green the other white with a note from Henry lying on the top saying 'Choose which ones you prefer!'. By the side lay the cutlery and on the side table were the glasses. She set to work discarding the white ones in favour of the

bottle green ones, laying out the table with six place settings. The dark red walls and matching heavy slub silk curtains the room had a cosy snug feeling. Having put all the cutlery and glasses out she stood pondering on how to add that extra special element. The table looked slightly boring, like a mediocre restaurant. With a rush of inspiration she headed into the kitchen searching for a pair of scissors before going on into the garden. The dusk was starting to fall and there were faint traces of her breath on the air, but in the excitement of gathering trailing ivy and large lush holly leaves she didn't notice. Around her feet Betsy snuffled away at the ground, keeping her company. With her arms full of glossy greenery she made her way back in to the warmth of the dining room, her ideas falling into place. She'd roll the napkins into fat sausages and fasten them with a strand of ivy to create the napkin ring. Then she would decorate the two candelabras with a mixture of trailing ivy and holly leaves, finishing off with a small garland of holly leaves fanned out around the centre of the table. She worked quickly and methodically so absorbed in her work she didn't notice Adam entering the room behind her. He watched her deft movements arranging the napkins on the centre of each under plate; rearranging the wound ivy for a few moments and then coughed discretely to catch her attention. She looked up at him in surprise.
"Have you been there long?" He shook his head. "What do you think? Too over the top?" Again he shook his head.
"It looks brilliant, just like one of those rooms you find in glossy house magazines."
"You don't think Henry will mind do you?"
'Personally I reckon you could paint the whole house in vivid purple and Henry wouldn't mind' Adam thought, but with unusual diplomacy he assured her that he thought Henry was bound to like it.
"Now if you've finished in here there's my final instruction to carry out."
"And what's that?" Josie asked intrigued at what else there was to do.
"To top up your glass and then let you have a nice long bath and get ready."
"But there must be loads to do." Josie protested thinking about the wine and the food.

"Henry said it was all under control. He should be back in half an hour, so you can check with him yourself then." He refilled her glass. "Now get going or I'll be in trouble for not having you got ready."

"Are you always this bossy to Henry's guests?" Josie asked archly.

"Definitely; I never have any of my own that I can boss round. Henry's left everything out for you upstairs that you might need, but shout if there is anything else."

She went upstairs, she'd only been up here once when Henry had shown her round. She walked over to his room, the tartan bed hangings decorated a newly made bed with fresh linen. Either side were two mahogany side tables, on one table a small pile of hardback biographies which was obviously the side Henry usually slept on. The other side had the latest copy of Bling & Boudoir. Her bags were on the ottoman at the end of the bed and her suit carrier was hanging behind the door. She walked through the bedroom to the inner door which opened into the bathroom. She hadn't been in this room before and the opulence surprised her. A large modern bath sat in the middle of the room, to one side was a decorative table obviously there for the bather to be able to rest their glass of wine and book. A pair of glass sinks sat on a floating shelf, reflected in the ceiling high mirror that filled the far wall, making the space seem even more cavernous. A neat array of bottles stood on the lip of the bath, wild orange blossom, tea rose and cocoa butter; selecting the latter she turned on the taps allowing the gushing water to create a mist of bubbles. As the water level rose the warmth of the bathroom began to steam up the mirrors and form fine beads of condensation of the small casement windows. Stepping out of her clothes and slipping into the bath she felt a tingle run through her as she lowered her body into the warm embryonic solution. Slowly she stretched herself out so that she was reclining fully; her head propped up one end and her pink painted toe nails just visible at the other. She sipped at her champagne, resting on the table and wondered whether people could really get used to living like this. Somehow it all seemed to a bit too perfect, Henry was everything any woman could want, the house was heartstoppingly beautiful. She'd never have to worry about money if she was with Henry. How different her life would be now if she'd married Henry instead of Nick. Her disloyal thoughts shocked her; she had never regretted marrying Nick when he was alive, so why was she trying to compare him against Henry? It wasn't fair; Nick wasn't here to even defend himself. And yet somehow Nick still seemed to have a hold over her, she felt slightly guilty at the enjoyment she felt when she was with Henry. Goodness only knew what would happen tonight when they went to bed together. Part of her longed to feel Henry lying naked against her, holding her body against his; but the other whispered she was being unfaithful, that she shouldn't even be considering it. She felt caught between the two, veering from one to another and back again. It all seemed so confusing.

On the same Saturday the icy wind whipped past and the surf droplets stung as the little sailing dinghy shot across the bay. Neil felt the rope bite into his palms as the sails strained against the blowing gale. There weren't many boats out on the sea today; you had to be experienced to know how to handle the dinghy in this weather, and Neil knew his well enough that he could predict how she would react even before it happened. 'If only the same was true of Claudia.' He thought. Except that wasn't true, Claudia hadn't changed at all. It was him that was going through this turmoil. He didn't quite understand what had happened, he didn't feel any differently to her, he still thought a lot of her, admired her tenacity and sheer balls, and they still had plenty in common. It just seemed that everything had been turned upside down. As though gravity had been reversed ad he was now floating along his life seeing an unfamiliar landscape. The little dinghy fell and rose, causing Neil to focus his attention on sailing. He couldn't afford a lapse in memory or he'd so easily be diving to a watery grave, and he certainly didn't want that. He pulled the rope tighter and then in one swift movement moved to the other side of the boat at the same time as he pushed the tiller and boom across. The speeding boat changed direction and they were now heading back towards the quay. His arms were aching from holding onto the sails, and his face felt raw from the stinging sea salt spray. But the cobwebs that had clouded his mind had been jettisoned away and he felt the London smog had been driven out of his system leaving him tired but refreshed. He was looking forward to a few pints with the others in the small harbour pub as everyone discussed their boats and sailing, the weather and sea conditions. Tomorrow he had planned to spend the day checking the dinghy over and pottering around fixing the sail that had a small tear appearing and checking the mast wires. Then he'd set off to London to be back by seven in time for work on Monday. It had been just what he had needed, a weekend away from everything, at least here he could escape and not feel guilty every time he looked at Claudia. He didn't know how it had happened with Josie, he'd always liked her, always thought she and Nick made a good, if unlikely, couple. There had never been anything else involved, no hidden flames or instant attraction between them, they had always just been friends. But since Nick's death he found himself thinking about her more and more, his offers to help her sort things out, just so they could spend time together, and now she was seeing someone else, and his emotions had reacted as though he had been physically assaulted. He was honest enough with himself to realise that he didn't necessarily want to give up Claudia for Josie, but now that she was going out with this new man a part of Neil felt as though she somehow still needed his protection; that having been through everything with Nick's death the last thing he wanted to do was see her hurt from a relationship that had been formed on the rebound. Just when he'd thought she was going to start doing something worthwhile with her life it looked like she was taking the easy option and living off someone, becoming their shadow and not taking the plunge to make her own independent life.

He let the rope slip through the palms of his hand, looking at the glistening crystals of salt that had gathered round the creases and folds of his fingers. Slowing his faithful nautical companion down he made his way into the harbour and across to his mooring point, carefully avoiding the other boats and dinghies already moored up. Tying her up securely against the tall stone harbour wall, he got out and made his way across the wooden platoon and along to the road. As the chill wind whistled through his damp clothes and tousled his hair, his thoughts flew to getting into a dry set of clothing and enjoying his first pint; after all this afternoon's strenuous activities he felt he'd earned it.

Despite all Josie's worries the evening turned out to be a roaring success. Everyone was relaxed and sociable, the men talked business and sport leaving Tara, Caroline and Josie to discuss fashions, shopping and the latest gorgeous film star. Josie was grateful that Henry had insisted on getting the girls in from the local deli to cook, they had also gamely agreed to stay on and serve as well as do the washing up, persuaded by the fat wadge of notes Henry had surreptitiously produced. Their lack of professional silver service combined with their casual clothes of skinny jeans and off the shoulder tee-shirts stopped the evening becoming too formal and stuffy. They had been invited to sit down for coffee towards the end of the evening, and helped to make the whole evening light-hearted and fun.

Josie had been secretly thrilled at Tara's open admiration of the house; she knew it was a shallow thing to be proud of, but the house was simply stunning. The two of them had walked around while Henry and Jeremy had stayed by the fire, Josie chatting animatedly about the house and Henry's various decorating efforts. Exploring the rooms and talking about redecoration ideas on the shabbier ones, until the door bell had announced Caroline and Toby's arrival. Caroline had greeted her warmly and conspiratorially whispered that she was pleased Josie was still talking to her and wasn't holding the dire cooking and child minding activities against her and Toby. Josie had laughed protesting saying how she had enjoyed it and asking after Max.
"Actually he was a bit upset when we left him; he didn't understand why he couldn't come along to see you and his Uncle Henry. Poor thing. Of course I'll remind him of this when he gets to the stroppy teenage years and refuses to go anywhere with us."

There had been a noisy appreciative reception to the dining room decoration, and Josie had felt a glow of pride, bolstered by the secretive wink Henry had given her across the table. They sat either end like an old married couple, with their friends between them, enjoying the company but also living partly in a world that only the two of them occupied, one which was shared with a loving look. Henry had already complimented her on the way she had managed to give a festive look to the room, but he proudly mentioned it again during the dinner.
"Have you ever thought about doing design as a living?" Caroline asked, thinking of some of the girls at her Swiss finishing school who had gone to be set up as an interior design by Daddy.

"I wouldn't know how to." Josie admitted, although the idea itself sounded appealing, but then working with fabrics and colours every day, what woman wouldn't want that?

"You could always train, there are loads of courses advertised in the glossy house magazines. You see them all the time."

"Would you like to do something like that?" Tara had never considered such an option for her friend before.

"Yes," Josie said thoughtfully, "the trouble is though I need to start doing something more immediate to earn some money." Her rising overdraft and dwindling capital raced across her brain, doing several circuits on the way.

"Henry would be able help you, wouldn't you Henry?"

Hearing his name from the other end of the table he broke off his conversation on the state of the stock market and looked down to where the three women were sitting.

"Did I hear my name?" He asked jovially, the excellent red wine increasing his feeling of well being.

"I was just saying to Josie that you would be able to help her if she really wanted to go to college to learn about interior design." Caroline repeated.

"Judging by this room I'm sure Josie is good enough already." He said gallantly, earning himself extra brownie points from Tara.

"But if she wanted to do it, you'd help her wouldn't you?"

Henry looked at them, Josie was quietly cringing, Caroline was watching him expectantly and Tara was looking amused at the whole idea.

"If Josie wanted to do something like that I'm sure there are loads of people who would be willing to help her." He said diplomatically, not wanting Josie to feel he was acting as some kind of Victorian Lord and Master who ruled what she could and couldn't do.

"Why do women always want to go off and do things? Why can't they be happy to be a wife and a mother?" Toby asked as though puzzled by the antics of the modern woman.

"My husband, the cave dweller." Caroline murmured to the other two women. "You'll have to excuse him. I blame his mother and my mother for installing the 'home is best' philosophy when it came to the woman's role."

"Jeremy is just the same." Tara empathised. "As long as his meals are on time, and there's a clean shirt to wear, his life is fulfilled." They turned to Josie.

"You've got all this to come!" Caroline joked as Josie gave a look of mock horror, she didn't think Henry was quite so Draconian. They had never discussed it outright, but the support he'd shown towards her Knightsbridge Ladies Social Circle obviously suggested he didn't expect his women to be chained to the kitchen sink.

"What are you three plotting now?" Toby asked leaning across towards them.

"How to achieve world domination and still be back in time to collect the children from school, my darling." Caroline answered sweetly. "Speaking of which we really must make a move. The baby sitter will be wondering where we are."

Reluctant to break the evening up, but spurred on by necessity, they got to their feet and while Henry went off in search of their coats, Caroline kissed Josie on the cheek, pressing her and Henry to come over to them for supper next time. "Although it will probably only be spag bol, not a patch on this I'm afraid."

"Oh it's Henry that should take the credit for this one." Josie acquiesced on the praise. "It was all down to his hard work." Toby gave her a friendly peck and told her to keep the old dog in order, and they walked out to the hall, where they heard them saying their final goodbyes to Henry.

"Actually it's time we were going as well." Tara said having seen Jeremy starting to try and stifle several discrete yawns. "It's been a lovely evening." She dropped her voice and in a low whisper said to Josie "Give me a call when you get home tomorrow. I want to hear all the low down."

Henry re-entered the room and saw Tara and Jeremy standing up.

"You're not going yet are you?"

"Yes, I'm afraid so. Jeremy's taking several clients out on the golf course tomorrow morning." The four of them walked into the hallway and with a chorus of goodbyes, and waving until Jeremy and Tara's car had disappeared into the darkness, they were all gone, leaving the house suddenly feeling very silent.

"Go and sit down, I'll be through in a minute." Henry suggested, guiding her gently.

Josie went through to the sitting room, and sat on the sofa, pulling her feet beside her and gazed into the fire as she contemplated the evening. Everything had gone so well; her thoughts were disturbed by Henry appearing with a tray.

"I thought we deserved these." Two glasses of ruby red port stood next to a fresh caffetiere of coffee, and in the middle a plate of exquisite hand made chocolates. Josie's eyes lit up at the sight of the petit fours, and selecting a dark chocolate pyramid bit in expectantly. The bitter chocolate taste melted against her tongue leaving the hint of the praline centre.

"Delicious." She proclaimed, licking her fingers clean.

Henry sat down opposite her, just as he had done the first time she had visited here with Molly all those weeks ago.

"That all seemed to go well."

"Yes everyone had a good time."

They sipped their port and relaxed after the excitement of the evening, savouring the success. Josie eyed the plate and wondered whether she could take another one already without seeming to be too greedy. Through half closed eyes Henry said.

"Go on, have another one. I got them especially for you."

"I shouldn't, I know, but they are just so morish. Where did you get them from?"

"The local deli, where else? When they get a chance they make them, so I ordered a batch for tonight."

A wave of gratitude swept through her, followed by a warm fuzzy current of bonhomie from the port.

"Why don't you come and sit over here." She patted the sofa cushion next to her, apart from a long meaningful kiss earlier this evening they hadn't had any time together. He sat down beside her, feeling the warmth of her body, and she rearranged her position so that she was sitting in the crook of his arm, with the other hand on her lap, which she began to stroke.

"You're a very nice man." She commented out loud before leaning her head back onto his shoulder. He gently ran his fingers along the inside of her arm causing delicious tremors to run through her skin. His breath was warm against her cheek and she reeled at the sensations running through her body. She half turned to kiss him; a gentle probing embrace followed by a rougher, harder kiss. He pulled her towards him; holding her close against his chest, the buttons of his shirt pressed into her skin unheeded. The thrill of the clinch caused Josie's fingers to move across the soft cotton of the shirt and caress the taut silky skin of his collar bone. He responded with a tiny moan, gently nibbling her lower lip. She felt light-headed and giddy; is this the lust she thought before realising it was a more physical sensation that was starting to assail her; waves of pain were ricocheting around. Extracting herself quickly she took a few deep breaths, a sheen of perspiration had enveloped her body. She patted her upper lip with the back of her hand, the sensation she was feeling was definitely medical.

"Are you ok?" Henry asked shocked by her sudden paleness, It looked as thought she had been completely drained of blood. He held her hand as she contrived to calm her breathing and quell the nauseous feeling. Seeing only one lone chocolate remained on the plate she knew the cause was gluttony. Nothing more than an old fashioned case of gorging.

"I'm sorry." She started to say but her voice cracked, she was humiliated at her behaviour having ruined the evening.

"Well I have to say that women don't normally react like that to my kisses." Henry said giving her hand an affectionate squeeze. She responded with a watery smile. "Would you like to go to bed?" She looked at him as though trying to see if he was being funny.

"Not to have my wicked way with you." He assured her, taking her arm and helping her to her feet. "Come on I'll take you upstairs."

Half an hour later, after dramatically vomiting several times, she lay rigid in bed, clutching a hot water bottle and vowing never to eat or drink as much ever again. A glass of water stood on the bedside to her right and to her left Henry lay against her, cradling her with his arm, his deep breathing showing he had fallen asleep. It was much later that finally sleep came and she fell into a dreamless state.

She woke up with a start; disorientated and blinded by the sunlight. Holding one hand up to shield her sleep glued eyes she peered round the room. Then as the familiarity of the surrounding came into focus she fell back dramatically against the pillows with a groan as she recalled the previous evening. She turned to where Henry had slept, but the bed was empty and cold. There was no residual warmth where he had lain. Pulling the bed clothes up to her chin, like a child does to protect themselves from the outside world, she tried to think what to do. Had Henry got up and gone out to save both her and him the embarrassment of seeing him this morning; or was he so angry with her behaviour that he couldn't bear to be near her? She considered getting up and slipping quietly away, but her head still throbbed and she felt pathetically weak. How could she have eaten and drunk too much she berated herself over and over again. She should know better, especially after that debacle on her girls' night out with Tara. Each time this happened she didn't think that she had drunk that much, but she was obviously misjudging what her body was capable of drinking.

The door creaked open and a friendly golden face appeared around the door.
"Betsy." Josie said relieved to see a comforting friend; she dropped her hand down and the dog ambled over giving a loving snuzzle to Josie's palm. Feeling the downy fur against her fingers she felt less bereft and leaning down to lay her cheek on Betsy's firm head she whispered "Oh what I have gone and done?" A few minutes later a second face appeared round the door, followed by the whole body carrying a tray laden with breakfast. Henry paused just inside the door, checking to see Josie was awake.
"Morning." He said softly. "Did she wake you?"
Josie shook her head. "I was already awake. What time is it?"
"About eleven o'clock." Josie groaned, how could she have slept so late. "How are you feeling?" Henry studiously enquired.
"Fine," Josie lied, then after a moment's pause blurted out. "I'm really sorry about last night. I don't know what got into me. I don't usually behave like that."
Henry turned back to face her from where he was putting the tray down, his expression showing surprise. "What are you sorry about? I thought the evening was a great success."
"I meant about being ill." The memories made her cringe. "I should have known better than to drink so much. I can't believe I managed to ruin our first night together. I'll understand if you want me to go." Her voice came out slightly hoarse as emotion tightened her throat and the prickle of tears threatened.
Henry walked over to the bed and sat down on it. He'd obviously been up for a while as he was showered, shaved and dressed in his typical Sunday vegging out outfit of frayed levis and white tee-shirt. Leaning across and brushing her tousled hair away from her hot forehead he said.
"It happens. Don't worry about it, I had a wonderful time; and it's not every girl I get to play Doctor to. I really enjoyed last night, and

I think our friends did too. So no more talk of going anywhere please." As though realising Josie needed all the reassurance she could get, Betsy propped her front paws onto the bed and gently burrowed her head against Josie, as though to bolster Josie's fragile confidence.

"See even Betsy's saying 'don't worry'." Henry joked to lighten the atmosphere. He stood up and picked up the tray from the chest of drawers and brought it over to the bedside table. Josie saw that it was laden with coffee, orange juice, yoghurt, bagels, butter and countless jams.

"I would have treated you to my speciality of a cooked breakfast, for which I may tell you, I am famous. However I thought you may prefer something a bit lighter this morning."

Josie couldn't believe how kind he was being about everything and grabbing his tee-shirt she gently pulled him towards her and kissed him very hard, and very long.

"Henry B you are such a gentleman." She murmured into his ear, causing all sorts of excited reactions to go shooting through his body. He took her into his arms and kissed her back, this time with more finesse and care.

"Carry on like this, and I'm not sure I will be." He warned

The caresses lengthened as the passion started to rise. Their bodies began to push together, wanting to feel the other close against it. He dropped kisses onto her neck and shoulders, and her hands ran up and down his firm muscular back. They forgot everything and everyone else, caught up in their own private heightened sensual state, intent only on retaining the feeling, of the heightening desire; the quickened breathing and intense longing that swept over both of them. All thoughts of last night were forgotten as they hurriedly undressed each other, wanting to lie naked together, and as Henry started to make love to her with a passion neither of them had ever experienced before. Afterwards, as they lay clasped together, feeling breathless but fulfilled, Josie knew she had never felt so complete with anyone before as she did with Henry. It was as though he had transported her body to a place where she was floating weightlessly among the heavens; it felt like she had finally come home.

Chapter 8

Claudia looked down at the cheap chic section; the photographs Derek and Shane had taken flowed across the page. The country gardens theme was inspirational. Everyone was getting bored with the winter theme, and the weather wasn't supporting the spring either. So this was an ideal excuse for pure escapism. Her readers could think of planning romantic picnics, of remembering innocent childhood holidays by the sea and rambling through fields of waving grass without actually having to put up with the invading ants, damp smelly cottages or stinging nettle bites. She gloated to herself that Monica Manning may have had Flossie, the goat, but she, Claudia, had her very own pet designer. She couldn't believe her luck; not only had no-one else discovered Josie, but she hadn't even asked for payment and Claudia would have been prepared to pay five figures for this. Instead she had got it absolutely free. In an imitation of Scrooge, she rubbed her hands together gleefully. There was only one thing better than having the scoop of the century, and that was getting the scoop of the century for free. Babs popped her head round the door. "Clara's off on the cappuccino run. Do you want one?"

"Yes that's just what I need. I've just got the page proofs back for the Cheap Chic section; what do you think about these?" She swivelled the pages round towards Babs who writhed in ecstasy as she looked through them. "Viva are going to be sooo jealous. I've just about put up with Monica's team crowing at every press party this month. It was be so good to be wearing the bootie on the other foot. These pictures are just fab. Who did the photography?"

"Guess."

"Derek and Shane?"

"Of course."

"You have to admit those boys have style. Who would have thought of gardens at this time of year."

They looked over the copy together highlighting in red tiny typos and minor amendments.

"What are you planning for a follow up?" Babs asked as they worked away.

"Erm not sure. I've been so pleased about this month that I feel completely out of ideas for the next issue. I thought if we get this one to print and then maybe we could all have another creative session at The Ivy to get some ideas flowing." Babs' dark red painted mouth began to twitch as the thought of the food made her tongue start salivating.

"I'll get it booked." She offered helpfully, wanting to get it in the diary before Claudia changed her mind. It had been great finding an unknown talent this month, but how often could they go on doing that? There was a limit to the amount of discovery her editorial team could do. She hoped that Claudia would come up with a brainwave. Anyway if she didn't at least they had the lunch to look forward to.

Later on that afternoon, after the frenetic activity to get the magazine to print, a relieved calm permeated the office, wafting down onto the previously tense shoulders, massaging away the previous last minute panics. A small group looked at their de rigour Cartier watches and decided four o'clock was the new five o'clock and it was definitely time to leave the office and hit Marco's, the wine bar that had opened round the corner from their office. As they grabbed their handbags Babs poked her head round Claudia's door and invited her to join them.

"I'd love to, but I can't tonight. Neil's picking me up from the office later and taking me out to dinner." Babs looked impressed.

"How do you train him so well? I'm lucky if I get bought a take-away these days. Which is probably just as well. We can't afford to keep eating out and keep my shoe fetish going." It was a running joke in the office that Babs had recently had a loft conversion so that she could move the baby upstairs and have her shoes in the old nursery close to her.

"He's taking me to Nobu." Claudia couldn't help keep the note of pride out of her voice.

"Now I really am impressed. It's not your birthday is it?"

"No, he just said he wanted to spoil me."

Babs gave a groan. "Why couldn't I have a partner like that. Promise me you'll send him my way when you've finished with him."

"Get on with you! You know that you'd never give up on Teddy; not when he keeps building you extra shoe cupboards. Neil can't even hold a screw driver in fact he would probably order a skip to keep the shoes in!"

Babs laughed and held her hands up in defeat. "True, so true. But I could keep Neil for special days. Anyway have a lovely evening and make sure you have the black cod, apparently it is to die for."

As Claudia tidied her desk back into some semblance of order, she thought back over the past few weeks. Everything finally seemed to be coming under control: the magazine, her relationship and the future. She fondly recalled how Neil had come back from his weekend down in Chichester, a bunch of drooping lilies in one hand, a bottle of Pouilly Fume in the other, full of apologies for being quiet. He had talked vaguely about the pressures of work, how everything had just built up, but that the sea air had the done the trick and blown his cares clean away. They had taken the bottle of wine with them to bed and had a rapturous half an hour becoming reconciled. Afterwards, propping herself up against his shoulder she had gently run her fingers across his bare chest, considering whether to tell him about the news of her scoop of the century, debating whether she could confess, but in the end she stayed quiet. If she started to talk about how she had discovered Josie then she would have to explain about her fears of him being ill; or even worse how he might have been having an affair. She didn't want to upset anything. So she decided to savour the moment instead, enjoying the stroking and the chatting as they sipped their wine. Claudia had a fleeting hope that Josie wouldn't mention the incident of her just suddenly appearing at Josie's flat; she didn't think Neil would quite understand how she wanted to find out more about losing a partner. It was funny but he could be so sensitive about things sometimes, telling her to think of other people's feelings. Perhaps she had better prep Josie on what to say if Neil ever asked. After all the last thing they needed now was something like that to rock the boat, especially when things were starting to go so well. Everything she suggested he immediately agreed with. A couple of days later she had found the travel brochures they had been looking at earlier in the year and he had been so sweet saying she should chose exactly what she wanted, that he didn't mind. She was torn between the Kenyan safari with a combination of earthy excitement and genteel living from a bye-gone age; and the Maldives with the romantic beach walks and beautiful thatched houses. He was being so considerate at the moment that Claudia was convinced he really was building himself up to popping the question. For the second time that day she rubbed her hands together in joyful anticipation. Finally everything was coming together.

Josie looked round the room which she had spent her girlhood years growing up in. It seemed strange to think she had come full circle, ending back at her parent's house. She could hear Molly moving about efficiently tidying Josie's boxes away. All her furniture had gone into storage until Josie had secured somewhere of her own. The room had hardly changed since she had left it over ten years ago to go first to uni and then to move in with Nick. The pink chintz curtains with their delicate rose petals and entwining stems, that she had loved at twelve and loathed at sixteen were exactly as they had been; the only thing that had changed were the walls. Gone were her posters of raunchy popstars and glowering movie stars and in their place hung a series of Monet's Impressionist prints. Her mother had kept the room just as it had been when she had left home, and it was comforting to think that there was somewhere that was always home. Her mother had even kept Polly-Anna, the ragdoll with bright orange wool plaits, and embroidered doe like eyes and huge eyelashes, dressed in a mossy green needlecord dress with a tiny collar that was edged in white broderie anglaise. It had been Josie's favourite doll, that had gone everywhere with her until she was thirteen. Josie remembered the frequent childhood tears each time Polly-Anna suffered another stain or another tear, but Molly had always repaired her in time for bed so that Josie could go to sleep with Polly-Anna's bristly plaits tickling her cheek.
"Everything ok?" Molly asked from the doorway. Josie nodded, and then holding out the limp rag doll asked.
"Where did you find Polly-Anna? I thought she'd been lost years ago."
"She's been carefully stored in my room since you decided you were too old for dolls. I plucked her out of the bin after you unceremoniously dumped her there having been teased by Dawn Smythe for still having a toy to sleep with." Molly reached out and affectionately and caressed the wool bunches. "You'd been so attached to her it seemed cruel to just throw her out. I couldn't help but rescue her. Then it was nice to have her around once you left home, it made it seem like you were still around, especially after your father died."

Josie gave her mother a quick hug, surprised at the emotional vortex she suddenly experienced at the guilty thought of her mother suffering from empty nest syndrome. "You never said; I didn't realise you felt lonely after Dad died. I mean; I know having been through it, but somehow I never made the link."
"Of course you didn't; your father and I were really happy, and of course I was devastated, but there was no reason to load it onto you. You were young and getting used to married life with Nick. I couldn't burden you with my difficulties." Josie felt a glow of pride at her mother's emotional resourcefulness; her own situation had been very different, with embarrassment she recalled all the intense support she had required from friends and family. Molly patted Josie's hand. "Shall we go down for coffee?"

Their days had fallen into a pattern; breakfast would be a leisurely affair together in dressing gown and slippers in the kitchen discussing the day ahead, over their toast and coffee. They would then get dressed and Josie would start thinking about new designs, phoning suppliers and catching up on paperwork while Molly would busy herself with light housework or pottering in the garden tidying up her flower beds and shrubs; then they would meet up for a light lunch, often soup that Molly had prepared with a roll before going their separate ways again. Molly to her bridge club or the local Women's Institute meetings; and Josie to sewing. The evenings would be spent in front of the TV or out with Henry, and the weekends were spent at Drayton Beauchamp staying with Henry and Betsy. Henry had phoned her last night to tell her they had been invited to dinner with Caroline, Toby and Max, and he just wanted to check whether she wanted to accept. 'Of course' she had responded with alacrity, she enjoyed meeting up with them. She thought about the forthcoming weekend with a flicker of enjoyment, everything seemed to going well finally. Walking into the dining room, which she had commandeered as her work studio, she made a mental note to do some tidying up later on. Every available surface was covered in fabric and accessories; small cuttings she had ordered were piled up, the small butterflies and blowsy flowers scattered around on top. Rolls of fabric were propped up against the end of the table, waiting transformation into one of the new designs, some still covered in the plastic postage bag. At the end of the table sat her burgeoning pile of paperwork, waiting to be processed, which Jeremy would have had a small fit about. It had been a piece of good luck that she was now running her own business, designing and sewing home accessories. It had been the sudden intervention of the friendly hand of fate that had precipitated everything. Josie had completely forgotten meeting Sally at the Knightsbridge Ladies Circle until she was wandering down the Kings Road en route to Chelsea Harbour and she had caught sight of Sally inside her interior design shop. Sally was quietly dressing the window with the season's new accessories, laying out the lights, furniture and cushions in colourful bands of vibrant red, orange and pink. In Josie's excited astonishment she completely forgot her manners and rapped loudly on the glass, much to the surprise of the unsuspecting Sally and several passers by. Sally had beckoned her in and hugged her warmly before gently chastising her over a cup of strong steaming tea for not getting in contact.

"So how is business going?"

"What business?"

"Your design business."

"Oh I haven't really done anything since the Knightsbridge morning. I didn't sell quite as much as I thought I would. I was thinking about taking the spare bits I made to some of the local car boot sales to see if I could get a bit of money for them."

"You have to be joking – why aren't you selling them to other designers, or setting up a website and selling them on-line?"

"I hadn't thought of it." Josie admitted. "I didn't think anyone would want to buy them."

"Well I do for a start; as long as I can have an exclusive deal, and you don't sell to anyone else on the road."

"Are you being serious?"

"Never more so. I wouldn't be able to take any of the make up bags or little boxes but the cushions and the photo frames would be fabulous."

Josie was taken back. She hadn't even thought of trying to sell her items into other shops. Sally, mistaking Josie's silence for a hard negotiating pause, went on hurriedly. "We would pay for our order up front, but we'd expect a 20% discount to cover our profit." She explained apologetic at the business-like talk.

Josie managed to control the impulse to throw her arms around Sally in gratitude and instead retained the business-like attitude. Trying to think how Jeremy would have handled it she said tentatively. "I'd need a written confirmation of your order so I can raise an invoice."

"Yes no problem, I can get a purchase order organised today."

"And you would need to choose which colours you wanted. How many were you thinking about?"

"Probably five of the cushions and four of the photo frames. You don't have table cloths or place mats do you? With summer coming everyone wants new things for outside eating, you know big bold flowers, that kind of thing."

"I could make you some up, that wouldn't be a problem. How about I bring a selection of cushions and frames for you to choose from tomorrow, and then you can decide what design you want the table cloths and mats to be in."

"Brilliant." Sally enthused. "It's just what we need for the new season launch."

So in between moving out of the flat and back to her mother's Josie had trundled down the King's Road laden with goodies for Sally to choose from. In the end Sally had selected ten of the pastel coloured cushions and matching frames, and ordered five sets of a pale pink rose design for the tableware. Josie had walked back to the flat on a bed of air. Suddenly she felt everything was sorting itself out.

Chapter 9

"Do we really have to go out?" Henry whispered into Josie's hair as they sat together on the sofa reading their books listening to music. They were snuggled up together, having been out earlier for a walk with Betsy in the fields in the cold air, coming back with frozen fingures and tingling ears. The afternoon had slipped into early evening unheeded as they relaxed, chatted and read, neither of them realising that time was stealing on so quickly. It was only when Henry heard the Grandfather clock strike seven o'clock that they realised they needed to be leaving for Caroline and Toby's.

"I'm afraid we do." Josie said regretfully; as much as she was looking forward to going out, it felt so warm and comfortable being here that she didn't want to break the moment. Henry leant across and started to kiss the nape of her neck teasingly, tempting her to stay. Immediately her pulse started to race and she responded, curving round to kiss his lips, gently nibbling the lower lip. Momentarily all thoughts of going out were thrown from their mind, until Henry, managing to regain some control apologetically pulled back.

"If this carries on, we definitely won't make supper tonight." Laughingly agreeing, Josie watched Henry stand up and hold out a hand to help her up.

"I just need to get changed." Josie said, following Henry as he lead her out of the sitting room.

"Why, you look fine?" Henry was amazed at just how many clothes Josie owned.

"Because I've been tramping round the meadows in these old jeans. I want to put on my black cargo pants and new cashmere sweater."

"But we are only going to Caroline and Toby's." He complained.

"Exactly, Caroline will be wearing something trendy." They went upstairs to the bedroom and quickly changed, discarding their clothes on the floor and the armchair. Josie touched up her make up in the large mirror in the bathroom, watching the reflection of Henry walking up behind her. He put his arms round her and their eyes met in the glass.

"Have I told you how beautiful you are?"

"I don't think so." Josie said coyly. "Tell me again."

"You are very beautiful." He said seriously, then planting a kiss on her cheek, he patted her on the bottom. "But don't let the compliment go to your head, you're still making us late."
"Oh you old romantic, how can a girl possibly be expected to concentrate on her make up with all those compliments."
"Well I'd better leave you to finish if off then, while I go and find a bottle of wine to take with us."
Josie waggled her fingers goodbye before returning to her mascara; tonight was going to be a great night.

"Where's Uncle Henry?" They could hear Max bellowing to his mother above them, and then Caroline's more muffled response.
"If only he was so enthusiastic about his father." Toby said balefully. "Would you believe this morning he refused to walk with me to football practice because I was too uncool. Can you credit that?"
"I can't think why – you weren't doing your David Beckham impersonation were you?" Henry quizzed.
"Erm, maybe." Toby admitted shamefaced.
"Well what can you expect!" Henry exclaimed. "I'd refuse to walk with you, if you kept doing that." The sound of pounding feet running along the wooden floor, the sudden throwing open of the door, and a fiery little figure projected himself headlong into Henry. Winded slightly from the impact, Henry held Max away and swirled him round until Max begged him to stop.
Giddily the boy swayed on the spot, chatting vigorously to Henry and Josie, telling them all about his day, and the den he had built with the other boys at the end of the garden. Eagerly he was pressing Henry to come and see it, when Caroline intervened and reminded him how dark it was outside, and that anyway they should be sitting down to eat. Turning his attention to food, Max took Henry's hand and led him through to the large kitchen where the long table was set up for the five of them to have dinner. Although it was the same size as Henry's the similarity ended there. Caroline's kitchen was smart and bold; it was all low level American Walnut cabinets with concealed handles, so there seemed to be just an expansive of smooth solid wood. In the middle stood a huge stainless steel range that wouldn't have looked out of place in a top chef's kitchen. There were no cabinets on the wall, only a modern extractor hood that rose up to the tall ceiling majestically.

At the far end were double French doors leading out onto a terrace, and to the right hand side a glass and chrome dining table with brown leather chairs had been set for dinner.

"I know it isn't as smart as your supper party, but I thought we could just eat in here." Caroline confided to Josie. "It's never going to be grown-up with Max around."

"It's much better in here." Josie agreed "So much more cosy."

Toby directed Josie and Henry to the other side to the other two chairs, when Max shot round and stood between the two of them.

"I want to sit between Henry and Josie. Mum, can I sit here. Pleeease." He wheedled. Caroline raised a questioning eyebrow to the two of them.

"That's fine." Henry assured, pulling another chair round. Max sat down between them, beaming away, continuing to chatter away about his latest adventures.

"If he starts to wear you down just tell him to be quiet." Toby advised as Josie was required to be a dedicated audience to another tale.

"Oh he's fine." She said, smiling across to Henry as she ruffled Max's hair lightly. Caroline noticed Henry smiled back, the kind of smile lovers exchange when they enjoy the first flush of the affair, she thought enviously.

"So how is the business going?" Caroline asked Josie.

"Really well," Josie enthused "I've found someone my sister used to teach in the village who turns out to be a real computer whizz kid. He's helping me to design a website at the moment so that I can start to try and sell a few more of the designs over the internet. I'm hoping its going to be up and running soon."

"Are you having to take photographs of everything for it."

"Actually I'm using the ones Bling & Boudoir took, they are far better than anything I could take."

"Who are Bling & Boudoir?" Toby asked, his brow furrowing at the strange name. Caroline gave Josie a conspiratorial sigh.

"They're the magazine who are featuring some of Josie's products." Henry said proudly, leaning behind Max to give Josie a friendly squeeze.

"You're being mentioned in a magazine. You never said!" Caroline was open-mouthed in amazement.

"Well it was a bit sudden really." She suddenly wondered how she could explain how she knew Neil and Claudia without mentioning

Nick. "It was a friend of a friend who is the editor. She visited the flat and saw some of my designs and asked if she could include them in the magazine."

"I hope you negotiated a good fee." Caroline teased.

"Nope, actually I didn't even think about that." Josie curled up her nose in disgust at herself. "I was just so excited about some of my designs appearing in the magazine that I didn't think about asking for payment."

"So when is it due out?"

"Next week I think, I'll let you know."

"We've got the local paper shop saving us a copy haven't we?" Henry said to Josie. "Just to make sure we don't miss the big moment." Caroline was amused at Henry's attitude, she had never seen him so caring towards any of his previous girl friends; she wondered if the perpetual bachelorhood was in danger of being swapped for something more permanent.

Max gave a huge yawn, and tried to keep his eyes open, so that he could savour every moment of the stolen adult time past his bedtime.

"I think it's time you were going upstairs." Toby suggested.

"Oh no, it's still early." Max half heartedly protested.

"It's way past your bedtime, and you've got cricket practice tomorrow. Now say goodnight and I'll come and tuck you up in five minutes." Caroline persuaded. Reluctantly Max climbed down, and without any self-consciousness kissed Henry, Josie and Toby goodnight.

"Goodnight old man." Toby called to the retreating figure. "Sleep well."

Josie looked at Henry fondly. "He really is adorable isn't he." Henry nodded.

"Why don't we go and sit in some more comfy chairs and I'll make some coffee." Caroline suggested.

"Do you want some help to clear the table?" Josie offered.

"Oh no, everything can stay here until tomorrow morning. I can't be bothered to even think about it tonight." Caroline ushered them to go through to the sitting room while she and Toby made coffee; as she heard their footsteps retreating she turned to her husband and remarked.

"I haven't seen Henry so smitten before."

"Really? I hadn't noticed." Toby said as he arranged the cups on the tray.

"Toby how you could you be so blind! They could hardly keep their hands off each other. I remember when we were like that." She recalled wistfully. Toby walked across and enveloped her in a hug.

"But then we got older and wiser;" he started unromantically "And realised that married life circled around mortgages, school fees and paying your visa bills."

"It's not that bad is it?"

"Of course not. I know how lucky I am to have you. It's just the focus shifts to day-to-day realities, and you can't always cocoon yourselves away."

"That's very philosophical for a Saturday night." Caroline commented as they prepared to join Henry and Josie.

"I know, must be all that wine."

"So do you think it is getting serious between them?"

"I've no idea. Henry hasn't said anything, but they seem happy enough."

"I hope they do; it would great fun having Josie living in the village as well."

"Well if Henry raises the subject I'll let him know he has your official blessing." he said laconically, darting out of the way as his wife threw a pair of plaid oven gloves at him. "Come on we'd better take this through or they will think we've forgotten about them."

It was much later when Josie and Henry finally said their goodbyes and started the short walk home; the air was still but cold, overhead a moon shone brightly unimpeded by clouds or fog, lighting their way home. Henry put his arm around Josie and pulled her in to share his coat to keep her warm.

"I can't believe how late it is." Josie said between yawns

"It was a good evening."

"May be we should have stayed a little longer."

"No it was time to go; I'm only willing to share you for so long. Plus we've got unfinished business to attend to from this evening." He kissed the side of her head.

"What can you mean?" Josie said archly.

"Well, let's just say that if we don't get home soon I'll be forced to ravage you on the green." Giggling she took his hand and started to jog.

"We'd better get back so you can show me exactly what you had in mind; if we try anything out here we'll die of frost bite." Laughing they ran back home, fuelled by wine… and desire.

Chapter 10

It was a week later; Molly and Josie had just finished their lunch when Molly suddenly remembered.

"I forgot to tell you, I booked an appointment for you to go and see Dr Howson when I collected my prescription yesterday."

"Mum." Josie grumbled, more at the thought of having to go to the doctors than at her mother's interference.

"Josie you agreed you would go and see him. You're still not right, you're looking very washed out, and you never have any energy at the moment."

"I know, but I think I've just got a bit of a flu bug."

"Well go and get something for it. The appointment's made for tomorrow at eleven fifteen. If you want to change it then his number's in the book by the phone." She leant across and put a comforting hand over her daughter's. "I don't think it's anything serious, but you've been quite run down since Nick's death. And Henry said he was worried about you as well." Molly continued. "He really is a lovely man."

"I know." Josie said gruffly, although the idea of her mother and Henry ganging up on her, made her feel like a teenager. "Ok, ok I'll go." Her voice was sullen, ungracious in defeat.

"Sarah's bringing Olivia over this afternoon for her tea. If you're around perhaps you could help to look after her. Sarah and I have to pop over to the Convent and do the afternoon visiting at the hospice. Old Mrs Freeman was supposed to be doing it but her hip is playing up again. You don't mind do you?"

"Of course not." Since she had been here she had been helping out more and more with Olivia; it was intriguing to find out what new skills her niece had acquired. It was a source of wonderment at how quickly they seemed to learn. "If I'm on official Aunt-sitting duties this afternoon then I'd better get some work done." Josie said heading off to the dining room.

"Take a seat Mrs Carrington." Doctor Howson indicated a battered chair that reminded Josie of the ones from school, probably especially chosen so that you wouldn't get too comfortable and take up more than your allotted ten minutes. "It's quite a long time since I last saw you." He peered over the top of his half moon glasses at the shabby looking pile of notes in front of him. "I understand from your mother that you've been through a..." he paused looking for the right word. "tough time recently."

"Yes, my husband was killed in a car accident earlier this year." It felt strange to say it so matter of factly; she remembered when every time she had even thought about she had been reduced to tears.

"Well you do look a bit under the weather. What exactly is wrong." His sympathetic manner began to make Josie feel a fraud for letting her mother bully her into coming along. She knew there wasn't anything really wrong with her that a good night's sleep and a holiday wouldn't cure. "You've obviously been under a lot of pressure recently, you look almost exhausted. Are you not sleeping well?" His kindly tone suddenly caused Josie to become overwhelmed with emotion.

"I'm sorry," she sobbed "I thought I'd got over everything. I don't know why I'm like this." Her body seemed to be wracked as she gasped for air in between the chest wrenching sobs. Finally as the emotions subsided she took the offered tissues and wiped away the tears blindly while he discretely telephoned through to his receptionist and asked not to be disturbed for the next twenty minutes. A second wave of guilt hit her.

"I didn't mean to take up so much of your time."

"Now listen to me. You've been through a traumatic experience, and we need to concentrate on making you feel better. I can deal with in-growing toe nails and waxy ears any time, so don't even think about it. Now tell me what has been happening to make you so run down."

As she regained her self-control she briefly outlined how she had lost weight in the beginning after Nick's death, and had then proceeded to feel generally under the weather with occasional bouts of what could have been alcohol excess, except she was positive she hadn't drunk that much, that had caused her to be violently ill. How she was now putting on weight because she was always hungry, which was probably down to working all hours to start the business. He nodded as she outlined her ailments, taking her wrist in his cool fingers and checking her pulse, examining her eyes and her throat and feeling the glands behind her neck. As she came to an end he asked her to lie on the couch, and deftly he checked her stomach, gently prodding into the soft flesh. Finally he dug out a small glass specimen bottle from under his desk and asked her to nip into the ladies toilet and fill it. Dutifully she did, returning with the bottle half full. Taking it from her he went over to the white porcelain sink in the corner of the room and selected two of the tiny paper protected sticks from the range on the shelf above.

'Oh no," Josie panicked "They don't do this if you've just got the flu, I must have some kind of terminal disease." She watched in horror as Dr Howson methodically dipped the sticks delicately into the liquid and then hold them aloft as he studiously counted down time on his wrist watch. Finally with a satisfied 'humph' he set the two samples down on the side and sat back down in front of Josie.

"Well my dear, you certainly aren't imagining things." Her pulse began to race with anxiety, what was he going to tell her. "I'm not sure how to tell you this but you don't have the flu. The reason for the sickness and the weight gain is because you are pregnant."

The words took time to penetrate into Josie's brain, she couldn't quite take it in, all she could think was that she wasn't going to die. Then the reality took hold.

"But I don't understand." She stuttered, "Henry and I have always taken precautions."

Dr Howson looked at her, his eyes clouded with sadness and pity.

"I should say you are over five months pregnant. I would think it's more likely to be Nick's baby you are carrying."

Josie couldn't remember how she got home, she had a vague recollection of Molly waiting for her in the Doctor's reception full of loving concern at the sight of her shocked daughter. They hadn't said a word all the way home, but Molly had continuously taken surreptitious glances as she drove them down the country lanes back to the house. She couldn't imagine what conversations had going on inside the Doctor's surgery to induce such a shell-shocked state. Josie had never been one to hide her emotions, and Molly just couldn't work out why she was silent now. Surely nothing was so awful she couldn't speak about it. Actually Josie was still trying to register all the facts. She was verging between flat denial and disbelief. When she had first heard the news her thoughts had flown to all the times she and Henry had made love, and part of her wondered what Henry's reaction would be. But then Dr Howson had said the dates she realised it must be Nick's baby; and now it brought his death all back again. She felt the same guilt at being alive while he lay buried in a grave, only now the guilt had increased, that Nick had died not knowing he would be a father. It all seemed such a mess. She couldn't believe just as she thought she had sorted her life out, it had all erupted again. It would have been laughable if it hadn't felt so terrible.

Josie heard someone at the door and Molly speaking in a low voice to the visitor. A moment later and Sarah appeared round the sitting room door, followed by an extremely worried looking Molly.
"Hi there." Sarah said casually as she sat down in the plump armchair opposite where Josie was standing.
"Where's Olivia?" Josie asked distractedly.
"Edward's looking after her. He's got a free period this morning. I hear you went to see Dr Howson earlier?"
Josie threw her Mother an accusing glance as though to say "now how do you know that?" Molly's eyes were glistening with unspent tears. She sat down on the sofa and put out a beseeching hand to her daughter.
"What is it darling?"
As though in a dream Josie said. "I'm pregnant."
The news was so unexpected that Molly simply stared at Josie, her jaw dropping and opening, dropping and opening as she tried to get a coherent word out. Her gawping goldfish impression was so comical that both Sarah and Josie suddenly burst out laughing. The mirth broke the film of suspense and suddenly everyone was talking at once. "When is it due?" "How do you feel?" "What did Dr Howson say?" and they were animatedly chattering away. Molly kept hugging Josie and saying "Another grandchild. I can't wait to tell Daphne Hawkes at the Bridge Club." It wasn't a full fifteen minutes later that normality rained down and Molly and Sarah wanted to find out more.
"Well of course it isn't quite the done thing," Molly admitted, putting her hair back into place after Sarah's boisterous hugs, "But at least you know he'll stand by you." Molly's mind was already floating off, picturing Josie's wedding with Henry in his family tartan kilt in the Drayton Beauchamp church. Daphne Hawkes wouldn't be able to keep bringing out photos of her newly wed daughter if Molly had Josie's wedding to ward her off with. Josie was still smiling when she asked uncomprehendingly "Who?"

"Why Henry of course. I mean I know you haven't been seeing each other long, but you can tell the two of you are meant to be together."

The laughter died instantly. A chill spasm of pain bolted through Josie as the realisation that having this baby would mean losing Henry. Dully she said:

"It's not Henry's baby."

Sarah and Molly looked enquiringly at each other; today was certainly handing out more than its fair share of surprises.

"Who else are you seeing?" Sarah asked bewildered, racking her brain to think of anyone else Josie had mentioned. Then an awful thought occurred to her. "It's not Neil's is it? You didn't sleep with Neil did you?"

"What's Neil got to do with this?" cried Molly desperately trying to keep up with the twists and turns of Josie's revelations.

"Nothing." Josie said firmly. "I've never got together with Neil."

"Phew," Sarah gave a low whistle. "That would have been complicated. So whose is it?"

"Nick's of course." There was silence, neither of them knew how to congratulate a widow on her pregnancy knowing that the father was dead. The looked at one another for inspiration, the silence expanded into awkwardness.

"What will you do?" Sarah asked finally.

"I don't know," Josie admitted "I'd just started to get things sorted out. I'm not sure what happens now."

"And what will Henry say?"

Josie shrugged her shoulders unable to speak; she was trying to shy away from thinking about the impact her pregnancy would have on them. The only thing she knew, that she was certain about, was that no man would want to watch his girlfriend bear another man's child. It was as though she was having to make some kind of mythical trade-off. In order to keep the baby growing inside her she had to give up Henry. It was so unfair, why did she have to lose the best man she had ever known?

It was funny sitting here Josie mused, the same café they had gone to after Nick had died, and here she was four months later back in the same position.

"So what was so important you that you couldn't say on the phone?" Tara demanded as they sat drinking their skinny lattes on the pavement at the Marylebone High street café. "I mean honestly. All this cloak and dagger style subterfuge. Life outside London obviously doesn't suit you."

"For your information I'm getting used to rural life." Josie said archly. "There's a lot to be said for enjoying walks in the fields, friendly postmen and waking up to the sound of bird song instead of the cacophony of car alarms I used to have."

Tara held up a silencing hand. "Enough of the party political broadcast on behalf of the Good Life Party." She studied her friend; she looked worse than ever. Her skin was pale, contrasting with the dark lines under her eyes which showed she wasn't sleeping. Her hair looked dry and slightly frizzy, and she was wearing a loose baggy top that completely hid her figure. "Come on tell me. Why are we sitting in a café having coffee instead of our usual chat on the phone?"

"I'm pregnant." Josie said dully, and for the second time she had a stunned mute audience. Tara took time to digest the news, chewing on the arm of her Jackie O sunglasses as she made sense of the revelation.

"And whose is it?" She finally asked.

"Nick's." There was a slight crack in Josie's voice.

"Oh sweetheart." The pity in Tara's voice was evident. "You poor thing."

Josie shook her head. "Don't be kind. It's fine as long as you aren't kind." Tears threatened to well-up at the back of her eyes.

"Well I certainly never guessed that. When did you find out?"

"Last week. I went to the Doctors thinking I had the flu, and I came out knowing I was pregnant."

"Well that at least explains your recent eating habits; better a baby growing inside you than worms."

"Tara!" Josie said in disgust.

"Josie you have to be honest you have been devouring food like a famished gannet. At least we know it is because you are eating for two. So why aren't you showing very much?"

"The doctor thought it was because I lost so much weight initially. He thinks it will suddenly start to show."

They lapsed into silence.

"You don't seem terribly excited about this. I thought pregnancy released a load of happy hormones that meant you wafted around with a self-satisfied smile for the whole nine months."

"I am excited; I can't wait to have the baby." Josie reassured cradling the tiny bump of her stomach protectively. "It's just so complicated. I mean I've found a new career, I meet Henry and I was planning to buy my new home; and suddenly I'm catapulted back to being an unemployed single mother with no home and very few prospects. It's not exactly the future I'd planned for a child."
"What does Henry say about this?" Tara asked knowing she hardly knew him, but that he certainly seemed to be the supportive type. A look of desolation shot across Josie's face, colouring it with sadness, her eyes had the haunted look they had had after Nick's death. Tara felt a pang of concern. "What is it?"
"I haven't told him yet." Josie said her voice husky with emotion. "I'm meeting him later to tell him."
"Well I'm sure he will be fine." Josie shook her head sadly.
"How can it be? Henry and I haven't been together long enough for it to be fine. Being pregnant changes everything. We can't carry on as we were waiting to see if things turn out ok for us. I've got to think about the baby and giving it some stability. I can't expect Henry to wait around until I've sorted my life out."
"It might not be like that." But even to Tara it sounded lame.
"Jeremy wouldn't want you having another man's child. So why would Henry? He can find any woman he wants and have a family with her. He doesn't need me and a second-hand child." Tara fell silent, acknowledging the truth of the words. She put her had out across the table and squeezed Josie's arm, noticing how cold she was.
"Promise you'll phone if you need me."
Impulsively Josie hugged her. "Thank you for listening." She whispered.

The warmer weather had abruptly turned chilly. People scuttled along the streets eager to get home and change out of their flimsy summer clothing. The scraps of paper that littered the pavements wrapped themselves round the lamp posts, getting caught on people's ankles. The young decorative trees were caught up in it, their spindly twigs waving manically as the wind pushed through them. The weather matched Josie's mood, she sat huddled in a window seat of the restaurant, torn between wanting desperately to see Henry and dreading the meeting. She had decided it was only fair to tell him in person about the baby; well it wasn't something

she could exactly hide now that the bump was protruding more. She didn't know how he would react, but either scenario "Oh no – just when we were getting on so well" or "Well it was only a bit of fun. I'm surprised it's lasted so long" weren't any source of comfort. She cradled her stomach as though trying to get some form of strength and reassurance, but nothing came, instead she felt vulnerable and alone. A waiter glided over "A glass of wine for Madam?" he offered. The thought was tempting, perhaps just the one followed by a swift whiskey chaser, but sense took hold.
"A glass of sparkling water please." He returned with the deep blue bottle of Welsh Water and solemnly proceeded to pour it for her into the cut glass tumbler. "Thank you." She tried to smile but she had lost control of her facial muscles. Her nerves were starting to show. She didn't know how she ended up being 20 minutes early, but the prolonged wait was definitely having an effect.

She finally spotted Henry turning into the street. His coat collar was turned up against the whirling wind and his tall frame leant forward slightly as if to steel himself against the force. In one hand he carried a bunch of flowers whose petals were starting to look a little battered. Her heart leapt at seeing him, she wanted to rush out into his arms but the remembrance of tonight's conversation caused her heart to fall leadenly back into place with such force it seemed to crush her insides. Wildly she wondered if she could go through with it, seeing him there and wanting so much to be with him, it seemed absolute torture. Josie hadn't realised how much she had grown to love him, the combination of boyish good looks and caring personality endeared him so closely to her that she had never fully understood the depth of her feelings. She watched him walk into the restaurant and be greeted by the Maitre d' while he glanced round the room looking for her. Having spotted her he held up his hand before taking his coat off and giving it to the waiting man. He was smiling as he walked over to the table, his inimitable grin lighting up his face, making his eyes crinkle slightly. Josie felt as though she was suspended in liquid as she watched him, trying to commit every detail to memory while internally the gut wrenching pain increased. He mouthed a 'hello' and bent forward to kiss her, but in the confusion and turmoil of emotion she ducked her head so that he ended up kissing her cheek. He was obviously surprised but he sat down opposite her and said pleasantly "These are for you."

Josie couldn't find the words to speak; and when she didn't respond he laid them on the table to one side. "Well they did look a bit better in the shop." He tried a half laugh. He studied her, trying to establish what was happening. They hadn't spoken much over the past two weeks, he had been busy with clients, and Josie had been travelling with work, and he had been looking forward to catching up with her, and hopefully persuading her to come back to Drayton Beauchamp tonight with him. On impulse he had put a bottle of champagne in the fridge for them. He studied the mixture of emotions that seemed to be crusading across Josie's face, and the way her hands were fidgeting with her napkin, something was obviously wrong, but he couldn't guess what. He knew she had been to the Doctors; had it been bad news that she was afraid to tell him, or worse had she found someone else. The fear of losing her ran through him, he hadn't considered it before, and it wasn't a pleasant thought.

Neither of them could remember how they got through the meal, food was only played with on the plates, neither of them wanted to eat. The waiters, hovering in the background like predatory birds waiting to pounce, heightened the atmosphere of unease between them. Over coffee Henry could no longer bear the suspense, Josie had hardly spoken a word, she wasn't even looking at him. Sadly he watched her, noting her curly brunette bob falling forwards shielding her face so that she was cut off from him. In the background other couples at another tables were laughing and chatting, some flirting, obviously on their first date and eager to impress, others were more relaxed and intimate. And outside the world was shrouded in darkness, but somewhere Henry knew there was home and Betsy, it was an age old adage but so true, you could always rely on canine loyalty no matter what.

"So what's wrong Josie?" His harsh toneless voice startled her and for the first time that evening she looked at him, taking in his hurt look and realising how much she would miss him. "You haven't spoken to me all evening. Is it something I said, or haven't said? At least have the decency to tell me instead of ignoring me."

"It's not you." She blurted out, forgetting the carefully rehearsed script she had been planning all day. "It's over. We're over." She said cringing at the finality of the words. Her hands sat in her lap clenched together as though praying, the skin of her knuckles was blanched.

"Why on earth is it over? I don't understand?" He sounded confused, like a small lost little boy.

"I went to the doctors. Henry I'm pregnant."

Henry's face dropped into a proud beam. "Darling that's wonderful. Gosh you must have been so worried about everything, but you don't have to be. It's a little sooner than we might have planned, but what does that matter?"

Feeling like a total bitch Josie shook her head and dispelled his happiness in one foul swoop. "The thing is...." She said. "Well it's not yours...." She tried to find the right words to explain but the look of rebuttal, anger and horror on his face froze her thoughts.

"Congratulations." The ice hung off his words, causing the air to instantly chill. He stared at her with an intense hatred, as the realisation that she had obviously had another man all the time they had been together sunk in. He clicked his fingers to catch the eye of the waiter, he needed to get out of here quickly either he would start breaking things in anger or begin weeping. "The bill please, I'm finished here." He said curtly.

Josie leant across the table to try and take his hand, but he moved it out of her reach.

"You don't understand..." she said hysteria creeping into her voice.

"You're quite right, I don't understand. I thought what we had was incredibly special, was something that ... well it doesn't matter now." He opened the elaborate leather bill holder and checked the amount before throwing a small pile of notes onto the bill and handing it back to the waiter. "My coat please."

"No. Henry you can't go like this." Josie cried out, oblivious to the turning heads of the other diners mystified by the outcry.

"Don't make things worse." He said coldly, attempting to keep his emotions under wraps, he pushed his chair back abruptly, the iron feet dragging on the wooden surface causing it to jar.

"Henry wait. Let me explain." Josie pleaded tears started to fall unchecked down her face; but he turned on his heel and walked out, a very different man to the one who had entered so upbeat earlier. The chatter of the restaurant resumed, discussing the scene that had just happened, making assumptions and passing judgment. Josie had never felt so alone, she tried to brush away the tears with her trembling hand and avoid everyone's eye as she sought to gain her self control. The mortification of Henry's loathing, combined with the very real sense of pain at losing him were a powerful demon.

The sheer feeling of frustration at the situation meant she wanted to scream abuse at someone, but there wasn't anyone to blame, no one to kick out at. It was just the hand fate had dealt.

Chapter 11

Work became her solace; so determined was she to create a new start for herself and her baby that she threw herself into it. No longer did she and Molly have their relaxed breakfasts discussing the day, or their cosy coffee mornings. Often Josie would get up before it was light to start sewing and designing new stock. Sometimes she would still be working when Molly popped her head round the door to say 'goodnight' on her way to bed.

"I'm worried about you." Molly would say. "You should be taking it easy."

"I can't;" Josie would say grimly in reply. "I've got to build a future. I've my own responsibilities now." And if she was tired it meant she didn't constantly feel the awful dull ache of missing Henry, of praying for every phone call to be him. She hadn't thought it was possible to miss one person so much. It was ironic that she should lose two people so close together, first Nick and then Henry, but she tried to block it out of her mind. It was only in the cold lonely hours of the early morning when emotions would catch up with her and she would shed a few quiet tears into her pillow. She longed just to be able to pick up the phone and try to explain everything to Henry, but the recollection of his cold unloving stare always stopped her. Instead she focused on work, she realised a monthly appearance at the Knightsbridge Ladies Circle wouldn't keep her; the buying whims of the ladies who lunched were too fickle. So she began to seek out other interior designers like Sally who would sell her stock in their shops. It was a time consuming process, first of all identifying them, trying to make sure there wouldn't be any competition locally between stores so she could offer exclusivity. Then driving all over the country to meet with the owners at their shops to talk through the finer details and show them the range. It privately amused her that she now carried a brief case for her paperwork and several boxes with labelled samples; to the outside world she managed to portray an image of an astute business woman successfully building her own business. 'If only they could see me a home sometimes' she thought picturing herself sitting at her mother's dining room table, with a growing bump, juggling her time between the latest sewing and filling out the VAT returns, dressed for comfort in a pair of loose drawstring trousers and a faded tee-shirt.

It was on the way back from one of the visits to a potential reseller that she had ended up in Drayton Beauchamp. It had been a hot humid day, and Molly's little red car, that Josie borrowed, was as hot inside as the air outside. There had been an accident on the motorway on the way home, and so Josie, her back sore from the baby's movements and fed up with the whole wasted day had decided to take a cross country route. Once off the open static motorway and into the leafy country lanes she began to revive a little, shielded from the blazing sun with a slight breeze coming in the open windows it became little more bearable. She thought back on the disappointing trip; the shop had offered so much potential, but the owner was a peroxide blonde who had been bought the shop by 'er 'usband because someone had once commented that his Shaz had a real flair for design. So when he had earned his money and they had retired to the genteel attraction of Gloucestershire on account of his health he had bought the shop for his wife. 'Nice little investment' he'd say with a wink to friends. 'Kills two birds with one stone. Stops Shaz getting bored with country life, and if she's making money she ain't spending it.' Of course the flaw in the plan was the real talent Shaz had for recognising what the other ladies in Gloucestershire would really appreciate in their homes. As an Essex girl through and through, Shaz loved bling, no matter how obvious or outrageous. Which resulted in her indulging in a seasonal orgy of buying anything big, bold and brassy, that would be shunned by the ladies of Gloucestershire in favour of more restrained palettes, meaning Shaz could claim the retail world was going through a tough time and promptly take the stock home to refurbish her house. Her only real clients were either American tourists or girl friends visiting from Essex who would ooh and aah at the fur and the bling extravaganza, invariably buying bits out of compulsion because Shaz assured them she'd reserved it just for them. Hazily through the thoughts Josie came off auto-pilot and began to take notice of her surroundings, they began to look vaguely familiar. She was certain she had been there before. Then as she drove past the ancient sign for Drayton Beauchamp station she realised where she was. Instinctively she turned off right down the tree lined roads as though pulled by some mystery force, she drew the car to a halt and sat looking at Henry's house. It still had its classical beauty, but the pulled curtains gave it a soulless shut up air that was radically different to the previous visits. Nothing stirred within the garden and shortly Josie forced herself to drive away; unaware that Henry was sitting in the kitchen nursing a glass of whiskey. He had left work early feeling low and dispirited, needing a shot of malt while trying to work out the meaning of life.

Drayton Beauchamp high street was unchanged; quieter only because it was the changeover time between mothers ferrying children home for tea before banishing them to bedrooms to watch TV, and fathers returning home from work hot and tired by the train journey. The bakers and butchers had cleared their precious wares away to cooler areas, the tea towels and decorative napkins in the tourist shop seemed to be wilting and the bookshop proudly bore the sign "Ring the bell if help required – owner in the garden". Nothing had altered; it was just as it had been after the Little Acorns Jamboree all those moons ago. Then she noticed the recent addition, a brash colourful sign hung out at right angles from the gentlemen's outfitters. The words 'For Sale' in vivid red stood out from the yellow background. Josie pulled over into the car park and hurried back to the shop. Someone had obviously made an effort to tidy it up; the windows had been cleaned and the old furniture removed; including the tailor's dummy she noticed. The space was a warren of rooms she could see, which would be difficult for any retailer to keep; she thought of the travesty of the wainscot panelling just being ripped out and burnt. She couldn't just let that happen; ideas began to tumble into place. After all she needed to have her own place so that she could start building a home for her baby, and if that ditzy blonde Shaz could run a shop there was no reason why Josie couldn't. In fact it would make perfect sense. She could sell her things from her shop, instead of relying on other retailers. Plus she could live above the shop so it would be like working from home. That would mean she wouldn't need to look at nurseries or crèches. The excitement bubbled up inside, causing her tiredness to disappear. Grabbing her phone out of her handbag she punched in the number from the board and listened to it ring.
"Hi," she said trying to keep her voice sounding casual. "I'm interested in the Drayton Beauchamp shop. How much are they asking?"

Tara picked her way through the cobwebs and dirt; gingerly trying not to let her new cream Donna Karen trousers pick up any marks. In bewilderment she saw Josie, Jeremy and a builder Molly knew huddled together earnestly contemplating a set of rolled up plans.

"Tell me why you want this?" Tara, Molly and Sarah had asked in total miscomprehension when Josie told them about it. "But you can stay living here." Molly had wailed. "You don't have to go and live in that hovel." Sarah had even offered to have the garage converted into a studio flat, but Josie had held firm. For once she knew what she wanted and she was going to stick to her guns over it. "I am grateful for everything." She had told a crestfallen Molly. "But I've got to start standing on my own two feet. You know we'll becoming to stay." she said patting her tummy. "But I need somewhere of my own, and this is the ideal solution. I can sell my things in the shop and this little bump here can be with me. That way I'm earning and looking after it."

"You seem to have it all thought out." Molly admitted grudgingly, still secretly hoping Josie would change her mind and stay at home.

Since contacting the estate agent Josie had gone into overdrive. In between fulfilling the orders that were arriving from the other shops selling her items, she had been busy doing her homework. She knew there was going to be fierce competition for the purchase of the building, so she had rationalised, cajoled and bullied the bank manager, builder and Jeremy relentlessly, which was why she was standing in one of the tiny rooms discussing floor space with Jeremy and Mick the builder. When Molly had initially suggested Mick she had described him in such glowing tones that Josie was half expecting a Brad Pitt look-alike to turn up. Instead he was a chunky 50 year old whose hair was flecked with grey and whose veins were a little too red. However what he lacked in looks he more than made up for in down-to-earth common sense. When Josie had originally outlined her plans for the shop and the flat above he had listened to what she wanted and promised to think about it. At their next meeting he had produced a rough sketch of the building including Josie's original thoughts with one or two clever additions to make the space work more effectively for her and reducing the cost. Jeremy had then been called upon to help identify all the costs, and the three of them began to make Josie's vision a potential reality.

They walked round the dusty rooms measuring which walls would go and what would stay. The idea was to create a large open space which would be where the main shop would be, then the two awkward little rooms would be knocked through to form Josie's workshop; which would have a set of dividing shutter doors that could either be shut for privacy or open if Josie wanted to help with the shoppers. Upstairs the rooms were a tiny bathroom, kitchen, a bedroom, nursery and sitting room.

"So when is the auction?" Tara asked as the others joined her outside in the tiny cobbled garden area.

"A week on Wednesday." Josie said counting down the days with anxious in trepidation.

"This will be lovely for you in the summer." Tara enthused. "A few terracotta pots with some herbs and some old wicker chairs – just the right place to relax with a bottle of wine after a hard day in the shop."

"Yes." Josie agreed dreamily. "Only trouble is most of the money will go on the shop; this bit is at the bottom of a very big list."

"But you will have a new bathroom won't you?" Tara asked in concern, thinking about the 1930s bath and limestone stained sink that had once been white but was now a mushroom colour. She saw Josie shaking her head. "Ergh;" she pulled a disgusted face "Now I know you are definitely mad."

Jeremy put a loving arm around Tara's shoulders. "Wouldn't suit you darling would it? You'd have it Philippe Starked in a flash wouldn't you." Tara smiled fondly at him.

"Too true." She happily admitted. "Now enough "shop talk"; are we going to for that drink you promised?"

"Not for me; " Mick excused himself "It's cricket practice tonight and I need to be making my way over to the nets to set up." He turned to Josie. "I'll try and get those prices for the flooring and the windows. Probably won't be until Monday mind."

"That's fine." Josie assured him. "Good luck with the cricket." They watched him trundle off, before making their way to the King's Arms.

The summer sun that had been beating down fiercely all day had mellowed into a warm embryonic temperature. The garden of the King's Arms was jauntily decorated with red and white striped umbrellas over the wooden tables and chairs. The windows of the bar had been flung open allowing the cheerful conversations inside to escape. The place seemed bursting with people; families and young couples were enjoying the sunshine, making the most of it before having to work the next day.

"Let's sit outside." Tara said indicating the free table she had spied by the hedge. "It's far too nice to be cramped inside on a day like this." She and Josie wove their way through the crowds and sat down at the table, enjoying the last remnants of the late afternoon sun while Jeremy headed off to the bar to order the drinks. Josie leant back in the wicker-backed chair, stretching her legs out in front of her, her freshly painted toenails glinted back, and she wondered idly how much longer it would be until she could no longer reach them. Instinctively her hand stroked her protruding bump, reassuring her baby that painted toenails were nothing compared to the bliss of being pregnant. She felt her shoulders untense, she hadn't realised just how uptight she was until now. It felt good to sit relaxing, not to be frantically sewing, or organising the work for the shop. She opened her eyes and caught Tara's amused glance.

"Sorry. I was just savouring the moment." Josie apologised. "It seems ages since I've just had the chance to sit and relax, not since…" She was going to say 'Since Henry and I used to spend the weekends holed up with the papers' but her throat clamed up at the memory. "… well not for ages." She finished lamely.

"So are you excited then?" Even though they were speaking regularly by phone, Tara felt her friend had subtly moved on, as though Josie had somehow become just beyond reach, and she didn't know what Josie was really feeling.

"At the moment I'm too nervous to be excited. I keep thinking supposing I don't get the shop; or worse; supposing I do get the shop and then it doesn't make any money and I end up on the streets. What will I do then? I keep oscillating between anticipation and panic."

"Don't worry; it will turn out alright." Tara consoled. "All your hard work has to pay off. You don't look too bad for all the stress and strain. Pregnancy obviously suits you."

"I still haven't quite got use to the idea. It's so hard to believe that I have another human being growing inside me who will pop out in a couple of months and then be completely dependent upon me. I can't wait to be holding my baby in my arms, but at the same time it's quite daunting because I will have someone I have to take full responsibility for. Forever. I just hope I make a good mother." Her voice was a mixture of anxiety and humility.

"You will; just as I am going to make a wonderful godmother. Take a look at these." Tara dived into her bag and pulled out a tiny tissue paper package; carefully she unwrapped the parcel and presented a pair of exquisite booties. They were a creamy satin with tiny embroidered roses across the toe and a frill of lace along the top. "I saw them in Gap for Kids and just had to buy them. I was trying so hard to wait until after the bump was born, but I saw these and my resolve just broke. I couldn't resist buying them for you. Just promise you won't tell Jeremy, he'll have a fit if he knows I've already started spending! He had the cheek to ask if I ever kept a record of my visa bill."

"Tara they're gorgeous. I know bump is going to love having such a trendy godmother. Just think you'll be like a Calvin Klein advert; you and Jeremy pushing bump in the park when you're baby sitting but without actually having to have a baby."

"Ohhh yes!" Tara became excited, she could picture walking down Marylebone high street with one of those smart three wheeled prams, wearing her favourite cool but causal clothes of cropped trousers and skinny ribbed tee-shirt to have coffee with friends. Babies were definitely going to be this season's must have accessory.

The pub had started to thin out as they prepared to leave, people were heading home to get ready for the Monday morning drag.

"Thanks for coming down, it's been really good to see you." Josie declared.

"Fingers crossed for the auction." Jeremy said crossing his fingers to show their solidarity. They started to make their way down the path when they suddenly came face to face with Caroline and Toby walking towards them. There was an awkward pause as Caroline and Josie spotted each other; eying the other one uncertainly. Josie was unsure of the etiquette of speaking to people after a break-up. At least when Nick had died everyone had wanted all the gruesome details so they had kept in touch, but this was different. Henry was still very much alive, and presumably still vocally berating her publicly for her actions as he had done at that last meeting. Tara froze, wanting to support Josie, but not sure of the line her friend was going to take. It was Jeremy who broke the spell by saying a loud "Hello" and asking Toby about a common friend; Tara then asked Caroline about Max and it kick started the conversation. Josie stayed in the background, catching Caroline's eye every now and again as Caroline darted a look of contempt, until the rage, that had been building up ever since Henry had told them that it was over with Josie, bubbled over. Turning on her heel away from Tara towards Josie she stood staring Josie firmly in the eye before blurting out.

"How could you!" Josie reddened and refused to meet Caroline's blazing gaze.

"I never meant it turn out like this." Josie mumbled embarrassed.

"Henry was heart broken by you. What was wrong? Was he not good enough for you; was he too boring and safe?"

"Oh no it wasn't like that." Josie began to defend herself, while inside her stomach churned at the mention of Henry with a combination of longing and hurt. "Henry was... Henry's..." but the words refused to come out. She couldn't put into words the depth of her feelings for him; it all ran too deep. The memories of him holding her, of kissing her flooded back unbidden; she could remember how it good it felt as he held her close at night. Tears began to fall down her face, angrily she tried wiping them away but they kept falling, tiny glistening channels that scarred her cheeks. With as much of her broken pride as she could gather she held her head high and stalked out of the pub garden over to Jeremy's car where she stood trembling like a young sapling in a storm, her legs feeling like water and her blood pounding in her head. She had always known that she would inevitably meet Henry's friends if she had a shop here, one day she would even have to face seeing Henry again somehow. But it all seemed so much harder in reality than she had ever envisaged.

Back in the garden a bated silence had fallen amongst the two couples, until Caroline said heavily to Tara.

"I hope she and her new man are happy; poor Henry is heart broken."

Tara raised her eyebrows. "What new man?"

"The one she left Henry for; she's obviously been seeing him for some time considering the size of her bump."

"You've got it wrong." Tara's voice was shrill in defence of her friend. "Josie wasn't seeing anyone else; she isn't the type to be unfaithful. It's complicated but she's pregnant with her dead husband's child."

There was a stunned silence from Toby and Caroline as they registered the news, they exchanged a confused look.

"But I don't understand Henry said she was seeing someone else."

"I think Josie was probably in such a state that she didn't explain it properly. I mean she was so distraught at having to tell Henry about the baby that I bet it came out all wrong."

Caroline looked concerned "But that puts a whole different interpretation on it. You mean she wasn't two-timing Henry? Oh no I can't believe I just yelled at Josie. She must think I'm a Class One bitch. Would you tell her I'm sorry?"

"Yes of course, but I think it's Henry she really wants to hear from."

"I don't think we can help with that one I'm afraid." Toby said apologetically. "He's adamant he never wants to see Josie again."

Chapter 12

The ante-natal class was a complete mish-mash; it was as though someone had tried to pick women from as many ages and backgrounds as possible. There was Shazzer, a sixteen year old from The Horton Housing estate who hadn't lost her teenage gaucheness or penchant for thick eyeliner and lipstick, and whose main topic of conversation was clubbing and the trials of getting her own council flat. At the other extreme was Margie, dressed head to toe in Laura Ashley, a dumpy matron who already had three other children and viewed the classes as a necessary evil. There were various yummy mummies who appeared in the latest designer maternity wear and wore their sun glasses constantly as a badge of their clique. But it was Martha who Josie ended up befriending. They had met at the first class, thrown together in the initial welcome, and were soon swapping wicked comments about the others. Martha was a throw back to mother nature and the 60s attitude of make love not war. She wore long flowing embroidered skirts that danced as she walked, with delicate cotton tops and little Indian slippers. She sounded like a faint musical orchestra as she moved, from the tiny bells on the bottom of her skirt through to her armful of bangles. Martha lived in a caravan in one of the villages beyond Drayton Beauchamp; she had been a traveller since she had run away from home at 14, but more recently had wanted the stability of living in one place. Josie never quite discovered how she ended up living in the farmer's field, but it seemed a permanent arrangement. The other thing about Martha was that she didn't have a partner, which meant it formed an immediate bond with Josie. Martha had explained how she had been seriously involved with one of the other travellers, an eco-warrior who lived to save trees, but wasn't interested in fatherhood. He had left the camp as soon as Martha found out she was pregnant which was when she had decided to take control and set up home somewhere; so she had hitched a lift with her caravan and ended up near Drayton Beauchamp.

Not having a partner to attend the meetings meant Josie and Martha became each other's support. Whenever the mid-wife talked about the dangers of partners becoming left out and feeling isolated they swapped smug smiles empowered by their single status. It was only when one of the others would start talking about romantic gestures their husbands had made that Josie would feel a pang from what she had lost with Henry.

"Coffee and cake?" Martha whispered in between huffs as they sat practicing their breathing.

"Yes but it will have to be a quick one." Josie hissed back before the mid-wife could chastise them like naughty school children,

Over a skinny latte and slice of banana cake they watched the world pass by outside.

"So what's the hurry?" Martha asked as she nibbled away at the crumbly cake.

"I'm meeting my builder to start planning the work."

"You mean you've actually got the shop? Congratulations." Enthusiastically she flung her arms around Josie and hugged her.

Josie beamed back, pride spilling out of her,

"It was touch and go," she confided " but at the last moment the council turned down the developer's application to turn it into a house, which meant a number of speculative bidders were put off. In the end it was only us and the auctioneer."

"Did you do the bidding?" Martha asked in awe, knowing she would never have been brave enough.

"No, my friend's husband, Jeremy, looked after that for me. I was far too nervous. I kept breaking out in a sweat and having to rush to the loo. If it had been left to me I would either have missed the auction or ended up bidding against myself!"

"So you are now the proud owner of your very own place."

"Yes, and it seems so exciting. I've got so much to do before we open; I've got to get the shop set up, and the flat habitable so that it's already for when this little one arrives." Affectionately she patted her tummy.

Martha shook her head. "You're supposed to be taking it easy, especially after the mid-wife told you that you weren't putting as much weight on as she had expected."

"But I feel fantastic; I've never been so happy or had so much energy." Josie assured her. "Look I promise once I've got everything sorted out I will relax and enjoy the last few week of pregnancy."

"Well if you're sure." Martha sounded unconvinced. "Just don't over do it."

"Fancy dinner at The King's Arms?" Adam asked when Henry answered his mobile.
There was a hesitancy "I'm not sure, I've got loads of work to do."
"Come on." Adam wheedled, his voice pleading "It's my shout."
"But you never have any money." Henry pointed out irritably. "And I always end up paying."
"Well come along tonight and I'll tell you everything. See you at seven." Adam smiled as he replaced the handset; if anything would tempt Henry there, it would be curiosity. Striking up a tune he whistled as he got ready.

The pub was jostling; people were flowing in to enjoy an after work pint and to take part in the quiz night. The teams had increasingly become more competitive lately, leading to several unusual disputes flying across the pub floor. The daily commuters had accused the estate agents of deliberately getting their star team member so drunk the night before the quiz a fortnight ago that he was still recovering from the hangover three days later. The estate agents had retaliated with claims that only locals could play, and that the commuters' star team member was actually shipped in for each quiz night. A claim apparently revealed by the star team member himself during the drinking session organised by the estate agents. Things hadn't been so competitive since the garden festival of 1972 when Wilfred Jones had taken on the long standing winner Bert Humphrey after they fell out over a certain Doris Downey.

Somehow, magically, Tina had managed to save a table for Adam, which meant he was already seated comfortably with the drinks in when Henry arrived ten minutes later still wearing his suit, but looking slightly crumpled and dishevelled. Henry's normal happy countenance seemed to be replaced with a permanent scowl and Miss Letty, the secretary he had inherited from his father, was in a constant state of nerves with Henry's shouting, cursing and door slamming. He was starting to look a little older, there was a hint of grey appearing across his temples, and his eyes were dull and lacklustre. Life certainly didn't feel good at the moment.
"Good evening gracious cousin." Adam said playfully hoping to lighten the mood slightly, aware otherwise the evening would turn

out to be just like the previous ones with Henry maudlin-like ranting about the unfairness of the world.

"Evening Adam." He dropped heavily into the other chair and took a long deep slurp from the pint glass, almost finishing it in one go.

"Steady on." Adam cautioned "Unless we're in for a session tonight?"

Wearily Henry wiped the froth from his lips with the back of his hand, and pushed his fringe back off his forehead. Adam noticed that the scowl had been replaced with an empty haunted look.

"I needed that." Henry's voice sounded hollow.

"So I can see." Adam said, catching Tina's eye and motioning for another two pints.

"I met Toby as I left the office earlier. He mentioned that he and Caroline had seen Josie."

Adam gave a grimacing smile. "Well it's a small place, they're bound to meet her at some point."

"I know that; the thing was Caroline asked after Josie and her new man."

'Ah' thought Adam 'This is obviously a pique of jealousy', but out loud he nonchantly asked.

"And?"

"Apparently there is no other man. It seems the baby's father was her dead husband." Adam gave a low whistle as he took in the irony of the situation.

"So she wasn't unfaithful to you then?"

"No." Henry said unhappily.

"But surely that's a good thing isn't it? I mean at least you know there was no-one else. You don't have to keep wondering who it was, and what they are up to."

"I guess." But the unhappiness was still in his voice.

"I don't understand. If she hasn't been unfaithful then there's no reason why you shouldn't get back together is there?"

"You're forgetting about the baby." Henry said intently studying the ceiling beams and avoiding Adam's gaze. "She finished it because there wasn't room in her life for me any more now that she had her baby."

"That sounds more like rejected pride than a rational argument."

"Oh go to hell." Henry said irritably making to get up. Adam put a restraining arm out.

"Sorry. I didn't mean to get you angry. It's just I've never seen you get on so well with anyone else. What you and Josie had was special. Isn't it worth giving it another go?"

"No. She has made up her mind, I've just got to accept that." Adam felt a wave of pity looking at Henry's crestfallen face. It appeared life had certainly dealt him a dud hand.

"So where did the money come from? Henry asked after they had finished their dinner of ale pie and chips. The pub had become emptier as the quiz night contestants drifted away; the vets for once triumphant were crowing over the remnants of the teams who had stayed on.

"In a way from Nanny Hargreaves." Adam explained. "Well you know that because you drew up her will."

"Yes but I had no idea what her worldly goods entailed. I presumed you'd be left with a few premium bonds, a lifetime subscription to The Lady and her funeral to pay for." Henry said in surprise.

"And had she died any earlier it may well have been. As it was, a distant cousin of hers popped his clogs the month before, and as Nanny Hargreaves was the only living relative she inherited the few pounds from her long lost family member and a small property here in Drayton Beauchamp."

Henry tried to keep up with the story. "So you have a property in Drayton Beauchamp?"

"I did have." Adam corrected gesticulating wildly with his arms to enhance the story telling. "Until last week when I sold it."

"Which property?"

"Do you remember the gentleman's outfitters on the high street?"

Henry's heart suddenly contracted as he was taken back to a cold crisp evening after the Little Acorn's Jamboree, stopping with Josie to have a closer look at the shop. "Josie really liked it." He said sadly to himself. Aware that any reminisces by Henry would completely kill the story, Adam continued steadfastly.

"I put it up for auction and some lady has bought it, snapped it up quick as you like. It was a pity we couldn't get the council to agree to grant a change of use to pure residential. That would have been a little more profitable. As it is I haven't done too badly at all. I've paid off the debts, so that's a good thing. Those chaps at the club were beginning to really start hassling me."

"They didn't get rough did they?" Henry was concerned.

"Of course not. They're grammar school business men, not Italian gangsters. They merely mentioned to a number of people, including my turf accountant and private gambling club that I was perhaps a little low on the old pounds, shillings and pence. Far more embarrassing and definitely more hurtful. Not the sort of thing one expects, although I think one of them did come from Croydon - probably explains it."

"Adam; you are a grade one snob." Henry said baffled by his cousin's cool demeanour. "Aren't you just a bit sorry that you've had to use the whole of Nanny Hargreaves' legacy to pay off gambling debts?"

Adam flinched at the word. "Honour, my dear boy, honour. That's why it needed paying. Nothing like the thrill and anticipation one gets from the cards. Just had an unlucky hand that was all, and you have to pay for your fun. The one thing my father taught me, it was always to honour one's debts."

"So what now?" Adam looked back at him blankly. "I mean, " Henry hurriedly explained "that having nearly lost everything on a crazy gamble, what are you going to do to make sure it doesn't happen again?"

"Oh I've no worry about that. I'm back on a winning streak now." The sincerity with which he spoke showed just how much he truly believed in himself; like the alcoholic who believes he can control his drinking, Adam really believed the debts had just been a run of bad luck. Henry shook his head slightly, he was about to start castigating Adam when his cousin's phone, which had previously been sitting silently on the table, began to ring. Both of them were startled by the flashing LCD screen as its ring reverberated through the pub. As he went to answer it, it cut off, only to start ringing once more. Again as Adam stretched out his hand to answer it the ringing stopped only this time a voice behind him said.

"Hello Adam. Long time – no speak." A tall middle age brunette woman moved across in front of them to the spare chair. The open phone in her hand suggested it had been the one phoning Adam's.

"Errrm, ohhh. Yes. Hello." Adam stuttered obviously taken back to see the woman. "How are you Patty."

"Patsy." The woman corrected smoothly.

"Of course. Patsy. Well it's lovely to see you again." He tried to turn on his normally bewitching smile but it only managed a flicker like a used light bulb.

"You said you would be here." She accused, leaving out all thought of small talk. "Three times I phoned, and three times you've not turned up."

Suddenly the penny dropped and Henry realised what was happening. This was obviously part of Tina and Adam's plan to lure more people to the pub. The newcomer was one of the women Adam had given his number to and subsequently arranged to meet at the pub, only to stand her up. This one was evidently a little more persistent. Tina's stories of Adam's infamous Casanova exploits had obviously fuelled the sparks of desire rather than quenching them. In amusement Henry stood and said.

"Well I'll leave you two love birds to it."

"No don't go." Adam almost sounded desperate, he had no wish to be left alone with the man-eating Patsy.

"I must; Betsy will be waiting for me." He added sotto voco in Adam's ear. "I'll get Tina to rescue you if she's still here in 20 minutes." Adam had a false grin pinned on his face and his eyes were glinting as he looked around for a form of escape, he looked as though he had been transformed into some kind of maniac. While Henry was leaning over Adam, Patsy had begun to appreciate his not-too-bad features.

"Well, if your friend wants to stay I could always get one of mine to come over and double up." She suggested flirtatiously to Adam while coyly watching Henry through her fluttering eyelashes.

"That is an offer I can definitely refuse." Henry said with finality, and turning on his heel left Patsy open mouthed and Adam still grinning innately.

The shrill ring of the phone woke Henry up with a start, he fumbled round trying to locate the light switch and phone successfully. Finally he found the handset and mumbled disorientatedly "Hello?"

"Thought you might want to know that I finally escaped. No thanks to you." Henry sunk back onto his pillow, convinced that it wasn't an emergency phone call.

"What time is it?" He asked longingly thinking of the deep sleep he was in only minutes ago.

"Half past twelve."

"And you've only just escaped. You must be losing your touch."

"No just losing my friends. I can't believe you deserted me when I needed you most. And Tina was just as bad. She kept laughing so much she couldn't get a word out. So I was there until closing time when I thought we'd say goodnight outside the pub and go our separate ways. But Patsy wasn't having any of that. Firstly she tried to launch herself at me and kiss me; apparently she read in some woman magazine that females today should take the initiative; and then started crying because she had made such a fool of herself. So we then sat for an hour in the pub garden while I tried to explain that it wasn't her it was just me. Which was really difficult to do considering I could hear Tina harumphing and giggling from inside the pub. I can't believe she was listening in and didn't come to my rescue."

"So Patsy's gone."

"Yes. And so has the phone. After she left I rang on the pub door until Tina came and opened it, then I handed it back and terminated our agreement on the spot."

"Well I'm glad you're ok. Now do the decent thing and let me get back to sleep."

"Actually old thing, in all the commotion tonight I seen to have lost my house keys. Can I bed down at yours?"

"Oh alright. I'll see you in a couple of minutes." For the first time since the split with Josie he smiled to himself, life was finally getting back to normal.

Chapter 13

The place was unrecognisable. Ever since the legal documents had been signed there had been a stream of people carrying, lifting, tidying and building all under the watchful eye of Mick the Builder. Where there had once been a warren of tiny downstairs rooms there were now two large open spaces interconnected by folding panelled French doors, and a tiny kitchenette slotted in the space under the staircase. Light poured in through the large plate glass windows at the front and back, so that customers could see the high street one side and the tiny terrace garden at the back. The careful use of mirrors meant the light was bounced around the room, and by adding several strategically placed crystal lights the colours of the prisms were refracted across the sanded pine floorboards causing hundreds of tiny rainbows to flicker against the wood.

They had managed to retain most of the mouldings on the walls and these had been painted a creamy white with the dado and cornicing picked out in a light cappuccino. Samples of the painted shelving lay to one side ready to be installed when the team arrived. Upstairs the tiny flat had been painted white throughout in an attempt to make the space seem larger. Each room had a different accent colour. The sitting room was cerise pink, with a dramatic outline of a rose on one wall. The bedroom was denim blue, with blue cotton curtains and matching bed linen. The kitchen was funky hot orange with terracotta herb pot on the window sill and burnt umber tiles on the walls. The nursery was the only non-white room. This had been painted a soft yellow, so that it always looked as though the walls were catching a glowing sun. The curtains had golden teddy bears jauntily wearing polka dot bow ties, and a farmyard mobile hung over were the crib would go.

It was one Saturday afternoon that Josie stood looking out of the crooked rooftop window in the kitchen out across the high street to the lush green common. Large specks were taking small specks for walks, appreciating the good weather. Inside the house was quiet, the tradesmen were all enjoying their day off so there was none of the usual sounds she had grown used to hearing. She tried the window catch and found she could now open it and shut it with ease. Running her hand over the old worktop she was surprised how much better the room looked with the new tiles. Somehow the old kitchen units and plastic sink didn't look so dingy. They would definitely do until she could afford the red gloss kitchen she had fallen in love with in Peter Jones. Checking her watch she realised Sally was running late; she had been due ten minutes earlier to collect new stock. It seemed strange that she had a new circle of friends forming with Sally and Martha. Tara was still her best friend of course, but something seemed to have subtly altered, as though they no longer had so many things in common. The last time she had spoken to Tara on the phone she'd been in full flow on the progress of the shop when Tara had pointed out "enough shop talk – I want to know about you". She hoped that once she had the baby that things would get back to normal. In the meantime she had Martha to remind her of the benefits of being single away from Henry, and Sally to help her set up the shop.

"Just promise you won't stop supplying me." Sally had demanded when Josie had told her about the shop. "Invite me over for advice any time, but keep letting me have your new designs. The Chelsea ladies are going wild for them." So Josie had invited Sally over to the shop and together they planned out the shop layout; making sure the larger items were displayed against the walls, and calculating how much low level display area was needed for the cushions, journals, memento boxes and picture frames. It had been helpful to hear Sally's thoughts and suggestions, she pointed out the simplest things that Josie hadn't even considered about placing the till where she could see it whether she was in the shop or the workroom; and fitting a large jangly bell above the door so she would hear customers as they entered. They had come across the original bell amongst the discarded bricks and rubble outside in the garden, looking rusty and worst for wear. Molly had gamely taken up the challenge to restore it; and in between her afternoon bridge and weekly WI meetings had sanded and painted it with black metal paint so that it now sat back in the pride of place above the door.

Josie decided to go downstairs and wait for Sally there; the flat was furnitureless and she needed to sit down and take the weight off her feet. She was finding that the sun made her pregnancy worse, she sweated from the heat and the exertion of moving around. Although her bump wasn't nearly as big as some in the ante-natal classes, she was beginning to notice how much less agile and energetic she felt; she'd even noticed that she was starting to walk flat footed as the weight of the growing baby increased. The floors were still covered in the dust sheets left over from the painting, and there were tools scattered round, abandoned on the day off. The stairs were one of the last thing to be completed, and her mother had instructed her not to use them while she was alone, but Josie loved watching the progress unfurl, each day bringing it closer to the day she could move in. She put one foot on the stair and leant across to reach the hand rail as she always did, but something distracted her. A distant noise caused her to lose concentration momentarily. But in that split second she missed her hold on the rail, and in doing so her weight went forward suddenly so that she became unbalanced. She felt herself start to fall, tumbling down the stairs, a series of unconnected bumps and bangs as she was bounced down the banisters. She lay in a crumpled heap at the bottom of the staircase, winded, confused and disorientated. Slowly she started to breath through her nose just as the midwife had taught her. She felt foolish for having made Molly's prophecy come true, she would have to eat a large slice of humble pie tonight when her mother found out. Stretching out her bruised limbs she wiggled her fingers and toes to make sure nothing was broken. With relief she realised how easily she could have fractured something. She pulled her legs round to the front and began to sit up when the first tidal wave of pain hit her. She cried out as a knife seemed to be stabbing her. Then an onslaught of pain ripples reverberated through her, increasing with vigour and intensity. Her hands flew to her stomach, to the unborn baby that was still so vulnerable. She cradled the bump trying somehow soothe it, but the pain and the waves of nausea remorselessly continued until Josie quietly fainted away with the pain.

Chapter 14

It was only afterwards that she found out what happened. She had awoken in a silent white sterile room with a start, and no-one was around. She began to panic, her thoughts were caught up in a foggy mist and she didn't know where she was. Her movements caught the attention of a passing nurse who swiftly glided in and attempted to calm an unsettled Josie. Molly who had just been getting another cup of undrinkable tea, in order to settle down for a long wait, hurried in after the nurse, flapping wildly with concern.
"Thank God you're awake." Molly blurted out and then promptly burst into tears as she hugged Josie tightly to her. Josie stayed placidly in her mother's arms still trying to piece the fragmented memories together from her woolly memories and work out where she was. She remembered being at the shop, and arranging with Sally to meet up. Had she seen Sally? There were gaps in her memory, big black frightening holes where she had no recollection just a set of fuzzy indeterminable images like a badly tuned TV set. Molly having realised Josie was ok, pulled back slightly so she could look at the pale face and confused eyes. Cupping her daughter's face with her soft plump hands as she had done a thousand times when Josie was a child, she wondered how she was going to be able to break the news. The past six months seemed to have thrown so much misery and sorrow Josie's way, that Molly had been surprised at the way Josie had coped. The new Josie had seemed so much stronger and more responsible, but would she be able to cope with this final blow? Molly felt her pity go out to her daughter, as yet unaware, and was ready to weep again.

The moment of tenderness was broken by the hovering nurse giving a discrete cough.
"I need to check the patient." She said apologetically and swiftly but efficiently checked Josie's pulse, took her temperature and examined her eyes. Her hustle was as sterile as the surroundings; tall and angular she had none of the cosy rosy-cheeked care of the comic book caricature who plumped your pillows and gave you motherly advice. She wrote down the stats on the obligatory patient board at the end of the bed with the same detached air as the examination, and clicked her pen shut with finality.

"The doctor will be here later." She uttered before leaving them alone.

"Why am I here?" Josie asked, concern rising as Molly's face crumpled again. "I don't remember what happened. I think I was at the shop."

"That blasted shop!" Molly retorted with force. "Nothing but trouble since you saw it."

"Mum, you're scaring me. What is it?" Molly took Josie's hand in her own, marvelling at the girl she had borne over thirty years ago had turned into this beautiful person, and perching on the green blanketed bed told Josie, as gently as she could that she had lost her baby, trying to comfort her as Josie's heart broke for the third time that year. "Sally found you lying unconscious at the foot of the stairs and had immediately phoned for an ambulance and then called me. I came immediately; I've left a half baked Victoria sponge on the side; I don't think I'll ever want to bake another one again." She stroked Josie's silent tears away. "When I arrived you were surrounded by men in green gowns and masks on a trolley, and there was a team of nurses who were shouting for people to let them pass. It was all so frightening. I'd never been so afraid of losing someone. It took me ages to find anyone who could tell me what was happening. They said you'd been rushed down to theatre so they could operate. Sally stayed with you in the ambulance and she waited with me until we heard you were going to be ok. The doctors said you may be unconscious for some time, and Sally had to get back to London. She said to give you her love."

"That was sweet of her." Josie said hoarsely, her mouth was dry and her throat felt sore.

A little while later the nurse reappeared accompanied by a doctor whose chiselled jaw and aquiline nose would have made him the ideal centre-fold model for the BMJ. "Dr Kildare I presume." Molly murmured to herself, wondering when medical staff had begun to get so young and so good looking. His looks obviously had the same effect on the nurse, gone was the starchy formal appearance replaced by a skittish almost flirtatious alter-ego. She handed the doctor Josie's notes and held a reverend hushed silence as he read through them.

"You had us worried today Mrs Carrington." Dr O'Donnell said, his voice deep and gravel-like, his eyes blue and sparkling as he took in

Josie's attractive face and slender figure. "Emotionally and physically your body's been through the wars today, and impossible as it might seem, plenty of rest and sleep is what you need to get everything sorted out." He smiled a slow languid smile that he saved for his younger, prettier patients and handed the notes perfunctorily back to the attentive nurse.
"Right lets have a sedative for this evening to make sure the patient has complete and uninterrupted rest and then we'll monitor her progress over the next couple of days." Turning back to Josie he flashed another smile and said half-apologetically. "Get used to this room, you'll be with us for a couple more days while we keep our eye on you." Then with the stately presence of royalty he swept out of the room, closely tailed by the nurse.

The strength of the medication and the monotony of the days meant Josie lost all track of time. She didn't have the energy to do anything, so she spent the time watching mind-numbing day time TV and dozing. She hated both; in her waking moments everything circled round babies, with every minor celebrity hitting the headlines for giving birth to their latest Bobo or Banana; Oprah talking to surrogacy mothers; or adverts for nappies; everything heightened the loss. When she went to sleep though it was worse. Instead of escaping to a restful slumber she was haunted by panic stricken nightmares. In her dreams she was always anxiously looking for her baby, running through pitch black rooms trying to find where her baby was, hearing the pitiful cries but unable to see where it was coming from; hunting down blind alleys, running through empty streets and searching deserted rooms in rambling houses. Often she woke herself up, dripping with sweat, throat hoarse from crying out, tangled in her sheets and shaking with fear. With no one visiting she felt she was slowly losing her grip on reality. She had no one to talk to about the loss, no one to be able to grieve with, and without these her thoughts spiralled down into deeper despondency.

It was four days later that Tara finally bullied her way in to see Josie. In Josie's slightly befuddled state she noticed a commotion outside her room in the corridor rousing her from a light sleep; she could hear raised voices shouting loudly.
"You can't go in there." A voice instructed shrilly.

"Just watch me." Tara's steely voice had answered and suddenly she appeared, a fairy godmother attired in Dolce and Gabana's latest denim jeans and jacket. "My god what has happened to you!" Tara was shocked by Josie's limp greasy hair and the vacant panda eyes etched with exhaustion into the gaunt pallid face. The imperious nurse hurried in after Tara.

"She's not to be disturbed; that's Doctor O'Donnell's orders."

"Then you had better go and get Dr O'Donnell and bring him down here pretty damn quick, because I have a few choice words to say to him." And when the nurse stood open mouthed at Tara's audacity, Tara followed it with a sharp "Now, I don't have all day." In confusion the nurse backed out and called across to another nurse walking by "Where's Dr O'Donnell?" Tara walked across to Josie and hugged her fiercely.

"We've been so worried about you. They said you weren't allowed any visitors so that you could get some rest, but I just knew that you'd hate that, thinking we had forgotten all about you. So I decided to bring the cavalry in." Josie clung weakly to Tara.

"Thank goodness you're here. I think I'm beginning to go crazy all by myself."

"I knew it!" Tara said triumphantly. She pulled away and studied Josie's pale complexion. "What you really need is a change of scenery and some good old fashioned sun."

"Just get me out of here!" Josie begged, anxious to be away from the hospital environment and constant reminders of her loss.

"Your wish is my command." Tara said now enjoying the moment. "Actually your mum and Sarah will be here any second." She dipped into her bag and pulled out, like a magician producing an award winning rabbit, two plane tickets. "This is two tickets to the south of France." She fanned the tickets gleefully in front of Josie's nose. "And I'm your fairy godmother who's taking you away."

"What about Jeremy?"

"He suggested it; he knew how worried I was about you. One of his work colleagues has a villa there, and he's organised for you and I to go and stay there – think of it as a bit of girlie break."

"But I haven't got anything to wear." Josie protested weakly, indicating the green gown she was wearing.

"You will have. Molly's packed a suitcase for you."

"Did I hear my name?" Molly's voice called out as she and Sarah came through the door lugging a suitcase and several plastic bags.

"Move over darling, I think I need Dr O'Donnell's careful attentions after lugging everything in from the car."

"Hah!" Sarah rebuked forcefully as she let the case drop to the floor with a thud. "You carry the sun hat and beach towel and leave me with the heavy stuff."

"Well I am getting on a bit." Molly said glibly.

"Maybe, but you're still as cunning as ever." Sarah charged. "Honestly Josie, if I hadn't been there this morning you would have ended up with three cases full of emergency contingencies from fleecy jumpers to ball gowns."

"Well you never know what you might need." Molly protested against the three laughing girls.

Amongst all the commotion and hurly-burly of conversations they didn't notice they had been joined by Dr O'Donnell and his lapdog nurse.

"Silence." The nurse shouted and clapped her hands for attention. Astonished the four women turned towards the newcomers and the silence that had fallen suddenly ended in a cacophony of questions and demands as each woman wanted to know how Josie was, when she could leave, and why hadn't they been allowed to visit. Dr O'Donnell felt like a lone zebra facing three very fierce lionesses intent on protecting their cub. Bravely he tried to respond to one, only to be attacked by another. He ran a finger around the inside of his collar which suddenly felt too tight, and noticed that his palms were starting to sweat. After fifteen minutes of grilling that even Jeremy Paxman couldn't have faulted, he signed Josie's release and was backing out of the room so quickly he almost fell over the nurse who was hovering in the background. The three woman turned triumphantly to each other and cheered before a brief round of jubilant hugs.

"You're out of here." Molly cheered. "Now see what we've bought for you to wear." The three of them pulled clothes out of the plastic bags and helped Josie to get showered and dressed. Sarah even insisted on doing Josie's makeup.

"If you are going on holiday you should look the part. You never know who you might meet." Finally they were all piled into Sarah's car and heading down the motorway to Heathrow airport. Radio One was blasting out the latest pop song and Molly was giving last minute advice on not drinking French tap water, not to speak to any strange men, and definitely not to drink too much.

"Too late on that one Molly!" Tara laughed as she and Josie sipped away at a shared bottle of iniquitous lemonade, topped up with Bacardi, in an attempt to get them both in a holiday mood. It seemed that in no time they had pulled up in front of the large glass fronted terminal building, and were hugging Molly and Sarah goodbye before checking in for their flight and sitting in the departure lounge drinking dry white wine.

"Here's to a week of sun, sea and serious drinking." Tara joked clinking her glass against Josie.

"Oh yes, I'll drink to that." Josie agreed heartily.

Chapter 15

Henry's in tray had never looked so neat, in fact the whole of his office was so tidy that even he had trouble recognising it sometimes. The usual stack of clients' files which spilled over the desk and onto the top of the cabinet had been cleared, the stack of billing sheets which usually languished on one chair for at least two months had all been typed up as invoices and sent out with the requisite polite note requesting payment within thirty days. Even the little mounds of dust motes and fine spindly cobwebs behind the large fern in the corner had been dispelled. Henry couldn't remember the last time he had seen the office so immaculate. Even after his father had died, Henry hadn't really cleaned up, he'd just preferred to move in and continue where father had left off. Now everything was going to be different. He'd made the decision in the lonely hours of this morning as he waited for the clock to slowly turn from 4 o'clock to 5 o'clock. He wanted a fresh start. Enough of the old, boring, dependable Henry, he was going to be a modern hip trendy Henry. Out was going the tweeds and the cords, he was going to model himself on James Bond, a character he had always secretly admired for his cutting edge style and his luck with the ladies. Carefully he guided his thoughts around the potential minefield of remembering Josie and focused instead on all the well dressed women Adam had introduced him to the last time they had visited London. Henry had been surprised at the number of gorgeous girls should had come over to say "Hi" to Adam; he'd been a babe-magnet all night. "How do you know all those women?" Henry had asked incredulously. "I've either been at Eton with their brother, walked out with their sister or had a brief flirtation with their mother." Had been Adam's jovial answer. Yes, Henry could see himself setting up as the man-about-town; maybe he could get a tiny flat up in town, just what every bachelor needed, a kitchen with a fridge for chilling champagne, a sitting room for entertaining and a bedroom for..." Henry smiled to himself, with the state of his love life hitting rock bottom his interest in sex had completely vanished. He hoped it was only a passing phase and nothing too serious, but it wasn't exactly the sort of thing you could just ask another bloke about. He tutted at himself, this was the old Henry speaking, the new Henry would be a winner with the women. He could see himself now, seducing them just like Sean Connery.

From greeting to bedroom in three quick steps, making conquests all over town. He left the day dreaming and opened the plastic bag on his desk to pick out a tin of paint, reading the label 'Guacamole Lime'. He'd been flicking through one of the house magazines, which Josie had left by the bed, this morning after he'd resigned himself to not being able to sleep. One of the features had been on 'boys and their toys' and had focused on rooms where men could relax, chill out and be the mature children they secretly were. One of the photos had shown a bright green wall covered with platinum records designed for the music mogul male, with wacky 70s style white chairs and a sheepskin rug dyed to make the walls. 'Seriously useful for seduction' the caption had read. There was something about the photo that offered so much, and that was so different to anything he had ever had before, that Henry had made an immediate decision to repaint his office in the green. Subsequently he had gone via the local hardware shop and picked up a sample paint pot. Striking while the resolve was still strong, the colour on the tin looked like a vibrant lime, just want he needed to become a new man, a hip trendy office and clothes to match. Maybe he could go shopping at the weekend and restock his wardrobe. He shook the can of paint just as a master barman shakes a cocktail, and then using his letter opener he prised the lid off. The colour was a little stronger in the tin than it had been on the label, but that was probably because it was wet Henry rationalised. He looked round for something to paint a small sample on the walls with. In the back of his mind something told him he hadn't really thought this through, the fact he was standing with a tin of paint in one hand, dressed in his best suit, scrabbling round for an improvised paint brush, but he quenched the disloyal thoughts and pounced upon the soft brush Miss Letty used to clean his keyboard with. He stuck the clean soft bristles into the gloopy paint mixture and with a reckless satisfaction dobbed a square of Guacamole Lime onto the wall. Uncertain whether he liked the blob of snot coloured paint he dobbed on some more until a ragged square two foot wide covered one immaculate magnolia wall. He stood back and critically appraised it; but it didn't matter how long he stared at it, the sample didn't look anything like the zany photo, it just looked hideous. The realisation of just how different it was from the desired outcome seemed to puncture his resolve. His plans and ideas seeped away leaving the steely grey silhouettes of reality. His temper flared up and he thumped the desk in frustration, nothing he felt was as he wanted it. He missed Josie, deep down underneath all the damaged pride he desperately missed her. When they had been together he hadn't felt the need to change, she'd never made him feel boring or parochial, not like the women Adam knew who looked down their Knightsbridge noses because of his lack of title and estate. His body flooded with an intense emptiness, chilling him to the core so that he felt he would never be warm again. With a heavy heart he dropped the paint can in the bin and slumped down in his chair, his head in his hands as waves of self-pity washed over him.

It was later that morning that Miss Letty knocked on his door and timidly entered with a pile of letters.
"Here's the morning post; sorry it's late but apparently Archie had trouble with his bike, something about a puncture. Anyway once you've…" She was stopped mid-sentence by catching sight of the lurid green decoration on her carefully washed walls. The square threw her into a kilter and she tried to formulate a cohesive question, but to no avail. Instead she mutely pointed, her delicate mouth moving but no sound was uttered.
"Oh yes." Henry said ironically "I was thinking of doing a bit of redecoration, but the colour was rather louder than I anticipated." He took the letters from her outstretched hand and was about to start opening them when he realised that his letter opener was now smeared in Guacamole Lime. "Could you get me a new letter knife and a strong black coffee?"
Still in shock Miss Letty went out, returning a few minutes later with a letter knife and a white porcelain mug of freshly brewed coffee. He watched as she gave the wall a look of utter distain before turning on her flat brogue heel and marching out, permed head held high. A small tut and "Josie would have known which colour to chose" quietly drifted after her as she pulled the door shut with more than usual firmness. The worst part was Henry had to admit she was right; Josie would have known the exact colour he needed. His thoughts flew unbidden back to their first supper party. He had been so proud of her, wanting to make the room look special for their guests. Every other woman he had known would have demanded Henry take everyone out to some smart restaurant. He rubbed his hand over his face, feeling tired and fed up as he leafed

half-heartedly through the post. There was the usual collection of client enquiries and payments, but a thick wad of photocopies caught his attention. A sudden injection of adrenaline ricochet through his body as he read the documents, instantly the feeling of tiredness had disappeared and he felt every nerve in his body become alive. He forced himself to concentrate, unable to take in what he was reading. He chewed on the edge of his thumb nail as he re-read the pages. Once he had finally digested the contents, he sat trying to work out what his next course of action should be. After all, he now had the answer as to why Nick had died.

Throughout the day he kept returning to the documents, checking the details, cross-referencing the notes. He couldn't believe how everything had come full circle. The innocent request of Mother Superior to look into Annie Carrington's will had been an unlikely catalyst, but somehow all the disparate parts of the jigsaw logically fitted together. The papers from the Public Records showed that Annie Carrington had given birth to Nicholas Carrington thirty three years ago, and that the same Nicholas Carrington had married Josie nee Patton three years ago. A distant memory of Molly enquiring whether Josie and Nick had processed the photos from the convent's open day, and the fact that Nick had died on the road to St Stephen's convent all joined together. Nick must have recognised his mother from the photos and decided to visit her, either because he realised she was dying, or to confront her about abandoning him so many years before. Whatever the reason he was obviously in a state; he hadn't mentioned anything to Josie or Molly about discovery, probably wanting to speak to Annie first. He'd waited until Josie was away before going to visit Annie. Henry had no idea why he was driving to the convent so late at night, maybe it had taken longer to pluck up the courage to confront the mother who had left him twenty years before. With all those turbulent emotions crusading inside his head, he may well have been distracted as he drove along strange unfamiliar lanes in driving rain. They would probably never know the real story behind it, but hopefully it would give Josie a degree of comfort. Or would it? Was he using this as an excuse to speak to her again? Maybe it would be better if he didn't say anything so that she wouldn't open up healing wounds for no good reason. But surely she would want her baby to know about its father. He dropped his head onto his clenched fists, the knuckles protruding white under the skin. The desire to do the right thing combined with wanting to see her churned away in his stomach. How would he be able to decide what to do?

Chapter 16

The original week had slipped into a fortnight, with Josie and Tara benefiting from the relaxation and quiet break. The villa was stunning, a low white washed building from the 1930's that looked out over the azure chiffon Mediterranean sea. Above the houses a few sea birds lazily circled round, dining off the easy pickings from picnickers and locals. Behind the house a line of tall poplar trees stood sentry in front of a backdrop of verdant green mountains. In the landscaped gardens that stretched down to the golden sandy beach a smaller white building sat behind a large fountain where Dominique and Pierre lived, the villa's housekeeper and gardener. The whole environment was one of a top class hotel, with the freshly cooked meals, laundry service and private pool. At first Tara and Josie felt awkward at having Dominique waiting on them, but her gentle persistence and maternal clucking meant they looked forward to each meal with relish. Their hosts had kindly offered the use of their wine cellar and so as the afternoon sun started to lose some of its intense heat, Pierre would appear with two chilled glasses of Sauvignon Blanc assuring the girls with a wink he had selected it as the perfect accompaniment to this evening's meal that Dominique was preparing.

The days had been long and languid, neither had wanted to venture out into the local town, instead they were happy to sunbathe, read books and occasionally swim in the pool to cool off. Both of them had turned brown, Tara with her olive complexion looked tawny, Josie with her lighter complexion was sun kissed. The gauntness and exhaustion was gradually draining away as Dominique's cooking and the summer sun worked their magic.

It was after the first week when they had decided to stay longer that Josie first raised the topic of the loss of her baby. They had been discussing how parents could be so infuriating and yet so necessary when Josie had suddenly started weeping. She hadn't cried once before, or raised the subject, so when the tears began to stream down her face Tara realised Josie was starting to come to terms with the loss.

"I feel so guilty." Josie mumbled through the tears, feeling the saltiness as they ran down her checks and across the corner of her mouth. "I should have been the one to look after my baby, and I didn't. I was so certain I could make a future for us both, that I didn't think about protecting it. I was so blinkered, all I thought about was work and the shop, and now look what's happened to me. I've been punished for not taking care of my baby, and it's been taken away from me." Tara was shocked at the interpretation Josie had put on the turn of events. "If I hadn't bought the shop then I would never have fallen down the stairs, and I'd still have my baby." Her tears increased to great wracking sobs; Tara pulled her close hugging her tight trying to soothe her friend. After a while Josie began to calm down a little, but she remained a wet heap in Tara's arms.

"Josie I don't know what you're going through. I've never been pregnant. But I do know that you did everything you could for that baby. You didn't hurt that baby, and you certainly shouldn't feel guilty. You should be proud of everything you've worked for to make a future." Tara thought about the conversation Dr O'Donnell had had with Molly over the reason for Josie's loss. "Josie, listen to me, What happened wasn't your fault. The doctors think that your baby was undersized; that everything you had been through since Nick's death probably meant the baby wasn't developing properly. You said yourself how small your bump was compared to the others. Dr O'Donnell thought it might have happened anyway. So don't go blaming yourself. It really isn't your fault."

"Do you really believe that?"

"Yes I do." Tara said firmly. "And that's what you've got to believe as well, because when we get back you've got a business to run and a shop to open. The Josie Carrington I know isn't going to let all her hard work just melt away." Tara felt Josie shudder.

"I don't know if I ever want to see that damned shop ever again."

Tara sighed. "Well that's up to you, you're a grown adult, you can make the decision to sell it, or rent it, or whatever you want. But remember why you bought it, it was a chance for you to start your future, and it still is. You can't just shut yourself away from life, especially not when you worked so hard for it."

"You don't understand." Josie flared up. "You've no idea what it is to lose everything. I haven't even had a chance to say a proper goodbye to my baby. It was just taken away from me, without me being able to even see it. Have you any idea what I have been through?"

"I know when emotion gets in the way of logic." Tara retorted, stung by Josie's comments.

"Oh just leave me alone." Josie cried out. "You don't care, you're only bullying me into doing it because you're too afraid to do it for yourself. Well I won't live my life for you."

Tara snorted "My life is just fine thank you. I certainly don't need to project my ambitions on you."

"Typical! You and your bloody perfect life, with your perfect husband, and your perfect home. You make me sick. You've no idea what it's like for those of us having to live in the real world where we don't have a husband's cheque book to support us."

"What you mean your new found friends Manhater-Martha and Simpering-Sally? Oh Perlease!"

Josie kicked the chair back and stormed off to the beach, scaring a flock of resting gulls as she rushed down the path, so the air was filled with their pitiful cries.

The sky had darkened as a storm blew in off the sea, the normal blue mirror finish was a churning froth of white horses and breaking waves. Tara sat curled up on one of the large squashy sofas, Sky TV on in the background trying to distract her from worrying, but her eyes kept being drawn back to the window on the look out for Josie. She had been gone for some time, and at first Tara had bristled with anger at Josie's comments thinking how unfair Josie was being about everything. Tara felt she had sacrificed a bit of her independence when she had given up work to become the little woman at home. It wasn't even as though Jeremy had acted draconically, banging his fist on the dinner table and manacling her to the sink. It was the realisation that if they didn't change something then the marriage probably wouldn't last; they hardly ever saw each other, they were socialising separately and then bickered when they were together because both were tired, stressed and disorganised. It had taken Tara some time not to feel abandonment every time Jeremy went off to work leaving her at home, but it had been worth it in the long term. By having her as his pivotal point Jeremy knew he didn't have to worry about whether she was free when clients suddenly flew in for a late meeting accompanied by their wives, nor did he have to think about collecting his shirts, organising the bills to be paid, or getting the food in. In the early days they had lived off cheap wine and pizzas.

Of course now Jeremy was earning more Tara did have help round the house, and why not she rationalised. The anger had slowly dissipated as the evening continued, turning into concern. She had eaten alone in the dining room for the first time since they had been there. She would have phoned Jeremy to hear a friendly voice, but he knew he was out with clients. Unconsciously she flicked through the channels, but nothing seemed to hold her attention.

A door creaked open and shut; the sound of wet feed pthuding against the marble tiles getting louder as they approached the sitting room. Tara looked up quickly and saw Josie silhouetted in the doorway, a drenched waif sheltering from the ravaging weather. Water streamed down her hair into rivulets that hit the floor in an orchestral arrangement, her skin was bluey white from the cold and her lips shivered involuntarily. Goosebumps stood up prominently on her arms under her soaking tee-shirt; her clothes clung wet and uncomfortably on her body, moulding her curves like a second skin. Her head hung down.
"I'm sorry." She stammered an apology, ashamed at her outburst. "I shouldn't have said those things. I know they're not true. I was just so angry."
"Where have you been? I was getting worried."
"Just walking along the beach; I was so livid with everything I lost track of where I was. Then when it started to rain, I realised how far I was from here, so I thought I'd shelter in the rocks for a bit while it passed. And then when I realised it wasn't just a passing shower I decided to make a start walking back."
"At least you're back now." Tara said lightly, not wanting to start another outburst of emotion.
"Sorry for worrying you, and sorry for shouting. You are right of course, just because one thing didn't happen doesn't mean I should abandon the rest of the plan. I mean, I'd already started to try and build a business before I knew I was pregnant."
Tara relaxed slightly, however tough each day would be, at least Josie was going to be prepared. She walked over and pulled Josie's icy cold arm through hers.
"Let's go and get you dry and then we'll see if we can persuade Dominique to rustle up some hot soup."

"That would be great, I'm absolutely starving." They walked down the dark corridor and a strange feeling of peace settled upon them; they were back to being the best of friends.

"Josie." Claudia screeched down the phone a continent away. "Where are you? You need to get back to London pronto. Our switchboard is working overtime because of you." Josie's face slipped into a grin
"Actually I'm sitting on my suitcase at Nice airport waiting to fly home."
"Who is it?" Tara mouthed.
"The Ivana Trump of the publishing world – Claudia." Josie hissed back, causing them to burst into a fit of childish giggles.
"Are you listening to me?" Claudia demanded.
"Of course." Josie lied soothingly, suppressing the giggles that were tweaking the edges of her mouth.
"Well we need to meet urgently. What time can you get here?"
"Claudia I'm flying to Heathrow at five o'clock tonight, there's no way I can meet you today, may be tomorrow."
"Right let's say nine-thirty tomorrow morning." Claudia cut in, desperate not to let Josie know how much she needed the meeting. "Ahem, you haven't had any other magazines contacting you have you?" She tried, and failed, to make the enquiry sound flippant and light hearted.
"No." Josie was amused by Claudia's questions. "You asked me once before, and I hadn't then. Why do you think I should?" She asked mischievously, down the phone she could hear Claudia having a minor cardiac at the suggestion.
"Nnnn...no. No." Panic garbled the words. "Look we'll talk about it tomorrow. Just be here for 9.30."
"Ok." Josie agreed, intrigued why Claudia wanted to speak to her again.
"What was that all about?" Tara asked as they shuffled forward in the slow moving check in queue. Josie shrugged her shoulders.
"No idea. She just asked me to be in their office tomorrow morning."
"Good thing you're staying at ours, or you'd never have made it up to town in the morning." They inched forward again, dragging their cases and clanking bags of local wine destined for presents. "May

be she wants you to decorate her office, a nice tasteful gold leafed and crimson flock."

"Or perhaps it's to make the wedding album now that Neil has proposed!" Looking at each other they were struck at the ludicrousness of the suggestion.

"Neil, propose? Nah!" Tara said and they felt the corners of their mouths start twitching again; then they saw the other trying not to laugh at the ridiculous notion, they wanted giggle even more. Suddenly Josie snorted with mirth and Tara couldn't contain herself. They leant against each other trying to stop the merriment, but each time one of the them got themselves under control the other would set it off again. The other passengers watched in silent bemusement at the two giggling women, not quite sure what to make of it. As they reached the check in desk they handed over their tickets with one hand and with the other wiped away the streaky mascara.

"Bet you're sorry you're going home." The British Airways check in assistant said.

"Oh no I can't wait." Josie said. "The real fun starts tomorrow." And linking her arm through Tara's they walked through to departures. "It was a wonderful idea to come away, but somehow its great to be going home."

"I know exactly what you mean." Tara agreed.

Josie almost skipped to Claudia's office the next morning; the sun was out and people were going about their morning activities, children to school and adults to work. It was one of the mornings that made you feel good to be alive. She was dressed head to toe in Tara's clothes, Molly not having thought of a work opportunity cropping up while on holiday. It wasn't something Josie would have considered either. The outfit was a long cream chiffon skirt and tailored shirt which looked too dowdy on the hanger for a second look, but Tara had teamed it with a wide chocolate brown belt and matching cling backs, and the whole outfit made Josie feel very elegant and Audrey Hepburnish. She kept surreptitiously at her reflection as she walked past the office windows, surprised at how much her tan enhanced the outfit. She was primed and ready for whatever Claudia had to throw at her. She was worried that there had been a number of complaints by the Bling & Boudoir readers at the magazine featuring her amateur designs. Hopefully

Claudia wouldn't be pressing for compensation, she'd never afford it. Her heels clicked as she entered the reception of Shaker Publications, the company which owned the magazine, it was an enormous glass atrium that rose up four floors and that was stuffed with enough exotic greenery for David Attenborough to feel at home. In the centre a dramatic edifice of boulders towered fifteen feet high, down which ran a constant cascade of water. The sound made her instantly want to go to the toilet, and she wondered how the receptionist coped sitting by it all day. She soon found out, it took several 'hellos' to get the platinum blonde head lifted up and acknowledge her. Casually the receptionist removed the iPod head phones from each ear.
"Sorry I didn't 'ear you." The girl was so heavily made up that her skin had lost all natural texture transformed into one matt finish. Her eyes were scored with kohl eyeliner making severe rings above and below her hazel eyes. The same technique had been applied to her lips so that they seemed even larger and more inflated and the blusher on her cheekbones were two distinct slashes of rose pink. "I said 'oo are yer 'ere for?" the girl repeated. Josie forced herself to concentrate.
"Oh Claudia Kingsey."
Efficiently the receptionist tapped a number into a key pad and said "Hi someone in reception for Claudia." She listened as the other person responded and then said 'bye' before hanging up. She looked back at Josie "Right go up to the fird floor – Allie will be waiting fer yer there." And pointed to the right to the glass elevators. She waited for Josie to go before putting her head phones back in quick before she had to listen to that dratted fountain any more.

Allie was the shy editorial assistant Claudia had almost reduced to tears over the cancer survival feature. Her tentative administrations, checking Josie had arrived ok, whether it had been easy to find, would she like tea or coffee, and apologising for being out of muffins, but she was certain there were some cookies if Josie wanted one, were so different to Claudia's approach she had a momentary panic that Allie knew how angry Claudia was, and was trying to make up for the tirade that was about to break. Allie ushered her into a large meeting room whose walls had originally been cerise pink, but were now plastered with initial featured outlines, magazine cover mock ups and reminder notes that only scraps of colour peeked through in odd places. The table was a glass sculpture worthy of Henry Moore. The legs were two huge hollow circles and the top was shaped like a blunted tea drop. The chairs were inflatable arm chairs in a gaudy array of reds and oranges. Josie decided to watch someone else manoeuvre themselves into one before she tried She didn't have long to wait, suddenly the door flung open and a gang of loudly chattering people rushed into the room and headed for their usual seats, dumping their Mulberry and Asprey notebooks onto the table before attempting to gracefully lower themselves into the glorified rubber sun chairs. Claudia followed on behind and spotting Josie gave a loud cry and kissed her on both cheeks.

"Everyone this is Josie." She shouted above the conversational murmur, keen to show off last month's answer to Declan O'Fara and his goat. A chorus of 'Hi', 'Yoh' and 'Nice to meet you' echoed round the room. "Sit down over there." She indicated a chair in the middle of the table, before sitting at the tip of tear drop taking the head place to reinforce her authority. "Before we start we'd just like to say how grateful we are you could make it today." Claudia smiled ingratiatingly, and the others, like sheep, smiled at Josie too. This was more alarming than if they'd been angry with her, uncertain how to respond Josie looked round the room once and then settled herself onto the inflatable chair. It bounced slightly as she settled herself and she found herself clinging onto the glass in an attempt to appear nonchalant and in control. "I don't think you know everyone in the room, this is Babs our features editor, Lucy the features assistant, Lotty, Dotty and Katy are editorial, Jaqs is photography and Allie is…"

"A waste of space." One of the others whispered spitefully. Allie flushed an unbecoming shade of beetroot and pretended not to care.

"Now, now." Claudia called the room back to order. "Lets focus on why we are here. How many calls have we taken on the Cheap Chic feature?"

Lotty or Dotty, Josie couldn't tell which since the two Sloane girls dressed in the de rigueur Joseph top and skirt with Jimmy Choos, cleared her throat and consulted her report before saying:

"As of yesterday we had two thousand, three hundred and thirty three calls." Josie's heart sank, that was an awful lot of disgruntled readers. "This is the largest phone-in ever following a feature."

Lotty or Dotty continued. "The nearest was the Bling Fling feature on glitzy romantic getaways, which received one thousand, nine hundred and eighty seven calls. This means that statistically 1.24% of our readership expressed an interest in the item which converts to..." Claudia cut in before the meeting became a quagmire of statistics.

"Thank you Dotty." She turned to face Josie. "Have you anything to say?"

Josie decided silence was the best form of defence and gave a non-committal shrug. Claudia noticed Josie no longer seemed the pliable girl she had previously been, a glint of iron determination was visible in the confident gaze showing an no-nonsense attitude. In an attempt to strengthen her argument Claudia asked Babs to talk through the circulation figures.

"Well we were up by 10% which means our market share increased to 26.4%, although in real terms it is a 4% increase, the other 6% relating to the circulation we lost to Viva with the Declan O'Fara feature." Claudia glanced again at Josie's impassive expression, God she was playing it cool, had one of her rivals started sniffing around? Claudia began to sweat, her foundation became claggy and she didn't dare wipe away the drip of perspiration forming on her brow. She had expected Josie to be her normal naïve self, and to willingly go along with their plans, preferably free of charge again. It looked like another strategy was definitely required; the room was waiting expectantly, so Claudia decided on the direct approach.

"As you have heard Cheap Chic was one of Bling & Boudoir's most successful features. We feel there is still mileage in this, and were thinking of a theme for this month." She looked across to Babs who jumped in.

"We were thinking of a bespoke Bling & Boudoir range of products for the summer, glitzy Chinese parasols and comfy garden cushions in this season's citrus greens and turquoises."

"And may be with the Bling & Boudoir logo subtly but definitely included." Lucy added, her cheeks dimpled in excitement. Still Josie's expression didn't change, she was vaguely trying to work out why they were talking to her about this.

"You'd be paid of course." Claudia found the words almost sticking in her throat, but the thought of another 4% increase in circulation lubricated it slightly. "We were thinking £5,000 for the product design and then a 70:30 split on revenues from the products you

make." Josie's antenna began to twitch into overtime, far from being called in for a castigation, they actually wanted to offer her a business deal. Her brain racked through the possibilities of how to handle it. Coolly she said:
"60:40 to me and we may have a deal."
Claudia snorted. "We'd never go below 50:50."
"Then let's call it 50:50." Josie said with a finality that closed the deal, leaving Claudia uncertain how she had lost that one. The others clapped hands excitedly and loudly began planning the next month's issue, when Josie suddenly realised about the timings for her shop opening and groaned.
"I've just realised I can't do this. I've got my shop opening to organise." A stunned silence crashed into the room. No-one dared breathe; Claudia actually looked as though she was going to cry. Then Babs started flapping her hands wildly as an idea germinated, formulated and finally flourished. "What about if we used the shop opening to launch the products! We wouldn't have to have much stock available for the opening day. Josie could always take orders. And no-one has ever had an opening party for their products before!"
Claudia would have kissed Babs if she had been in reach, instead she made to with a mouthing a huge 'thank you'. They all turned to Josie.
"If we lent you a couple of people to get the shop ready and organise the opening would you be able to concentrate on coming up with the Bling & Boudoir summer range?" Josie chewed her lip thoughtfully as she tried to calculate how long the initial sketches, sourcing the materials and sewing the mock ups would take.
"It will be tight." She warned "But I reckon we could just about do it. I'd need to get an idea of what you envisaged so I can get started as soon as possible."
"That's fine, we've got our suggestion boards ready next door." Lotty and Dotty said in unison.

It was much later in the day when Josie finally started making her way home, sitting on the rocking train, watching the changing scenery flash past she decided she really did need a car, it was ludicrous that at thirty she was still using trains and borrowing her mother's car, goodness she'd been doing that as a student. Her mind buzzed with the morning's discussions. Her notebook was crammed with scrawled notes and tiny diagrams as she, Dotty and Lotty had gone through the initial Bling & Boudoir designs. They had changed a few of the original designs, swapping chintz oven gloves (too Cath Kidson) for a hat box ("I'm thinking Ascot and Cartier Polo" Lotty embellished) and dropped the diamante jewellery roll and hand embroidered kimono as just too expensive to make. Josie flicked through the pages contemplating which suppliers she would need to contact for supplies. She yawned and stretched her arms out, feeling tired and travel cramped. She'd phone round tomorrow, this evening she longed for a soapy bath and glass of chilled white wine. As they pulled into the station she realised she hadn't given her mother a call to arrange a lift. Oh well she had her keys, she'd just grab a taxi and make her own way back. She managed to find an empty taxi and five minutes later she was standing outside Molly's front door feeling glad to be back. She put her key into the lock and let herself in.

"Did you hear something?" Molly cocked her head, positive she had heard something. Sarah shook her head, but instinctively they peered through the doorway into the lounge at Olivia. She was sitting happily in her play pen gurgling articulately to her favourite teddy bear. A movement caught their eye and they saw the door to the hallway open and Josie appear. There was a moment of sharp intake of breath, they had been careful not to mention Olivia since Josie had lost her baby, not wanting to upset her further by flaunting what she had lost. "What's she doing here?" Sarah demanded sotto voce. "I thought you said she was going to ring from the station so that I could take Olivia before she got back."
Molly shrugged her shoulders unhappily. "She must have decided to take a taxi instead." They turned their gaze back to Josie who, having spotted Olivia dropped her cases on the floor and wandered over to the playpen. Leaning over she picked her plump niece up, and holding her close breathed in the soft baby smell of talcum powder. "Hello gorgeous, have you missed your Aunty Josie? I've missed you." And cradling Olivia carefully on her hip she walked towards the kitchen. Sarah and Molly scattered, trying to look busy without looking guilty about accidentally snooping. As Josie walked through the door Molly called out brightly.
"Had a good holiday darling?
"Yes, it was just what I needed."

Sarah tentatively hovered. "Do you want me to…" she nodded her head towards Olivia.
"In a minute." Josie assured. "She's saying hello to her auntie at the moment, aren't you sweetheart?" She gently blew at Olivia's forehead causing the blonde downy hair to tickle; Olivia burst into delighted giggles at the sensation and waved her fat little arms in the air.
"We weren't sure if you would want to see her."
"Of course I do." Josie said distracted by the new hair blowing game, then realised what her sister meant and looked across suddenly to Sarah and Molly's concerned faces. "Oh you meant because I lost my baby don't you?" They nodded cautiously, worried in case they said or did the wrong thing. "Don't worry, there's no need, being away has helped put a lot of things into perspective. Now if there's any wine on offer I'd love a glass and maybe I can give you an update. So much has happened and I'm dying to be able to tell someone." Sarah pulled the wine out of the fridge while Molly got three wine glasses and in no time they were sitting round the kitchen table, listening to Josie recounting the holiday, including the argument with Tara and the temper outburst.
"Well at least it helped to clear your thoughts." Molly said "However painful it is having everything come to a head, at least you came through it."
Sarah agreed. "You've been through three griefs in a way; losing Nick, losing Henry and losing the baby. That's an awful lot of emotion for anyone to cope with. So what are your plans now?"
"Well…" She stopped to examine the empty wine bottle. "Think we need another one. Here, take your grand-daughter for a moment." She handed over the sleeping bundle to Molly's outstretched arms. "I'll go and get a replacement."

Once everyone's glass had been replenished Josie began the exciting recollection of the meeting with Bling & Boudoir that morning; not forgetting to mention the inflatable chairs and the Sloane triplets. Molly and Sarah alternated between giggles and amazement.
"So they are hiring you to design their range of products?" Molly asked incredulously.
Josie nodded.
"And you're going to sell them in your shop?" Sarah asked.

Josie nodded again.

"And the shop is supposed to be opening in three weeks?" Molly said dubiously.

Josie felt like she was resembling one of those nodding dogs you saw in the back of cars. "How on earth are you going to manage it?"

"With a little bit of help from Lotty and Dotty and a lot of help from friends and family! Actually I was wondering whether you two would be willing to help? I know you've done so much already, I feel awful asking for even more."

"Nonsense." Molly said briskly on behalf of them both. "It's ages since we have an exciting project, besides I might even get to meet Lawrence Llewyeln-dooda at the opening night." Josie didn't have the heart to tell Molly of how remote that chance was.

"What do you need help with?" Sarah asked automatically flipping into school teacher mode and grabbing her pad and pen, her hand poised to start making notes and allocating tasks.

"Well." Josie was thoughtful, mentally thinking through the jobs that she had been worrying about on the train home. "The shop needs finishing and cleaning, then we'll need to get all my existing stock over there and set it up; I'll need to mock up designs for Claudia's team to approve, and then they will want to photograph them. Lotty and Dotty are helping to organise the shop opening, with the invitations and the catering. But I think we need to get some of the locals along, because the shop will have to make money outside of Bling & Boudoir." She dropped her head in hands as the enormity of the task became unveiled. "I'm never going to manage to do all this." She wailed.

"Nonsense." Sarah adopted Molly's attitude with frightening similarities. "First thing tomorrow morning we'll all go over to the shop and meet up with Mick to check what else needs doing. I'll get Edward to come over, now that the schools have broken up for summer holidays, he's already bored. We can get him onto the painting."

"And I'll organise the WI ladies to help with the clean up." Her daughters raised their eyebrows questioningly. "I'll tempt them with the prospect of meeting Lawrence Llewyeln-dooda!" She exclaimed wickedly. "We won't be able to help with the setting the shop up though, judging by some of the artistic talent in the WI flower arranging competitions we would lose you more customers quicker than you would win them." There was a quiet contemplative pause as each thought of a solution.

"I know – what about your friend Sally?" Sarah's cheeks dimpled in the excitement. "She must know all about setting up a shop."

"Good idea." Josie agreed. "I'll give her a call tomorrow."

"Getting some local interest, I can do. Between the School's PTA and the local nursery there should be quite a few volunteers. That just leaves the fetching and carrying down to you."

Josie felt a lump forming in her throat at the willingness they were showing to help her. "Thanks for all this." She squeezed their hands.

"That's what families are for darling." Molly comforted. "Now enough shop talk. Tell us are there any good looking men in France?"

Chapter 17

Looking back those three weeks seemed a blur of activity, but because Sarah was so diligent at organising everything and everyone in such an understated way it felt like being part of one long party. Everyone who helped out was offered a ticket to the opening, with the promise of an introduction to L.L-dooda if he was there. "I didn't realise he had such a following." Josie had joked to Lotty and Dotty as they discussed the canapés and drinks. "Oh yes, he's very big with the ladies." One of them said seriously. Even though they were talking almost daily, Josie still hadn't worked out which one was which. The shop was progressing, all the building work had been finished and now it was just waiting for Sally to come down from London to advise on the cabinets and shelving layouts. Edward had started on the painting, roping in several of his mates from the 5-a-side football team to help. They had happily slapped on the paint listening to the world cup on Radio 5 and sipping the chilled beers Sarah had thoughtfully provided. Molly and her elite core of WI volunteers were champing at the bit, eager to get on with the cleaning. They had begun synchronising cleaning kits in order to get the best results, almost resulting in a handbags at dawn between Mavis Connor and Edna H-V over whether bees wax should be applied with an old rag or a new duster. The invitations had been designed by the Bling & Boudoir team and were made to look like a sumptuous fat frilled cushion on the front, with all the invitation details on the back. A boxful had been handed over to Sarah who had deftly distributed them amongst her PTA and nursery helpers, each given distinct areas and explicit instructions on who should be given one so that no villages were missed out, but only potential customers received one. On one of her flying visits to the magazine offices in London, Josie had caught up with Tara for lunch and had spent all the time regaling her with the antics. Tara had offered to hand out invitations to the wives of Jeremy's partners, and although Josie doubted anyone from London would trek out to Drayton Beauchamp for the opening of her shop, she was touched that her friend had offered. She had been thinking if she should invite Caroline along, but wondered if it would be seen as an insult. She had asked for Tara's advice who had bluntly pointed out that she was running the shop as a business, so she would need every customer she could lay her hands on. There was an unasked question over whether she had contacted Henry, that hung heavily on the air. Eventually Josie finally answered with "What do you think I should do about Henry?"

Tara thought for a moment and then suggested:

"I would send the invite, but send it to his work with a covering note. Make it from one local business owner to another. That way if he doesn't want to come along he can make some polite excuse and you needn't feel let down."

Josie felt doubtful "Maybe." She agreed dubiously.

"Enough of this shop talk! Let me tell you all about this fabulous boutique that I've discovered off St John's Wood high street. They sell the most amazing clothes. Poor Jeremy doesn't know what's hit his credit card. Maybe I could give them a few of your opening invites in exchange for one of their gorgeous clutch bags." Josie smiled, things were definitely back to normal.

Later that evening, after a great deal of thought, she had crafted a short note to Henry. She still felt uncertain whether to send it out, and placed the invitation on the hall table to postpone the decision making until another time. Seeing the phone she realised she hadn't spoken to Martha since the miscarriage and in a rush of guilt gave her a call.

"How is it all going?" She asked Martha once the berating for not being in contact had been quelled.

"Terrible. I don't have anyone to make snide remarks to any more. I even considered wearing paisley to fit in with middle-age-Mary. Can't you stuff a pillow up your jumper and come and keep me company?"

"I'd love to, but I'm pretty busy at the moment."

"Not still working on your shop are you?"

"Oh yes." Her voice was warm and glowing. She launched into an abbreviated account of the last few weeks.

"So will you still have time to be my birthing partner?" Martha enquired.

"Of course I will. I can't wait to see little Tarquin enter this world." Martha snorted down the phone loudly. "He's not going to be called Tarquin." She said loudly. "I was thinking about River or may be Shadow."

"Mmm, they sound... er interesting. Anyway make sure you come along to the opening and support me. It may well just be you, me and the Drayton Beauchamp WI."

A couple of days before the opening Josie arrived at the shop to find the usual hive of activity had unbelievable increased. In one corner Molly and Edna were polishing the window panes energetically while discussing the merits of adding vanilla essence to bread and butter pudding. Lotty and Dotty were flitting around discussing canapé routes and wine refuelling points. Sally was artistically positioning Josie's stock of pillows against an old chaise long Molly had been storing in the garage. Edward was finishing off the last touching up of the paint, and Sarah was berating an unlucky nursery mum for not getting the invitations out on time. It was all finally coming together. The Bling & Boudoir photographers Derek and Shane had ventured out of their studio in W1 to come and photograph the Bling & Boudoir range of products in-situ at the shop, which meant Mick and Edward had worked several late nights in order to get the shop ready for the photo shoot. Derek had been almost orgasmic about the shop, clapping his hands together and sighing like a love sick teenager. Shane had been dispatched to the local deli for two skinny lattes, and returned with slices of melt-in-the-mouth chocolate brownies as well causing Derek to declare that there really was civilisation outside of London. Claudia had sent some of the sample shots down by courier so that Josie could choose some for the shop's catalogue. They were waiting for her on her workbench, like an unexpected Christmas present.

Josie walked in and said a general hello and received half-acknowledged grunts while everyone's focus remained firmly on their task in hand. Wandering through to the area that was gradually becoming her workroom, she dropped the boxes of sequined photo frames and chintz memento boxes onto the floor ready for Sally's magical touch later. As she greedily tore open the stiff backed envelope and began to devour the photos, her attention was caught by a polite cough behind her. Spinning round she caught sight of Henry standing in the doorway. Instantly her mouth went dry and her pulse seemed to suddenly increase, he looked as handsome as ever, and she could smell the familiar scent of his aftershave. She had dreamt about meeting him so often, but now that it was actually happening it felt uncomfortable. She had pictured them falling into each other's arms, declaring undying love, not standing like two distant strangers. They looked awkwardly at each other; the contrast between their other meetings burnt into their minds; where once there had been kisses and tender expressions, now there was only hurt and embarrassment.

"How are you?" She asked finally, aware of the sudden cessation of activity next door as the others tried to subtly watch with interest.

"Oh, fine." There was another long pause. "And how are you?"

"Tired, stressed and feeling over worked, but hey. I keep telling myself it will all be worth it." Josie said deliberately keeping her voice light and upbeat.

"I had to come and see you." Henry said awkwardly, averting his gaze from her.

"Did you?" Josie felt a rush of emotions surge through her as hope roared up.

"Yes, it's to do with a client's case, and I didn't think it was appropriate just to write to you."

"Oh right." The steel shutters of disappointment slammed down inside. So he had only come to talk business, he didn't have any interest in her.

"Do you have a moment?"

It was on the tip of her tongue to refuse, but somehow she couldn't face having to see Henry again if it was going to be this bad.

"Yes of course." She ushered him into the workroom and pulled the heavy shutter doors across to give them some privacy, trying not to catch the anxious eyes of Molly and Sarah as she did so. "So what is it?" She asked, her arms folded defensively across her chest.

He cleared his throat and pulled out several sheets of paper out from inside his suit jacket. Josie noticed it was the suit they had chosen together one fun afternoon in London and her heart did an involuntary crunch.

"I think I know how Nick died." Henry said slowly. Josie was stunned. Whatever she had expected it hadn't been to discuss her dead husband. Henry watched the frozen expression on her face and regretted having to open up the old wounds, but he forged on. "You see one of the patients at the Convent Hospice died, leaving no-one in charge of her estate. Mother Superior asked me to get involved because there appeared to be a discrepancy between the name the lady used and the name on her legal documents. As it turned out she was an Annie Carrington, married to a one Tom Carrington with one son Nicholas Peter. That Nicholas married one Josie Patton three years ago. You see you were that Josie Carrington. I don't know why I never guessed the connection before. I suppose I'd always known you as Molly's daughter and somehow associated you as a Patton."

Josie was in a daze, fumbled behind her feeling for a seat and sat heavily in the chair.

"Nick never really remembered his mother." Josie mused.

"I think he must have seen those photos your mother took at the Convent open day and recognised his mother. I don't know why he left it until late in the evening, but I think he wanted to see her while he still could."

Josie tried to take in all the information.

"So you decide to come along and calmly tell me how my husband died? What is it with you? Do you get a kick from this kind of thing?" Her voice was shaking with anger.

"No of course not." Henry was indignant. "I actually thought I was doing the right thing coming along to tell you, rather than having some official sounding letter."

"Why tell me at all, are you trying to bring it all back?"

"Of course not. There were two reasons, firstly I thought it might help to answer a few questions so you wouldn't spend the rest of your life demonised by Nick's death, and secondly because although it's not much there's a small legacy. As Nick's wife you inherit the money Annie Carrington left."

"And that's supposed to make me feel better is it? That although Nick died it's all ok because now I get his mother's money! What do you take me for – some kind of fortune hunter?"

"Of course not." Henry's reasonable tone infuriated Josie.

"Get out of here. I don't want any money, and I don't want your pity. Just leave me alone."

The door burst open on them and Lotty and Dotty tumbled in "Help!" they cried "We've just found out that..." They stopped suddenly when they caught sight of Henry.

"Don't worry we've finished." Josie assured them, her voice sounding hard and brittle. She held the door open indicating to Henry the way out. He scrutinised her closely and then started to leave but before he had got far he turned round and held the invitation Josie had written and left on the hall table.

"Thank you for the invite, but I don't think it's really my kind of thing." He turned on his heel and walked smartly out without walking back. This time it was Molly who refused to meet Josie's glare.

It was later that evening that Molly found the courage to ask about Henry's visit.
"Can you believe him." Josie fumed indignantly. "He wanted to tell me how Nick had died and how I was now the recipient of money left by his mother."
"Sounds as though he was trying to make it more bearable for you." Molly said reasonably.
"Goodness you sound just like him!" she retorted.
"That's because we both care for you, we've got that in common."
Josie sighed "Oh no you're wrong on that point. He was only there for business, he made it perfectly clear that there was nothing personal about the visit." Her voice sounded hollow.
"It's such a waste, the two of you were good together."
"Was that why you sent that invitation?"
Molly nodded. "I'm afraid my interfering didn't do any good judging by his response to you. I thought that as you had written it, you must still have some feelings for him. I just wanted you to have a bit of happiness again." Josie moved closer to her mother and slumped into her arms, just as she had done countless times before as a little girl.
"I thought I would have got over him by now, but seeing him there brought it all back so vividly. I still love him, that's why it hurts so much."

Chapter 18

The opening was going with a swing. The shop had been full from the moment they had opened, a combination of interested locals and Bling & Boudoir readers all eager to be part of the celebrations. Sarah in her typical school teacher mode, had organised several of the other nursery mums to handle the till and the ordering, leaving Josie free to talk to guests. Initially Josie had felt put out that she wouldn't be doing everything, but she now recognised Sarah's logic, it left her free to circulate. Her feet ached in her Manolo Blahnik sandals, but she was so pleased she didn't care about a few blisters. Lotty and Dotty's careful planning had paid off, the canapés and drinks continued to flow as new guests arrived. Derek and Shane appeared in matching denim cat suits and a tiny Shiatsu called Lulu and ecstatically greeted Sarah and Sally bitching wickedly about the clothes most of the other women were wearing. Claudia greeted, air kissed and waved at people as she took the congratulations from everyone for coming up with the brainwave.

As the afternoon wore on she wove her way over to where Josie was standing, champagne glass in one hand, salmon blini in the other. They clinked glasses conspiratorially.
"It's going rather well isn't it." Claudia was proud of how the day was turning. The magazine was going to have another bumper month.
"Yes it is. Thanks to you and your team. Actually I had a call earlier today. You won't believe it but it was Monica Harkness."
"No! What did she want?"
"To run an article with Declan O'Hara's goat visiting the shop. But I told her – I was a Bling & Boudoir exclusive girl."
Impulsively Claudia gave her a hug "Thank you. Revenge is just soo sweet sometimes."
"How are you and Neil getting on?"
"Much better, he's taking me to Antigua next week. I can't wait, two weeks of total pampering."
Josie spied Caroline entering the shop and they swapped friendly waves. It was funny how things sorted themselves out, in the end it had been Max enthusiastically running over to her as she had been walking across the green to have a few quiet moments that broken the silence between the two women. Max's bubbling chatter of

what they had been up to, and his questions about Josie meant that any previous embarrassment slipped away.

"I've just received this." Caroline said jovially bandying the invitation to the shop opening in front of Josie.

"Well I jolly hope you're going to be there. I need all the support I can get." Josie had instructed "Max you make sure your mummy comes along."

"Oh she will do." Max complied happily. "Daddy says she never misses the chance to shop."

Josie and Caroline exchanged a conspiratorial "what-do-men-know" look.

"I take it Toby is keeping well."

"Oh yes, busy with work. You must come over for supper some time. I know we both want to hear all the news." She was quiet for a moment and then said in a sympathetic tone. "I was really sorry to hear about..." She held her hand out towards Josie, instinctively her hand flew to her stomach still unaccustomed to its flatness.

"That's life." Josie said philosophically.

"I don't suppose you've heard from Henry?"

Josie shook her head. "That's one thing that hasn't quite healed yet."

"I'm sorry that it's turned out like this. I've never known two people so well suited."

Since that encounter Caroline had joined forces with Sarah on the promotion of the shop, setting up 'exclusive shopping days' for her well-heeled friends in the following weeks, so that Josie wouldn't be swamped on the first day.

"Isn't that Lord Shaker's daughter?" Josie heard Claudia saying in a tight excited voice. "Oh I must go and say 'hi', I'll catch you later." Josie watched in rye amusement as Claudia swept off to rapturously greet the daughter of her boss, greeting Caroline like a long-lost sister and commandeering her attention.

"Are you enjoying it?" Tara asked from behind her; as Josie turned the smile was still in place, as it had been all day. "Don't bother answering, I can tell you are. Well I think today had been wonderful. Just don't go forgetting your old friends now that you've become a successful business woman."

"Don't be silly, you can't get rid of me." Josie chided kindly.

"Make sure you stay in touch, I'll phone you later just to check you're ok. We have to start heading back or we'll never get back to town." She kissed Josie on the cheek goodbye, and as they moved towards the shop front she said. "It looks like someone is in need of rescuing." Josie followed Tara's stare and saw Henry nervously standing in the doorway looking helpless round at the thronging crowds of women. "I'll leave you to it." She gave a quick squeeze and went off to say goodbye to Molly. Josie walked slowly over to Henry, all of sudden her heels, which had been so well behaved all day, seemed to become too high and unwieldy, and it took enormous effort to just walk across to where he was standing. He smiled shyly as she approached, accepting two glasses of champagne from one of the passing waitresses. Handing one to her he said.

"It looks like a good turnout."

"It's been a fantastic day." Josie was glowing with pride. "Everyone has been so helpful. I'd never have managed it without them. Tara's here somewhere. She brought some of the London crowd down, and my mother is in her element. She actually had her photo taken with Lawrence Llewyeln-dooda."

"I bought you this to say 'congratulations'." He handed over a bottle of champagne, and she noticed it was her favourite. "I thought maybe you could celebrate once everyone has gone." Their hands touched momentarily as she took the fizz, and the sensation sparked a familiar longing in the pit of her stomach. "I'm so proud of you."

Josie was taken aback, after the cool business attitude of their last meeting she hadn't expected any personal talk. Slightly choked with emotion she admitted.

"It hasn't been easy, but I'm getting there."

"I wanted to phone you as soon I heard about... well you losing the baby. I know how much it meant to you."

The constriction in her heart tightened a little more. 'Oh why didn't you.' She wanted to ask. 'You were the one person I needed more than anyone.'. Instead she just tenderly patted his arm, unable to find words.

"I've missed you." He said so low and quietly that it was almost inaudible. There was a momentarily silence as the two tried to understand this emotional cyclone against the backdrop of the nosy party. "Josie look..." he began to say urgently, but he was interrupted by Derek and Shane who were hunting Josie down for a final photo shoot.

"In a moment." Josie promised desperately trying to return back to Henry.

"I can see you're busy, go and enjoy your party." He called. She thought wildly about grabbing his hand and running off with him to somewhere quiet, but even as she thought about it the moment had passed. Molly and Sarah had spotted him and were bearing down on him with joyful greetings. She was led off, gently but persistently by Derek. Throughout the rest of the afternoon they had caught each other's eye across the room, but somehow they were never close enough to speak. The moment they had shared once again had obviously gone.

Chapter 19

The chiming clangs of the church bells rang out across the warm summer morning, calling the congregation to the Sunday Service. With the launch of the shop and the Bling & Boudoir range of products successfully underway she was settling down to running the shop and starting to fulfil the orders which the nursery mums had so carefully taken down. The shop had been busy every day since the opening, and Josie was glad of the Sunday; she felt tired and exhausted, but for once extremely happy. It felt as though her life was finally slotting into place. Slowly she was moving her things into the flat above the shop and it was beginning to feel a little more like home. Molly would occasionally pop over to cook for them both, and Sarah, Edward and Olivia would call in to say hello.

Yesterday she had received a cheque from Henry, hand delivered by Miss Letty, on behalf of Annie Carrington's estate with a short note from Henry congratulating her on the shop opening and asking if she would like to go to dinner sometime. She had phoned Henry, using the cheque as an excuse, expecting to hear his deep voice but there had only been an answerphone, and disappointedly she left a short formal message thanking him for sorting everything out so efficiently.

She walked down the gravel path of the convent chapel listening to the rhythmic singing of the choir float across the air, wandering off the path past the ornate Victorian Cherubs and marble statues to the corner where the new more discreet headstones sat closeted by the hedge and an ancient yew tree. Picking her way deferentially through the graveyard she read the names, looking out for one in particular. The simple granite headstone read "Annie Carrington 1941 – 2005. Finding Solace in God and the hereafter". She knelt down on the springy grass in front it, her hands on the stone cold face. It felt strange that she was here tending a grave of a complete stranger, and yet they had so much in common, they had shared an important person in their life. Arranging the chrysanthemums that she bought with her, their bright cheery faces gleaming out in the sun, she contemplated the strange paths that life provided. Twelve months ago she had been living with Nick, thinking of having a baby, and no idea her mother-in-law was so close. Now here she was with her own business and a home that she had created just starting out on her adventure.

"I hope you and Nick finally meet up wherever you are." She wished to the unknown lady with whom she had shared such a important part of her life, before standing up and brushing the moss from her hands. Thoughtfully she retraced her steps across the cemetery and back towards the lynch gate deep in contemplation. The day stretched before her with so much possibility, there was no more planning for opening days, mocking up designs or work on the shop. She was free to grab a Sunday paper and spend the day lazing in her tiny sitting room. At first she didn't notice the tall silhouette against the bright sun, so deep was she in thought; it wasn't until she drew level with the gate that she noticed the back of someone leaning nonchantly against the lichen covered stone wall. As she passed through the gate, the figure turned, and she recognised Henry dressed in a crumpled suit, his tie half askew.

"Hello." He said warmly as though they met like this every Sunday.

"Morning." She replied "I think you might be a bit late for church."

"Oh I'm not going to the service, I've only just back from town. I was up there for a few days on business. I was supposed to be there until Tuesday, but suddenly I felt I needed a day at home."

Josie thought of her previous call and realised with relief that it hadn't been that he was ignoring her, unbidden a grin broke out on her face, lighting up her eyes.

"So you haven't been avoiding my calls then?" She asked involuntarily, then blushed wildly as she realised the desperation in her voice.

Taking courage from the outburst Henry quizzed. "So you did call then?" He was secretly pleased at her admission. He had deliberately sent the note knowing he would be away, but had been unable to bear the waiting, not knowing whether Josie would ever phone.

"Well you mentioned supper." Josie mumbled feeling her cheeks burn even brighter.

"How about breakfast instead?" He offered. "Have you got anything planned for today?"

"All I was going to do was relax and read the papers."

"Sounds like an excellent idea. Do you think we could combine forces and read together?" He asked hopefully. Josie eyed him, noticing the half-eager expression tinged with a fear of rejection, and her stomach set off into a series of somersaults.

"I can't see why not." She said lightly.

"Actually it was you I came back to see, I thought you might be here."

"How did you guess?"

"I worked on the assumption that when you had received the money you would want to try and say some kind of thank you to Annie. How else than by flowers on her grave? What did you choose; lilies?"

She shook her head. "Oh no, far too funereal. I chose chrysanthemums, they seemed so much more cheerful."

"I'm sorry I didn't get a chance to speak to you properly at the shop opening. I should have thought about the timings, but it was a bit of an impulse. I just hadn't realised how many people would be there."

"I was glad you came. I wanted to say 'sorry' for being rude to you before, I know you were only trying to be kind. It was just that I wasn't expecting it. It felt like a complete blast from the past when I wasn't ready."

"No it's me who should be sorry. I should have handled it better, but in a way I was so desperately for an excuse to see you that I didn't think it through properly." There was a silence, Josie pleated the fabric of her skirt and outlined a small circle with the end of her pump.

"Did you mean it when you said you missed me?" Josie asked in a small unconfident voice.

Henry moved across in front of her and lifted her chin up gently so that they were gazing into each others' eyes.

"Yes. I behaved very badly when you told me about your baby. There is no excuse other than I was totally jealous. I love you more than I ever thought it possible to love another person. Being without you made me realise what I had lost. I don't know if we can make it work, but I certainly want to try."

He bent forward and kissed her on the lips with butterfly tenderness. She responded, kissing him back lightly as though afraid it would turn out to be a fantastic mythical dream. Almost in slow motion Henry stroked her cheek, his long fingers caressing the soft peachy down of her skin. Then pulling her closer, holding her body against his, both of them experienced the familiarity of attraction come flooding back. He kissed her with more passion, as desire crashed through them with an urgency and intensity. Josie clung to Henry, feeling the curve of his muscles and the outline of his spine, she moulded her body against his tightly, all rational thought gone. The kissing began to get more urgent, and it was only the sound of the church doors opening and the congregation spilling out that brought them back to earth. Weakly they pulled apart, hardly able to believe what happened.

"I've missed you so much." Henry whispered into her hair, one arm still around her shoulder keeping her close.

"Me to." Josie admitted, afraid that the moment would burst into a thousand pieces.

"Shall we go and buy those papers?" He suggested urgently.

"Somehow I don't think we're going to have much time for reading." Josie responded archly.

Taking her hand, Henry started to lead across the fields back to the high street and her flat.

"Sounds just fine to me." He assured her. Laughingly they broke into a run, racing to get back away from the crowds, and the curious glances. Everything was going to be alright.